SUPERHUMANS FROM THE PAST

A Superhero Epic

Jaime Mera

Dedication

I dedicate this book to my friends: Rich Richardson, Aaron Smith,

Mullins and Lee Forrest. Your friendship extending across the world has

been profoundly wonderful and I hope this book represents all of your

best qualities.

Published books:

A Superhero Epic Series

Creator (2004, 2014)

He Is Known as Ego (2006, 2014)

Guild Without a Name (2014)

The Galaxy Is Ours (2014)

Masterminds (2014)

Superhumans from the Past (2016)

Ultimate Assassins (2016)

Non-fiction

Jesus and the Paint on the Wall: What Do People Live For? (2012)

Doomsday Prepping and Survival: From Civil Disturbances to Biblical Proportions (2014)

How to Write eBooks & Printed Books: Traditional and Self-Publishing (2016)

Preface

The world of enlightenment and self expression dominated the late 1960's and early 70's. For some, it was war and scientific success or defeat; for others it was a time to indulge in what could be gotten away with. Movements of all kinds were in the making to include racial and gender equality. The Korean War was over, but now the Cold War caused many people and countries to look at the USA and USSR flex their political and military might, no matter who it hurt or helped. The government entered the Vietnam campaign under the guise of governmental aid to South Vietnamese democracy and advertised it as a new war against communism. But in reality, it was a partially self inflicted egoistical struggle to claim land and people who were already rebelling against colonial oppression. Whatever the cause, the CIA was in full swing as they started many secret projects which involved experimentation, covert assassinations, investigations into alien activity and investigations into what would lead to the superhuman phenomena. The CIA's special operations section assigned to superhuman investigations started small, but received great interest after superhuman superheroes came out into the open during the late 1970s.

The small covert group was all but forgotten as the founders of the Special Investigation Agency (SIA). The truth behind their success hinged on a young woman determined to find proof of superhumans willing to fight for truth and justice. The mission, which started her career as Director of the SIA was classified, but if it were public knowledge, it revealed very little because the superhuman who saved her life disappeared, never to be seen again.

The European elites pushed large amounts of money into Super Soldier and ESP programs. Allegations and convictions for retribution of human atrocities ensued because of the many failures resulting in the death of the experimental subjects and those near them. International laws protecting humans and superhumans from experimentation held strong in many countries. But there were a few countries with the technology who sanctioned the activity and supposedly stayed within the law. One being the United States under the misled impression they could conduct safe experimentations. The growing pains of their endeavor mirrored that of Europe and many humans horribly died. Superhumans on the other hand fared better. A few companies had positive results until some overstepped their boundaries. Joshua Marks was one of several superhumans who fought back, making sure companies like the Founders were destroyed or disbanded. Unfortunately, experimentations in the past had already made their mark in history and the future.

Australia became a haven for superhuman outcasts and villains fleeing the northern hemisphere and South America. They focused on improving superhuman abilities without brutal and extreme scientific exploitation. Superhumans flooded government positions and it was clear to the United States that Communism was the least of their worries in the Australian region of power. The CIA erupted into all corners of the world trying to keep up with the ever growing underground superhuman influence. This gave ground for Director Asher to beef up the SIA and be allowed to legally and easily cross international borders. But the road to change was long and what people feared was the unknown. The question of where superhumans came from was revealing itself as history, legend, science and unyielding mystery. But the full effect of superhumans on the planet would be revealed in the future, not the Cold War era. A future where superhumans with godlike powers would have to pick their battles carefully, or be destined to repeat the follies of the past and possibly cross the line of total destruction of planet Earth.

This story, however unfolds on the battlefield of another planet called Arlos and a time far from the reaches of diplomacy or nuclear apocalyptic concerns. It was a time when Queen Cassandra placed all hope in the hands of five Earthlings to save a galaxy far away from their own and the Earth's future. This is their story.

Contents

List of Characters

Stargazer / Steve Messer – Leader of the group known as the Five Ghosts, nicknamed "Star.", ex-CIA agent

Ghost / Albert R. Hansen– Member of the Five Ghosts, ex-mathematician

Rat Bastard / Gus Madex – Member of the Five Ghosts, ex-drifter

Spot / Aaron Fisher – Member of the Five Ghosts, ex-sniper (Alias: Abaddon, Ra, Set, Solar)

Master / Benjamin Dempsey – Member of the Five Ghosts, ex-student

Queen Cassandra Leavan – Ruler of Arlos and Andromen Empire, daughter of King Alexmarks

Captain Rashell Lix – Imperial Special Operations Leader

Gina Pollas / Gina Asher – CIA Special Agent and Regional Chief for the Western States

Kevin Aries – Security Task Force Commander, CIA

Randolph Maximilian – CIA agent, team leader and weapons specialist

Admiral Novis – Commander of the Andromen forces

Arbitrator – Cosmic traveler, from the House of Cilos

Commander Exleter – Commander of the Vorgoling Space Station

Major Krodis – Historian aboard the Vorgoling Space Station

Cyer – Destroyer of Ordis, Harbinger of Death, one of a kind genowraith

Chief Executer Bhala – Lead Scientific Research Commissioner, creator of the genowraith project

Emperor Korvax Bac'dir – Leader of the Arkemis Covenant and Emperor of the Kalar Race

Realgar Knights – Three genetically enhanced Kalar super Soldiers loyal to Korvax, having survived the Osuris Wars

General Mihod – Kalar general in charge of special defense projects and chairman to the Counsel of Covenants.

Pananthra – Orphan teenage girl from Siglar Moon Base

Richard Octavian / Creator – Leader of the Eternal Champions

Elizabeth A. Octavian / Isis – Member of the Eternal Champions

Larcis G. Draven / Night – Member of the Eternal Champions

Erica – Member of the Eternal Champions (Super Artificial Intelligence computer)

Burik'dir – (meaning: the specters of change) prophesied as the saviors of the Andromeda galaxy

Superhumans from the Past, A Superhero Epic

Chapter One

Not on File

Southern Nevada, March 11, 1971

Steve Messer sat in a comfortable leather seat enjoying the company of a very attractive CIA operative. They had never met before this trip and the team which he was now a part of all had their established relationships. As far as he could tell from conversations and wedding rings, the only single and available people were him and Ms. Gina Pollas.

Steve was handsome, tall and clean shaven with sandy blonde hair, cut short and tapered in the back. The other men in the team however, grew out their facial hair and half of them made it seem like the new hippie trend had invaded the agency. The only other female in the group was in her late thirties wearing business attire as if she worked for the IRS instead of Langley.

Gina by contrast was young for an operations agent, with primary strengths in nuclear physics and biological warfare and secondary in actual espionage experience and skills. Her attire was less businesslike with long black pants, a long sleeve turn down collar light blue shirt and low heeled shoes. Her smile was uncanny with an abundance of attractiveness and mystery. She was strategic with her conversations about all subjects, which made Steve cared more about her as a person than her profession.

Steve kept quiet for the most part, letting people talk themselves into whatever came up. But when asked questions, he steered all conversations to her, asking her opinions and views on life. It worked for a while, but she kept her distance as if she did have a boyfriend or just wanted a professional relationship without getting personal. So Steve went along, but eyed her for most of the flight when not speaking directly to her.

The flight was long for a Lear jet, but extra fuel tanks on the wings extended the range of the plane. As the plane started to reduce altitude; Steve knew they were nearing their undisclosed destination. His attention veered to the horizon as he faced the front of the plane with the right and left windows out to his extreme fields of view. He peered through the plane and bodies in front of him. His extraordinary vision allowed him to see through matter, thousands of miles away, but he only concentrated on the red sky and dark forming desert ground from the setting sun.

The jet flew towards a set of mountain ranges, but then banked parallel to it as the plane went below the highest peak. Steve buckled his seatbelt and relaxed on the seat as his vision focused back on Gina. She noticed his stare and then looked at the buckle.

The fasten seatbelt sign lit up. Gina slightly tilted her head as if wondering how Steve knew the sign was going to turn on. "I see that you like to follow rules." She smiled.

"Only the ones that matter." Steve smiled back and took a mental picture of her smooth skin, long blonde flowing hair and pearly blue eyes. Her left ear was slightly lower than the right, but unnoticeable to the average person, especially since they were covered by hair most of the time. They were beautifully shaped and any other imperfections on her face or body would have been considered perfectly human. He looked back outside hoping to calculate the exact time they would touch down to show off his predictive knowledge. "But don't worry, we'll be landing in about…"

Steve saw the landing field and several empty buildings. Dead bodies lay in a room of one of the buildings, but what startled him most was the bright exhaust of a surface to air missile. The missile came from the north somewhere on the mountainside or at its base. There were seconds before the missile hit. Before he could say a word, the plane was taking evasive maneuvers as one of the pilots must have spotted the light of the exhaust in the dark background. Or perhaps it was the newly installed prototype radar system in the plane, which warned the pilots to some degree.

The passengers' calm faces changed to confusion and horror, thinking the plane was crashing. Gina hadn't clipped her buckle so she and three others violently flew out of their seats towards the ceiling and to the right. But the direction abruptly changed towards the floor as the plane rolled left and looped as hard as the pilot could pull on the control yoke.

Steve adjusted to the direction changes and G forces with his flight abilities. He grabbed his belt buckle with one hand and reached for Gina, who was now at his side of the wall and window portal. The buckle broke off the fabric as he ripped it with superhuman strength. Instead of releasing the latch, the excitement of the situation left him reacting to make sure the seatbelt didn't prevent him from getting a firm hold on Gina. He straddled her against the wall, keeping her from bouncing around at the same time protecting her from the interior debris with his body.

Gina's body dangled between him and the wall as the jet looped and twirled. Steve looked around over his shoulders at the chaos, then back at the heat seeking missile as it hit the tail end of the jet. One engine burst into pieces and flames. The concussion of the blast violently pushed the jet into a yaw. The body of the jet broke up into large sections. Heat and air rushed inside as two agents and added debris darted outside. Moans and screams were muffled into nothingness as the rush of air overshadowed most sounds. Steve instantly analyzed his options. The jet would soon blowup once the heat interacted with the fuel tanks, or at the very least disintegrate into pieces before it came to sudden stop. He was sure to survive the fragments, heat and anything else in the air, even hitting the ground, but this wasn't about him at the moment. Steve thought quickly on how to save the people in the plane. The expanding open areas to the outside gave him a shot at a rescue of one or two people.

The seconds seemed like a slow motion video to Steve as he grabbed Gina by the waist and flew towards the large open fuselage. With his free hand, he grabbed one of the other agents by the arm on his way out. He rotated in flight trying to avoid debris and plane sections as the jet plummeted to its doom.

The three of them cleared the burning ball of soaring jet wreckage in the nick of time. The night air was cool, a drastic change to the last few seconds of terror. Steve flew swiftly towards the desert sand. He felt liquid on his hand and arms as he laid the two agents on the ground. Steve looked down at the liquid, ignoring the explosion of the jet on the landscape several hundred meters away. He could see the chemical compounds of alcohol, water, blood, urine and minute traces of jet fuel on his arm. His hand however, was drenched mainly in blood. Agent Nelson was profusely bleeding out of a large gash on his arm. Steve could see the brachial artery pushing life out of the man, as he placed his finger deep into Nelson's forearm and stopped the bleeding.

Steve quickly scanned them with his vision looking for other life threatening injuries. He rushed the scan and then looked up in the direction of the missile attack. The desert foliage prevented his vision from seeing the details of the hostiles. The one disadvantage to his vision was in the composition of plant life he couldn't see through which he could never figure out how to overcome. But he did spot a vehicle leaving the scene over the ridgeline. He sighed and looked at the other two agents. Nelson would die if he let go of Nelson's arm to pursue the fleeing attacker. Both were unconscious, had concussions and multiple fractures. Nelson had two in his arm and rib cage. Gina's right leg and foot were broken. Their lungs were expanding as normal as could be expected, but Nelson's heart contractions were weak from the large amount of blood loss.

Steve looked at the airfield buildings less than a mile away. The ten dead bodies in the room he saw earlier were still there. There were no signs of anyone else in the area, but he wasn't looking for people. His first look from the jet told him that, but what he scanned for this time were small and numerous. His vision jumped from room to room looking inside cabinets and storage rooms. The things he needed were there and that was the problem.

Steve sat Nelson up and wrapped his legs around Nelson's waist from behind. With his free hand, Steve grabbed Gina's wrist and flew off the ground about ten feet. He sped towards the airfield structures keeping note of the two agents' vitals. The warm rushing air massaged Gina's face and body as she went in and out of consciousness.

The pain of her foot and leg making contact with hard ground woke her up from limbo. Her hair covered her face as she felt a hand brush it aside. Her bruised hands instinctively went up to feel her head and body. "What, aaghh?"

"It's alright Gina. It's Steve."

Pain surged through her body as the memory of bouncing around the plane became a reality. "What?"

"Gina! What's your full name?" Steve asked.

"Gina Victoria Pollas." She managed to reply with a grunt.

"What's your service number?"

"3923-4800-92." She replied wide eyed and alert.

"That's good." Steve said as he thought something else. *'If that's your real service number I wouldn't know, but a number is better than nothing I guess.'*

Her back was against a hanger metallic wall. Steve knelt between her and Nelson. "Your right leg and right foot are broken so don't try to move them. But I need your help." Steve grabbed Gina's hand and put two fingers inside her palm. "I need you to squeeze my fingers as hard as you can?"

Gina squeezed tightly. "Good, now here. Keep your thumb inside Nelson's forearm so he doesn't bleed to death. I need to get medical supplies." Steve plunged Gina's thumb inside Nelson and stood up with wet and dry bloody hands.

"What if he wakes up?" Steve heard Gina say as he was already out of sight inside the hanger. He sprinted and flew through the hanger rooms, collecting the needed items for an emergency surgical procedure and comfort items for the two patients.

Gina felt her fingernail buried inside Nelson's flesh. Blood continued to seep out of the long gash as she reached with her other hand and applied pressure on the wound. She looked around out into the darkness, except for the burning crash site and mixture of a quarter moon and stars in the distance. She heard movement inside the hanger Steve was in, wondering if he could find anything in the dark. She could barely make out herself and Nelson, how could Steve see anything? But that thought quickly disappeared as Steve ran outside by her side with several large parachute cargo bags, one being a medical bag and a few mop poles. Steve turned on two large flashlights placing one on the ground next to Gina and another on the other side of Nelson.

Gina held her tongue as Steve moved with lightning speed setting up three I.V.s, utensils, medications and sanitary covers. Steve didn't stop to read anything or decide on what items to use or place in preparation for stopping the bleeding and caring for the two of them. Before Gina knew it, Steve removed her hands and thumb from Nelson's arm. All she could see was Steve stabbing into Nelson's arm, blood engulfing everything. "Do you know what you're doing?"

"Yes. Hold his arm still." Steve calmly replied.

Blood poured out from where the two metallic prongs entered; soaking the large sterile pads Steve had placed around the gash. In less than ten seconds after Steve removed Gina's hand from Nelson's arm, the bleeding stopped. "How did you do that?" Gina's tired eyes widen.

"Did I tell you how lovely your voice sounds?" Steve said, as he took another set of instruments and thread, stitching the seven inch gash in a matter of seconds.

"What the hell?" Gina said in shock.

Steve positioned Nelson's arm and pulled on it, resetting the bones and wrapped them with torn sheets and wooden stilts in less than a minute.

Gina looked at her leg and tried to bend over to touch her fracture as if it would make things better.

Steve rapidly pushed her back against the wall. "Try not to move." Gina felt the I.V. needle enter her arm like a quick and small sting before she could object.

The I.V. bags were already hanging on a makeshift standing mop pole. She looked up once again at the I.V. bags as her leg reeked with pain. Or was it her foot, or both? Steve held tight onto her fractures as he splinted her foot and leg. "I know it hurts, but they don't have morphine or anything close to it. Please be as still as possible."

The 3D transparencies of Gina's blood, bones, tendons, muscle fibers and many smaller particles were Steve's guide in making sure the bones were set properly leaving no blood clots or strained ligaments.

"Aarrgh… Ookaay." Gina panted. She watched Steve inject Nelson with medication and then her. "What's that for?"

"It's so you don't get an infection and it helps with the pain."

"I thought you said there weren't any strong pain killers?"

"It's a weaker alternative. Luckily, chemistry and medicine were some of my strong subjects in school." Steve smiled as he whipped out a few blankets from one of the large bags. He laid out a spot for Nelson and sat him at an incline on the tar mat and hanger wall. He looked around every now and then, instinctively wanting to avert anymore dangers in the area.

"How do you move so fast? And how did we survive the plane crash?" Gina's voice was calm.

Steve finished positioning Gina on top of her blanket and bundled pillowing. He had lied many times in the past about his abilities and superhuman attributes, but he could only stare powerlessly into her mesmerizing eyes.

"We didn't crash with the plane. I grabbed who I could, which was you and Nelson, and flew out of the plane as it broke apart after the anti-aircraft missile hit it. We landed near the crash site and I flew you two here so I could save his life."

"You flew? Like Superman?" Gina almost smirked, but the fact of their survival begged an explanation, even if it seemed outrageous.

"Well, no. I can't fly that fast or back through time like he can, and I was born here, so I'm not an alien." Steve said as he looked around. "Sorry, I can't talk anymore, but I need to get the power working and we need to contact someone so you and Nelson can get needed medical attention." Steve said and flew off out of site into the desert darkness.

Gina stared at herself and then at Nelson. His chest was slightly rising and falling. He would wake up sometime, and she needed to be ready to calm him down if he did. She didn't notice any injury on Steve, and hoped that this super person would soon figure out how to get

Nelson and her to a hospital.

Steve flew directly to the main electrical junction box. The main cable was cut, but he grabbed the cable and spliced it back together with his fingers. A strong electrical current passed through his body and into the ground, but he endured the minor tingle as his metal hard like fingers restored the cable to normal. He flipped the levers and the hanger came to life. The two flashlight beams were overwhelmed by the hanger lights coming out from the inside, exposing a large portion of the tar mat and other buildings in the distance.

Steve flew back in front of her like a speeding race car. "There are a few beds in the back of that building. I'll get them and place both of you inside the hanger while I look for a working radio or phone."

"Who would do this to us?" Gina said out loud to herself, realizing it was never brought up until now.

A rifle shot came from the darkness in the distance, and the round mushroomed on the back of Steve's head, sending his chin into his upper chest. Steve slightly moved forward, but caught himself with an instinctive flight reflex. Steve instantly looked back for the origin of the gunfire. He saw a sniper in the lowland brushes several hundred meters away. He saw the sniper clearly, down to him, squeezing the trigger, releasing another round. Steve quickly guessed the trajectory, but to make sure, he flew up into a horizontal position in mid air getting between Gina, Nelson and the sniper; the round hitting his upper leg.

A torn streak was made on Steve's jeans as the round bounced off, his skin staying completely intact. Gina instinctively moved for cover by trying to lay flat, but the pain from her leg and other parts of her bruised body made her scream in pain.

Steve twirled around to see Gina in pain from moving and quickly assessed the situation by scanning for foreign objects inside or next to her. In an instant, finding nothing was wrong; he twirled back and flew as fast as he could at the sniper. Another round exited the sniper rifle, but Steve had flown to the side away from Gina, so when the round left the barrel, Steve didn't care if it hit him or not. The round passed Steve by a few feet, fifty meters away from the sniper. Before the sniper could move or fire another round, Steve plowed into him like a high powered harpoon.

The sniper rifle caved into the man from the impact of Steve's body, but primarily, Steve's fists which were extended in front of him. Steve and the rifle tore into the sniper's head, all the way through his body. Blood, bone and flesh littered the desert ground as Steve came to a complete stop far from where the sniper used to be. A shallow trench of bloodied desert ground trailed behind him. Steve grumbled under his breath in disappointment. He stood up and shook his hands and body, trying to get the newly added blood, sand and guts off of him. Blood splattered all around him, removing a large portion of blood and entrails, but it also served in spreading blood to all parts of his body.

He looked around for any other sniper or enemy that may have returned. He saw Gina huddled next to Nelson, as if she could somehow protect him from another attack. Steve flew straight up and scanned the area. The metallic properties of the buildings, unoccupied vehicles, remains of the sniper's equipment, plane wreckage and mineral ores in the ground told him there were no more enemies in the area. So he hoped for sure this time.

Satisfied, Steve flew back to Gina. "It's clear."

"Who the hell is trying to kill us… and why are you all red?"

Steve knelt next to her and looked down at her neck, instead of her eyes. "Yeah, about that. I didn't think about slowing down before I got to the sniper so I flew into him."

Gina's eyes squinted. "You killed him?"

"If you haven't noticed the extra blood, here it is." Steve said as he moved away and wiped his clothes and exposed skin with clean towels he had gathered.

Gina stared in disbelief or confusion, Steve wasn't sure. "Why are you looking at me like that? Did you want me to let him keep shooting and maybe get lucky in hitting you?"

"No, of course not. As long as you know the difference, I'm alright with that."

"Just so you know to set the record straight, I didn't like killing the guy." Steve stood erect in a moment of relaxation.

"Who are you?" Gina calmly asked.

"I had special powers since childhood. I grew up wanting to be an agent, but I guess the cat's out of the bag now. But let me focus on getting the beds for now."

"Are you sure there're no more snipers?"

"The people who shot at the plane left the area to the north once the plane crashed. That sniper must have been positioned prior to the attack to confirm the damage assessment. I'll go after them once I make contact with headquarters for help. Unless you want me to stay with you until help arrives?"

"Let's talk about that once you get a hold of anyone."

"Well, in the meantime, think about the possibility that someone in the agency might have helped in this attack." Steve replied and flew off once again.

"What?" Gina said towards an empty audience.

Steve quickly entered the hanger locker room latrine and washed off most of the blood and dirt, using up two bars of soap in minutes; wanting to make sure he didn't expose his patients to more unnecessary infections. He grabbed a shirt and fatigue pants from a locker, easily breaking the padlock with his hands. Without delay, he grabbed two beds and flew them next to Gina and Nelson. He made sure to take the bed frames since they kept the mattresses from folding into unwanted positions.

Steve placed both of them on the beds and moved them one at a time inside the empty hanger. "We have a problem. The radios in the one aircraft on the other side of the airfield, and the two radios in the temporary control tower have been destroyed." Steve said as he gently elevated Gina's leg with pillows.

"I'm sure the pilots got out a Mayday or some type of signal, so someone should be looking for us right now." Gina stated.

Steve sat at Gina's bedside. "You think the agency is that good to be looking for us, out here in Nevada?"

"Well, if we're in Nevada, I know they will be, but how do you know we're in Nevada?"

"I can see very far, and saw where we were flying, to include the destination orders the pilots received in the cockpit. So that brings up the question. Someone had to know we were flying at this time and who was on board. Someone in the agency is a traitor, or there's a leak somewhere and someone is taking advantage it."

"It doesn't make sense. We're supposed to be a think tank initiative to locate and monitor nuclear and chemical weapon systems. Aren't there more important projects they could sabotage?"

Steve stared into her eyes. "Maybe it was a person or people they wanted to get rid of?"

"You mean people like you?"

"No, I'm pretty sure no one knew about me, but you and the other brainiacs are another story. Besides, if they knew about me, they would have sent a lot more firepower."

"Thank you." Gina half smiled.

"Does this mean we can go out on a date later?"

"Aooh, I was wondering when you were going to ask me since we started talking on the plane." She smiled in pain.

"After I get the bad guys and you recover some more of course. If, that's okay with you?" Steve lightly held Gina's hand.

Steve's hand was warm and soft. Gina felt at peace, but excited as well. How could this man in front of her withstand a missile attack and bullet, but yet feel so tender and smooth against her skin? "Can I ask you a million questions while we wait for someone to find us?"

"I would love that, but Nelson won't last too long if we just do nothing, or hope someone is really on their way."

"Yes, I suppose… So, what do you suggest we do?"

"I can scan towards the four cardinal directions and look for a building with a phone. If there's one within a hundred miles, I should be able to fly there and back in about fifteen minutes, including making the call."

"So what's the hold up?" Gina asked in wonder.

"Just because I can see far, doesn't mean I can find something easily. The further an object is, the easier it is for me find for some reason. I can't explain it very good but a few hundred miles is close to me. But if something is nearby it is easier for me to find if I know generally where to look within a few miles; it's like I have a dead zone from within a mile to a thousand miles."

"You mean like a telescope?"

"Yeah, sort of, I guess. That's why I haven't started flying, since I haven't spotted anything so far towards the west."

"Oh." Gina replied.

"Oh, wait. There're six helicopters thirty miles out, coming towards us."

"Do you know who they are and how long until they get here?"

The silence of the area was broken by aircraft engines. Steve looked up higher into the sky and spotted three F4 Phantoms. They were soaring high, circling like vultures. "The jets are Air Force it seems; a recon maybe?" Steve looked back at the helicopters.

Steve examined the crews as if he were looking at a close up movie action scene in great detail. "They're CIA. At least they're wearing agency gear and some of the identification cards and tags that I can make out... confirms it."

"You mean to tell me you can read an ID card from this distance through everything in between?"

"Well, as long as it's in English or Spanish." Steve smiled. "Do you want me to move you to a safe location until we find out their intentions?"

"No, they're a rescue team."

"You seem so sure... How do you know?"

"I'm the new regional chief for the western states." Gina slowly replied.

"So you would know their reactionary SOPs, and not tell me anything important like that until now?" Steve looked at her with a strict face.

"I guess, I might have been the target." Gina's said with a reflective straight face.

Steve thought about her past facial expressions and words, rolling over and over in his mind. She gave no indication of surprise or deception on the plane or when they were talking about who it was that attacked them or possible targets and motives. "For being the chief, you're kind of clueless as to our location, or did you know that too?"

"I was supposed to stop here in Nevada and continue to L.A."

"And you couldn't tell me the truth after I saved your life twice in the past thirty minutes?"

"I'm telling you now, instead of keeping the charade. I want you to know I won't tell anyone about what you can do and what happened here."

"Huh, you think I can stay and work for you?" Steve stood up facing her.

"With the things you can do, we can change everything in law enforcement and the country."

"What makes you think I'm the only person on the planet with these powers, or that I will agree in helping you or those people who seem to be trying very hard to kill us?"

"So you know there're more people like you?"

"Yeah, you can find them in the wanted ads looking for a job as we speak. How should I know? And besides; if there were, they wouldn't advertise it. I lived most of life hidden from people like you, until now."

"Steve, if that's your real name. Why did you join the agency?" Gina's tone raised as Steve turned to walk away.

Steve stopped walking and stared at the hanger's interior. "I wanted to make a difference, to learn about the world of spies and see if I could save lives, without a cape or Speedos." Steve half smiled.

"Nothing has changed Steve. I will help you and you will help me do what's right for this country and many people around the world."

Steve faced Gina, her bloody and soiled tangled hair blended in with the rest of her appearance. A dirty beggar/zombie kind of look, but a very beautiful one to him. "They'll be here soon. I'm going to go look for the people who fired the missile. If I return, then count me in. If I don't return, it's because I'm dead or decided to leave the agency."

"I will look for you, no matter what you decide."

"You'll won't find me if I want to disappear. But anyways, send a helo to the north after me. It was one vehicle and four people from what I could gather. Take care of yourself, Gina Pollas." Steve came up to her, bent over and kissed her on the forehead.

Gina quickly grabbed the back of his neck with both hands and pulled herself up to him, kissing him in the mouth.

Steve let her hot lips and tongue dominate him, as he gently squeezed and supported her upper arms with his hands.

Gina pulled away after a long moment, letting go of him. "Remember me at least, if you don't see me again."

Steve smiled. "My first day on the job and the boss falls for me. I would have joined a long time ago had I known." Steve turned away and silently flew out of the hanger.

Gina stared out into the opening, horizon and stars beyond. Then her attention moved to Nelson. She stretched out her hand and felt for a pulse. It was weak, but thankfully it existed.

The roaring of the jets high above continued, being overwhelmed by the rotors of three Chinooks and three Huey gunships. Spotlights blared over the tar mat within minutes, and agents armed to the tee stormed the hanger.

The agents secured the area and lowered their trained weapons on Gina and Nelson once they were identified and found safe.

"Ma'am, I'm Agent Kevin Aries. What happened here?" Kevin asked and motioned for medics to tend to both of them.

The middle aged man was massive in stature, resembling a professional NFL linebacker. His face was camouflaged black like the rest of his night Delta Force outfit.

"Our jet was shot down while descending. Agent Messer saved us and went after the attackers. I need you to send a team to help him out, towards the north." Gina twitched in pain as the medic touched her injuries.

"Sir, she's stable for now, but we need to take some x-rays and she'll need a cast as soon as possible." The medic reported.

"Get them ready for departure. Team four leader, come to my location now, and prepare for new orders." Kevin said on his mouth piece. "Ma'am, I'll send my best team to the north. In the meantime, we need to get you out of here."

"Wait… I need to talk to you alone right now."

Kevin motioned the agents to take Nelson away on a stretcher, and the security team to give them space. He bent over next to her head and turned off his radio.

"How loyal are your men?" She whispered.

Kevin turned his head towards her. "Ma'am, we will die for each other any day of the week?"

"I knew I would like you after I read your file back at Langley."

'Then you should know my men and I will back you up with our lives, you're safe with us Ma'am."

"There's a leak or a traitor in the agency. I need to disappear for a while for me to recover, and find out why we were attacked."

Kevin stood up and spoke out loud. "Consider it done Ma'am... Maximilian, I want you to meet our new boss."

A young agent carrying a sniper rifle as his main weapon, ran up to them. "Madam, I'm Randolph Maximilian and extremely honored to meet you."

"Max this is my best team leader. His team will search for the attackers and the pursing agent Messer. Is there anything in particular he should know before he goes?"

"They have ground to air missiles, so I don't know if sending a helicopter is the best idea. But I'm sure that agent Messer will have neutralized that threat by then."

"How long ago was it since agent Messer left in pursuit of the vehicle?" Max asked.

"A few minutes ago."

"A few minutes ago?" Kevin echoed, a little confused.

"It's hard to explain, but by the time you get there he will have done most of the work for us. There is also a dead sniper out there so you need to clean up the scene before your last man leaves here."

"My guys found ten dead agents in the other hanger, remains of several people from the plane, but we haven't accounted for all the passengers, which might be scattered for several miles. In the meantime... Attention, all personnel, code name Shakespeare. Repeat, Shakespeare." Kevin said over the radio as he gave the okay hand and arm signal to Max as he ran off to hunt down the attackers.

"Shakespeare?" Gina asked as Kevin faced her.

"It's our internal codename for this kind of contingency. We'll make a cover for what happened here with no survivors. The attackers will all also be reported as killed, even if we get prisoners. We'll take you to our main office in the TS levels where we can attend to your medical needs and hide you, Nelson and Messer."

"Are the helo pilots your men too?"

"Yes, Ma'am. The pilots in the jets as well. We pride ourselves for being independent from outside assistance. We are always ready to react when new personnel come to this site, but honestly, this was a total surprise. I didn't know you were on board the plane until the Mayday was flagged by Langley, then us."

"Well, at least it makes it easier for you to report me dead without any weird explanations."

"I would normally agree with you, but is agent Messer going to blow this cover?"

"No, he's special… he's some kind of superman."

Kevin looked at her and then at the empty makeshift medical beds. "So, you're saying he's some kind of superhero like the Flash? I was wondering how all of this was done in the amount of time it took us to get here?" he said waving a hand.

"Superman would best describe him."

"I'm not going to disagree with you Ma'am seeing that you're alive, but you know there will be many people that will call you crazy or want proof."

"Yes, I know and that's why everything here has to be covered up until I can get agent Messer to continue helping us, and find the people trying to kill me and the project."

"I agree, and with that, I'll call you agent Lincoln from now on." Kevin said as three agents grabbed Gina and moved her on a stretcher.

"And don't worry, this place isn't on file and you don't exist." Kevin said as he focused on getting all his men on board with the cover plan, to include leaving a reception team for Langley's replacement of the people to occupy the secret airfield and strengthen its defenses.

North of Area 51, Nevada

Steve flew short of the speed of sound over the mountain range. The plant life seemed to create a sheet of a solid three dimensional topographical layer on the ground. There were many patches of spaces where he could see into the earth, but he didn't try to concentrate on these patches or plants since he was flying too fast and close to the ground. The vehicle left tracks, but he didn't want to slow down to analyze them. Instead he sped up knowing that if the people made it to taller trees or a highway with other vehicles and directions, then it would make finding them a lot harder. Steve looked out twenty miles as he flew, scanning slowly from side to side at a 45 degree span. Ten miles out beyond the mountain's base, a few dirt animal trails appeared, but no sign of people or a vehicle. Steve looked back and could barely make out pieces of helicopters at or around the tar mat. The fighter jets continued to circle the area ready to provide an air strike if needed. The foliage was too great for him to see through the mountain in fine detail, and he hoped Gina was right that he hadn't left her and Nelson to be killed or captured by the bad guys.

He turned his attention to the front, ensuring he flew a hundred meters above the ground as not to get hit by insects or debris from the desert night air currents.

Finally, the vehicle he was looking for was struggling to speed through the rugged terrain. The lights were dimmed which reduced their speed and made their getaway more difficult, but they had covered over twenty-five miles which was impressive when compared to a highly trained military special operations team. Steve could make out details of the attackers as he soared silently through the night sky. They were wearing mercenary gear, a mixture of military and civilian hunting uniforms and equipment, with commercially and privately customized modified weaponry. Steve's in-depth research on weaponry and world militaries paid off to some degree. However, he still couldn't make out if they were American, European, or Hispanic. But one thing was sure; they weren't from the Orient or African.

Steve focused on any face, but it blurred the more he concentrated. At his speed, he would soon be on top of the modified large jeep. It seemed like an African expedition vehicle with a back mounted launcher system. The two prong launcher held one ten foot missile, the same as the one which hit the plane. It was retracted so the warhead was facing towards the front of the jeep. Steve's clear vision was now going in and out of focus. He shook his head and rubbed his eyes as if trying to reset them, feeling like an electronic camera with dying batteries.

Steve took a deep breath and zoomed out so he could just see the vehicle popping up dust in its wake. The passengers of the elongated jeep thought they hit a big freaky rock as they heard and felt a very loud thump underneath them. The jeep lifted up forty feet and swirled multiple times. One of the mercenaries shot out of an opened door as the centrifugal force took him by surprise. The men yelled in fear as one would expect when facing disaster at the hands of gravity and uncontrolled extreme velocities.

Steve groaned as the weight of the jeep almost exceeded his max lift capacity. The spinning didn't help either, something he hadn't planned on so he tried to fly in the opposite direction he came from and land the jeep on solid ground. The jeep hit the ground sideways and would have flipped several times, but Steve held tight to the underbelly of the vehicle, stopping the first flip. The jeep rested upside down with the missile warhead going off skipping everyone's near death experience into a worse situation.

Flak and heat burned the three passengers alive, if they weren't already dead from the vehicle's harsh stop, missile explosion, or secondary explosions of grenades in the vehicle.

Steve was blown backwards into the air. "You got to be kidding me!" He yelled as his T-Shirt and fatigues were half burnt or torn off his body with the under carry of the jeep keeping the explosion focused on the passengers and ground.

All three men were dead so Steve turned in the direction of the one guy who didn't wear his seatbelt. He flew towards him, scanning his body at the same time. The man was unconscious with two broken shoulder blades, several nasty ruptured vertebrates and abrasions all throughout the back of his legs and back.

"What's going on!" Steve screamed in frustration or was it bad luck, as the man was also on top of a toppled cactus arm.

Steve grabbed the man at the most effective points on his body without injuring him further and moved him to a clear spot on the ground. "Well, it's a good thing I'm here, cuz you're going to live."

Steve removed all of the hundreds of cactus needles in seconds, and positioned the vertebrates to maximize reduced pressure. He flew back to the burning jeep and recovered pieces of metal and scrapes to make a frame for the man. In a few minutes, the man's upper body was immobilized by a cage looking network of car parts. The abrasions were a little different. Steve didn't have the medical bag or things to help the man's open cuts, so he used the remains of his T-shirt to cover most of the wounds and reduce bleeding.

"Now that I think about it some more, you're this way because I am here, or was it because you came to this desert, or following your destiny? Hmm, it's a conundrum I or the CIA will most likely never be able to answer."

Steve looked down at the man and then in the direction of the hanger. "Lucky for you the good guys are coming this way. But they're going to take too long to find you, even with the fire blaring."

Steve looked around making sure no wildlife around would attack the helpless bad guy while he left the man there alone. Once satisfied, he flew off towards the oncoming helicopter.

'Steve, I need your help. Come to me before it's too late.' A young woman's voice said in Steve's mind.

"Gina?" Steve said and thought, but the voice didn't sound like Gina's voice.

A surge of mental pictures and memories blinded him as he flew aimlessly into the ground, then back into the air. The horizon and everything around him seemed to go in circles as he fell into unconsciousness.

Maximilian and his team spotted the burning vehicle in the distance. Their night vision goggles assisted greatly from such a stretch of land, but they failed to see Steve laying face down in the midst of desert foliage; two miles from the dead mercenaries and soon to be Prisoner 1 of the Special Investigation Agency.

Chapter Two

❖---✳ ✪ ✳---❖

Not Feeling It

A lbert took a sip from the rum at his side. It ran smoothly down his throat. The icy alcohol dispersed into his entire body as his cells filtered any destructive properties. Albert's black hair extended down to his shoulders which gave him a much older look with a pirate type of appeal. He was young however, especially compared to the collection of veteran gamblers around the exclusive table.

"What are you going to do with all that money if you have to go to Nam?" A gray haired well rounded gentleman asked, on Albert's right.

Albert turned towards the bearded man who seemed to have come from a Louisiana plantation. In fact he was a wealthy plantation owner. His white overcoat and very small circular silver and black designs on his vest made him stand out among the group. Not to mention his pearl white wide tie, stained with sweat from several hours of playing.

"I'm not sure, but I'll deal with that if it happens."

An elderly but rough looking man across the table eyed Albert. "He's a toothpick; the Marine Corps will eat him alive."

"Didn't you say you were a scientist?" A modestly sexy red haired lady asked as she hugged the old man's arm.

"Yes, I did. In the field of synthetic computer systems. And I call." Albert said as he flipped over his remaining cards, leaving three kings and a pair of jacks.

The last two players flipped their hands in defeat.

"Mr. Hansen's hand wins." The dealer announced as a mixture of moans and awes erupted audibly and mentally.

Albert almost smiled as he saw the thoughts of the eldest man. *'He must be gay or something. He's not paying enough attention to Elena's boobs and exposed cleavage.'*

'He reminds me of James, when he was younger.' Elena thought.

The Louisiana Plantation owner breathed heavily with anxiety. *'I can't lose any more money. Please, God, help me!'*

'I'm going to have to keep an eye out for this guy. He doesn't seem to be cheating.' A heavy set man in his mid forties wearing a very expensive brown suit thought. One of the players who was taking the opportunity to learn from the masters.

Albert read the thoughts of the two mafia connected players and the other very experienced players trying to figure out how to get out of their losing streak. He wasn't worried about winning and possibly being a target by the mafia for extortion of some sort. If it had crossed his mind, it didn't register to him one bit.

They were invested for the most part and the eldest, James

McCormick, was willing to lose all of his budgeted half a million dollars just for the pleasure of the gamble.

Albert was already at $300,000 winnings, which should have been enough for him, but today was the day he would be the ruler of his own destiny. The many statements of a book he recently read kept him motivated to accomplish the goals he had set his mind to.

The long hours at the table started to take its toll as a new dealer started the next round. Claire was in her mid thirties with a pleasant face. Her long brown hair was in a ponytail and her elegant glasses gave her a sense of an experienced dealer at the high stakes poker table.

Albert concentrated on Claire's thoughts, but it wasn't like the past several hours. The thoughts were sporadic at best, as if there was a fast forward button and he couldn't clearly see the video.

Claire dealt quickly as Albert drank water, hoping his mind reading ability got better.

His hand was a strong one, and he knew the initial hand of the other players, but for how long? *'I need to raise the stakes before I can't read anyone's mind'* Albert thought.

Raising and checking brought the pot to $250,000, but to Albert's dismay, the thoughts of the people around him had completely faded away into a fuzz of nothingness.

He concentrated on James, Elena and then on Luther, the plantation owner, since James and Luther were the only ones not folding or simply trying to stay in the game. *'Nothing?'* Albert thought to himself in alarm.

James stared Albert down. "You don't seem to be playing like before... I'll raise, all in."

Albert thought about James' initial hand of two queens, and he traded in three cards. Albert had four of a kind, four nines. There were no wilds or jokers, so the odds of him having the better hand was in his favor.

"I fold." Luther replied.

"I call." Albert smiled, his unshaven face gave him a roughness and attraction some women admired.

The crowd silently waited after an expressive awe once Albert turned over the last nine of diamonds.

James eyed Albert and nodded as if agreeing to an invisible contract or rite of passage. "I enjoyed it while it lasted. Thank you." James turned over his remaining cards: four queens.

Albert dumbfounded, stared at the cards and then at the chips moving away from him. "Well, it was a pleasure Mr. McCormick. I was just not feeling it." He sighed and smiled.

Albert didn't waste any time leaving the immediate area, but once he got through the crowd and near the roulette tables, he slowed his pace in deep thought.

His room was paid for already and he still had three hundred dollars in his pocket. So he looked around for a while as if mapping out the casino floor. He went up to his room on the eleventh floor and sat at the head of the bed. His blank stare at the turned off television changed to a tighten jaw as he looked on top of the nightstand.

He grabbed a black book next to the hotel clock. It read: "What Would I Do If I Could Read Minds? By Carl Hawking". Albert took a deep breath and stood up with the book in hand. He pitched it in the trash can as he walked up to the room's front door. Instead of opening the door, Albert disappeared. His phantom like body instantly moved through it. He flew down through the floors as if they didn't exist. Before long, Albert was floating in front of the casino vault. It was closed at the moment and it would be opened when money would be counted and consolidated on the routine schedule.

But, Albert floated there for a while, thinking about his own ideas of what he would do next. He had lost all of his savings and income from selling all he had, trying to follow the book of proven 'Success'.

He flew inside and placed his hands among money stacks. The money mixed in with his phantom like body properties, allowing him to grab bands of money and also making them invisible and intangible. Fortunately, the inside of the vault was lit for him to see and there was a camera, but Albert's invisibility gave no warning or evidence of a crime. He approximated three to four hundred thousand dollars and then flew out of the vault and back to his room. He counted and bagged the money in a backpack, checked out and left Las Vegas, flying invisibly towards California.

Albert made a modest purchase on his own Los Angeles beach front property two months later. The four bedroom home was very elegant, but what made him happiest was the deck facing the pool and ocean. The night salt air brought peace to him as he drank a pineapple smoothie with a little kick, out on the wooden deck with a pile of notebooks on a patio table.

The quarter moon made the ocean glisten as the sound of the waves soothed his thoughts of starting a computer company business. The dreams of the future changed in a matter of seconds as darkness enveloped him.

'Albert, I need your help. Please come to me before countless people die.' A young female voice blurted in Albert's head.

Albert tried to speak, but he couldn't and found himself outside of his body. 'Is this a dream? I don't remember falling asleep.' Many flashes of memories surprised him, taking him away from the deck and into a pit of sounds, people and places.

Aliens and battles in wars were seen in seconds, nothing distinct popping out at him except Capitol Hill in flames and the sky scorched by a green Sun. He wasn't sure if the visions were all from Earth, because there were aircraft and ships he never saw before except in science fiction movies or shows. Rock creatures from what seemed to be hell, fought against him and other people he also never saw before. He blacked out and awoke face first on the deck floor.

The sound of the waves helped bring him back to his senses. His forehead was bruised from hitting the table's edge and floor, but it was minor since it would completely heal within the hour. Albert got up and looked around as if he was being spied on. There were no people in his view. The neighboring houses were occupied, evidenced by the lights and noise of music in the far distance. "At least I'm not alone." Albert said, thinking he had experienced an Omega Man apocalyptic event.

Albert touched his smoothie. It was still cold, so he couldn't have been passed out for very long.

'Please Albert, I need you.' The female voice said in his mind, but this time he didn't get dizzy or anything.

"Who is this?"

'I'm Cassandra Leavan, Queen of the Andromen Empire. The mental visions I gave you will gradually become clear and organized, but what's important for now is you need to follow that tug you're feeling in your heart.

"I don't know you, how do I know you're not lying?

'You don't, but the more you resist this craving you're feeling now, the stronger it will get. In time you will not be able to function properly, even with your special powers.' Cassandra replied, making Albert feel as if she was emotionless by her cold tone.

"Well lady, I'll go only because it seems I have no choice. But you're going to have to keep your panty on while I make arrangements to leave my new house with a house sitter." Albert walked inside the house mumbling to himself.

'You know I can hear every thought you have right now?'

Albert stopped and looked up at the ceiling. "Sorry, I didn't mean to call you that."

Albert waited for a response, but nothing. "Hello, are you there?"

Silence.

"Well, maybe I did mean some of it." Albert smiled as he started to lock down the house and make calls to his few friends.

An hour later, he flew off to the west. The moon was gone, but he could make out the dark water underneath him and the stars above. The LA coastline also gave him a reference of the horizon behind him, but soon there was nothing but darkness below him and a partly cloudy sky with stars above.

The craving like an addiction was in his blood and helped him keep to the right direction as it got stronger when he turned in the wrong direction. At least he hoped it was the right direction where ever he was going. He hadn't seen any ships in a while and if this was a wild goose chase, he would have to wait for daylight to fly towards the morning Sun to get back home. Well, that was if he was flying west all this time.

Albert was invisible and intangible the entire two hours of his flight. He must have flown at least 400 miles. But the rising Sun in front of him told him otherwise.

'What's this? How the hell?' Albert thought as an island appeared on the horizon along with daylight.

The craving left him once he was within rock throwing distance from shore. The island measured a little over three miles, which made it easy for him to fly around looking for whatever he was supposed to find. He flew high above the trees and spotted a tall man and teenager sitting on a log in the shade along the shoreline to the north.

Albert flew down a few meters above them so he could ease drop on them and see their faces.

"How long do you think we have to wait here?" The teenager asked, looking at the dirty sand next to the log.

"If I knew, I would be the genius." Gus said with a very heavy voice, being at least six and a half feet tall and extremely muscle bond.

Benjamin looked at Gus. "Hey what's that?" He pointed across his chest towards the trees.

Gus turned to look. "What? I don't see anything."

Albert also saw nothing from his vantage point.

"Have you ever had the feeling you were being spied on?" Ben stood up and faced the west towards the jungle.

"No, never." Gus turned back to the front enjoying the blue and white waves.

"I'm telling you that someone is watching us."

"Should I give them my famous pose?" Gus stood in a front double bicep stance.

"Ahhh... this isn't a contest. We're in the middle of nowhere because the lady told us to come here. Well! Here we are Your Majesty! Now what?" Ben walked out turning in all directions towards the water.

Gus stopped posing and smiled at his best friend. "Well at least there's no lake around here to worry about, so we wait."

"What? What lake?" Ben asked with a goofy frown.

"If there were a lake I would be expecting Excalibur to pop out. I thought you were the genius?" Gus smiled exposing his bright white rows of perfect teeth.

"You know you're right!"

Albert made a puzzled face, but no one could tell.

"Since there's an ocean and not a lake, we should be expecting Leviathan, or better yet, Godzilla!"

"Hmm, yeah, I prefer Excalibur, but for now, we'll have to settle for that guy."

Ben and Albert with slack-jawed faces looked at Gus, but then turned to where Gus was looking, out into the ocean.

Steve had flown at top speed, but slowed down greatly as he approached the three of them. He came within twenty feet from them, floating above the sand, with the waterline behind him. "Greetings. Now, who's in charge?"

"That would be me." Ben stated.

Steve folded his muscular arms, standing in midair. His tattered dirty and bloody fatigues, topless and no shoes made him look formidable. "What about that guy back there?"

"Who, Gus? He's strong and all but I'm the brains." Ben replied.

"No I was talking about the guy acting like he's one with the bushes."

Ten meters in the wood line, a man stood up as if he were a bush. The colors of his skin and clothing changed to that of a normal human. He wore a Special Forces sniper uniform, but carried no weapons. His boonie hat and shades covered his face as he walked up to Gus and Ben.

"Hello, I'm Aaron."

"I'm Gus Madex and my young friend is Benjamin Dempsey." Gus stuck out his hand.

"Aaron Fisher, good to meet you Gus." Aaron shook his hand and waved at Ben and Steve. "Good to meet you all."

"I'm Steve Messer, but all of us aren't here yet." Steve said and floated down on the ground next to Ben.

"No, everyone's here." Ben said. He was five feet five inches tall and slender. His curly dark brown hair gave him the image of a nerdy teenager, but his demeanor was that of a military tactician.

"Really? How do you know?" Steve asked.

"Because I'm the genius and there's still someone spying on us."

'*Who's this kid?*' Albert thought as he looked at all of the people below him. He read Ben's mind, but he was thinking of many things at the same time, confusing him.

"Well, you heard Ben, show yourself, whoever you are!" Gus commanded.

Albert became tangible and visible above them. He wore a tropical long sleeve white shirt and pants, with casual canvas shoes. "How did you know I was here?"

"I'm a genius and since I saw five people in the visions, calculating the time the four of us have met, I knew there was another person here with special powers."

"You fell for his bluff." Aaron commented.

"He made an educated guess." Gus smiled.

"Who are you?" Steve asked.

"My name is Albert Hansen. Cassandra told me many people were going to die, including me, if I didn't follow her orders."

"She told me she was in danger and worlds would be doomed if she died." Aaron contradicted.

"She told us we were going to save the galaxy." Gus said.

There was an eerie silence from the group even from the ocean as if it was Steve's turn to speak.

"What did she tell you Steve?" Ben asked.

Steve looked at the group with a straight face. "She told me I was the leader."

Ben squinted his eyes a little and almost grunted with aggravation. '*I should have thought of that.*' He thought.

Albert smiled as he could see everyone's surface thoughts. Steve lied and everyone knew it or had doubts but didn't want to lead, except for Ben. Albert knew best from what he could see that Steve was best suited for leadership. "I support Steve as leader and suggest we reveal our history and special abilities so we can do whatever the lady in distress wants us to do."

"Is that what you want us to do Steve?" Gus asked, treating him as the leader already without a vote.

"Yes, that's exactly what I want, so I'll go first." Steve said and told the group about his training with the CIA, short lived work as an agent and all his special abilities.

Albert saw that Gus and Ben were most impressed by Steve's claim to being almost indestructible and seeing through solid and liquid matter millions of miles out.

"If you can see that far, have you ever seen aliens?" Gus asked.

"No, I don't look up at the sky all of the time, but even if I did, I'm sure I or all the observatories around the world would have reported a sighting." Steve answered, unsure if Gus was serious about the question.

"Ah…" Gus glanced at the ground in disappointment.

"I think I'll go next, because this is taking way too long, and I don't want to hear the same thing twice. I can turn invisible and intangible." Albert said as he floated down with his legs disappearing into the sand.

"Nice." Ben awed a smile.

"I don't have to eat for a very long time, or sleep for weeks, I can fly as fast as a commercial airplane, I can transmute small non-living objects into a jell-like matter, and I can read minds." Albert put up his hand to stop Gus and Steve from speaking, floating back up to normal altitude on the sand.

"And yes I know what all of you have been thinking. Aaron, you're a Special Forces sniper. You left the jungle of Nam to come here. Your powers are similar to Steve's except you're not as tough, you can't see as far or through objects, but you can see in the darkness and your other four senses are enhanced. You also have energy powers to make a force field for protection and... a laser beam comes out of your hands."

Aaron nodded approval. Albert failed to inform the group that he was a killing machine for the military with thirty-eight confirmed assassinations, but now Aaron was given the opportunity to do something besides killing for the government.

Albert turned to Ben, "Ben is a genius and heals very fast, but you have to eat a lot. Gus, you are strong enough to lift several tons, very tough and... are, a flying rat?" Albert didn't believe what he was reading in Gus' mind.

"Yes, well when I'm a rat, I can fly and destroy many things with a sonic screech. I can also tunnel through the ground very fast." Gus added.

"Of course you can." Steve smiled.

"Ben, how did you get here?" Aaron asked.

"I flew with Gus, why?"

"Oh." Aaron imagined a teenager being held by a small rodent flying through the clouds.

Albert laughed. "Gus, can you please turn into the rat so everyone understands and doesn't freak out later."

Gus instantly turned into a three-foot black rat, his tail making him six feet long. His eyes were different as if glowing white while he looked at the group members, perched on the log. "I heard all the rat jokes, so don't worry, I will make fun of you guys too."

"Now that introductions are out of the way, now what?" Ben asked.

"We search the island together and find out why we were all led here." Steve said.

"Why don't you use your vision to recon the island?" Aaron asked.

"Because he can't see through plant life." Albert replied.

"Ah." Steve glanced at Albert in approval for answering the question. "I have been looking in all directions since I arrived and we don't seem to be stationary. So what we're looking for might not be on the island at the moment. But, I might be wrong." Steve stated.

"How are we not stationary?" Albert asked what Aaron and Gus thought.

"I can't see beyond fifty miles and if you haven't noticed yet, there used to be clouds, now there's not a cloud in the sky." Steve stated.

"The Sun is directly above us. Where did the hours go?" Gus added.

"We seem to be in a time shift, or displacement field." Ben theorized as he squeezed grains of sand in his hand.

"Is that a good thing?" Aaron asked.

"It all depends if Cassandra was telling the truth. But I think we should check out that ship sticking out of the ground to the south." Steve said.

"What ship? I didn't see it there when I got here." Albert said as he saw Steve's mental picture of a half buried battleship in a clearing near the shore.

"Follow me." Steve said and slowly flew in that direction, picking up speed as he saw everyone fly behind him.

Steve landed on a grassy spot centralized in front of the ship. Aaron and Albert landed next to him. Ben with a rat on his back flew towards one of the turrets. "Stop, don't touch it! It's radioactive!"

The teenager swirled around holding on to Gus's front limbs. "Why didn't you tell us that before?" Gus's squeaky voice was loud.

"Follow me, means follow me, not go ahead of me!"

"Oh, I see how this is going to work. Are we going to have to ask permission for everything? Ben asked as Gus flew them down in front of the trio.

"For now, yes. We need to work better together and build trust so we don't have problems like this later." Steve explained.

"I understand the mechanics of leadership." Ben countered.

"What's with the attitude then?" Steve replied.

"Can I interrupt?" Aaron jumped in.

"I like you Steve. You reacted like I had hoped." Ben said, as Gus changed back into his human self, standing behind the teenager.

"Good to know. Go ahead Aaron." Steve said.

'If the ship is radioactive, why is there green foliage on it?"

Loud thunder responded to Aaron's question, and the ground quaked violently. Gus instantaneously turned back into a rat and flew up a foot above the ground. Everyone else did the same, except Ben who fell on the grass trying to get on all fours. Gus quickly picked him off the ground, which shook for fifteen or so seconds.

"Look!" Albert pointed at the sky.

A bright light flickered into a beam of light. A rainbow effect trailed a black dot, streaking into the ship. The thunder and tremors instantly stopped as a loud hollow clang ended the event.

"It's a man with a skateboard." Steve said, looking at the new visitor and then concentrated on the ship's structure. "And the ship isn't radioactive anymore."

"Maybe it never was. But it doesn't matter. Let's go see if this guy needs our help." Aaron said, referring to the vines at the base of the hull, then at where the visitor disappeared from normal view.

The group flew on top of the ship's 16 inch forward gun turret. The gunhouse metal was aged as if the ship had been exposed to the elements for decades. A man-sized hole was on the lower deck wall.

Steve saw a medium height man wearing a silver and red space suit. The space suit was similar to an old black and white science fiction movie, except the helmet was of a jet fighter pilot helmet design. He didn't have a backpack and his mouth and chin was exposed. The man had an African-American complexion, with an Afro a few inches long. The skateboard was four feet long, with thirty-two small wheels. Its makeup was of a weird alloy, which he had trouble seeing through.

"We'll wait here for him. He's dazed, but he's getting up just fine."

Steve said.

"Stranger, we're friendly! Come out when you're feeling better!" Gus yelled.

"If he speaks English, he'll be so willing to talk to us." Ben sarcastically placed his hands on his waist and walked around at a slant, examining the ship.

"I'll go get him." Albert said and disappeared.

"Okay… Ben, what do you see?" Steve asked.

"The ship has been exposed to the air or buried for at least a few years. You would think there would be more corrosion with the salt water, but this doesn't make sense. Can you tell me what kinds of materials are inside the rooms?" Ben looked at Steve.

"Looks like all of the rooms at ground level and below are filled with earth. The rest is filled with air. There are no skeletons or equipment either." Steve slowly said at the end of the sentence.

"It has to be a displacement field then."

"You mean the ship was teleported?" Aaron asked.

"Yes, very good Aaron." Ben smiled with surprise.

"You know, this reminds me of a show of the Bermuda Triangle, I saw on In Search Of." Gus commented.

"I can't see any identification. Aaron, Ben, please go to the bridge down there and find out anything you can about this ship. Gus and I will wait for Albert and our new visitor." Steve pointed down to a large box with portals half buried in the ground.

"Hop on my back Ben." Aaron turned away from him.

"One of these days, I'm going to make myself a Jetpack or something." Ben said as he piggy backed on Aaron's back.

Aaron flew down to the bridge, while Steve slowly flew to the opening. "Albert has revealed himself and I think he's done talking to the visitor." Steve said with Gus floating next to him.

Steve entered the room covering up any light coming in from the new hole, but Gus widened the hole with his bare hands when it was his turn to enter.

"Steve, this is Arbitrator from the land of Cilos." Albert said as metallic bending and cracking sounded in the background.

"Cilos? I never heard of it."

"It's a wondrous place far from here. But let us get out of this room so I can meet all of you." Arbitrator said with a Jamaican accent, as he held his skateboard under his arm like a surfer.

Gus stepped into the slanted room with a prideful grin, turning gloom as Steve motioned him to go back outside. "Sorry big guy, but thanks for the large whole." Steve said while Gus smiled once again.

"You're welcome Steve." Gus allowed Steve to pass and waited for Arbitrator and Albert. "Nice to meet you, Arbitrator."

"You must be Lord Rat Bastard?" Arbitrator revealed a bright and perfect white smile while extending his free hand.

"Ahh, yeah, I must be." Gus' confused face said it all, trying to be his usual polite self and shook his hand.

The four flew towards the ground away from the ship; Arbitrator stylishly using his flying skateboard. It wasn't long before Ben and Aaron joined them at Steve's beckoning.

"What happened?" Aaron asked as they landed.

"Aaron, Ben, this is Arbitrator. An alien from another galaxy." Albert stated.

"What? I thought you were from somewhere in the Caribbean Islands or something." Gus interjected.

"No. Lord Rat Bastard, I am as Lord Ghost has said. I'm from the galaxy you call Andromeda."

"Wow, I knew ETs were real!" Gus joyfully smiled.

"So it seems." Steve said with a raised doubtful eyebrow and crossed arms.

"Queen Cassandra Leavan instructed me to come here and take you to the imperial outer marker so you can organize an offensive against Korvax Bac'dir and retake the kingdom." Arbitrator floated inches above the sand as his body rotated looking into each man's and the teenager's eyes.

"I have long since waited to meet the five of you." Arbitrator knelt on his board. "My, Lords."

"What are we lords of?" Steve asked but looked at Albert, knowing he already knew why Arbitrator seemed to treat them as if they were royalty or legends of some sort.

"It is written that the five Lords from Earth would come to save the galaxy from destruction. The ancient writings were passed down by our king six hundred years ago, but I have seen with my own eyes the things which have and will come to pass. You are Lords of Arlos and the Queen's Champions."

"So I'm a Lord already, I don't have to do something to become a Lord?" Ben asked.

"Yes, Lord Master." Arbitrator slowly stood up.

"Master… I like that." Ben scrutinized Arbitrator's body language.

"If he's Ghost, Rat Bastard and Master, then who are we?" Steve pointed at the three, then at himself and Aaron.

"You are Lord Stargazer and you my lord." Arbitrator faced Aaron. "You go by many names, but many call you Lord Spot."

"So where we're going, does everyone know use?" Ben asked.

"Lord Master. Everyone does not believe in the legends, but once you arrive, there will be many who will rally behind you."

"So we came here to be taken to another galaxy to win a war we didn't start?" Aaron asked.

"Wasn't that what you were doing yesterday?" Gus countered.

Aaron stared at Gus, his strong jaws were relaxed, eyes as soft as a dove. "Yeah, you're right." Aaron half smiled.

"Sounds good to me, but one thing Arbitrator. I would like to be addressed as Master, no need to put Lord in front of it." Ben stated with a wide smile.

Steve smiled and uncrossed his arms. "Okay from now on, let's stick to one naming game and use Stargazer, Master, Spot, Ghost and Rat Bastard."

"I think it's time to go." Arbitrator said and pointed up at the sky. A hole in the fabric of the blue atmosphere revealed space and stars.

"Wait! How's this going to work? I still have some questions." Ben asked as Arbitrator floated a few feet above the ground. His skateboard hummed and glowed underneath as if revving up for a drag race.

"I was sent here with the queen's power and cannot control the vortex rift, my young Lord."

Albert stared at Steve. Steve's gaze bared on the horizon out at sea. "Are you alright?"

Steve paused to answer. "Yeah, I'm just wishing I had dated sooner." Steve turned to Albert with a weak smile.

Albert finished his grin. "It's okay Steve, we'll be back soon so I can be your chaperone."

"Thank you for caring." Steve almost laughed out loud and looked at Gus, motioning him to pick Ben up then turned toward Arbitrator. "Do we fly with you holding hands or something?"

"No, my Lord Stargazer. I will loop back around and teleport you to the rift, it will take you to the outer marker. If, I'm not there when you arrive, no worries. I will be with you as soon as I can."

"Why won't you be there?" Aaron yelled.

"I pop in and out as nature takes me." Arbitrator said as he flew off a few hundred meters out and quickly returned. "But you my Lords are not bound by nature!"

A white light appeared in front of Arbitrator. The group saw the flash and instantly were pushed into space. Ben held tight to Gus's arm as they drawn into a black hole the size of the moon. Steve looked in the direction of Earth now several hundred thousand miles away. The quick glimpse of the planet only confirmed that they had teleported into space and his thoughts went to Ben. Surely Ben wouldn't be able to survive in a vacuum. But, the time it took to take a breath, the blackness had erased all the stars. Steve and probably only Aaron could see the five of them floating in empty space. The coldness and heat of space was somehow nonexistent. Steve looked around as far as he could see, but saw only darkness around the group. He tried to speak, but it all seemed as if he was in a dream where the laws of physics and metaphysics baffled him.

The darkness swiftly faded away as the interior of a landing bay replaced it. The five hit the metallic floor at various angles. Aaron tumbled into an upright stance, while Steve slid on his back. Gus tumbled also, but it was an uncontrolled landing, breaking Ben's arm. Albert flew into the floor several feet before he flew out, standing on top of the metallic structure next to Steve.

"That was fun." Albert sarcastically mumbled as dizziness hit him for a few seconds.

All of the men felt the dizziness, except for Ben, who screamed in pain.

"Stargazer." Aaron warned as everyone else was looking at Ben's suffering. "We got company."

The landing bay was enormous, but there was only one spaceship looking craft a hundred meters away. A company size element of suited humanoids carrying weapons raced to their location from all directions. "Ghost, take the boy and hide. We will see if they're friendly." Steve ordered.

Steve looked at the people approaching and the surroundings they had materialized into. They were in a space port as if from a real science fiction movie set. But there were no cameras or fake props. The humanoids were human-like as far as he could tell, but they had fur or were very hairy humans at a glance. They were also wearing sophisticated body armored spacesuits. The weapons were a mixture of energy based or projectile, but they were too alien for him to fully determine. There were twelve decks up and five decks down that his vision would allow him to penetrate with great detail before open space. He looked at the spacecraft and it seemed to be under repair; a shuttlecraft of some sort, seating about fifty passengers. The open view of space in the distance indicated that there was some sort of energy force field keeping an atmosphere inside the bay. He finally focused on the approaching people while he stood up.

Ghost grabbed Ben's arm and they both turned invisible and floated through the floor. The dematerialized ghost form helped Ben cope with the now not so painful dangling forearm. "Don't worry, no one can hurt us or see us right now." Ghost said.

Master looked at Ghost. All common sense would say that he shouldn't be able to hear or see him, but he too was in another plane of existence and the laws of common sense were thrown out the window a long time ago.

They flew down into a gap between the landing bay floor and another compartment or deck below them. Ghost continued to fly down until there was light and he could see where they were. They entered a large room full of cargo in the form of large crates the size of houses. "We'll wait here for now. I hope the people in this place are friendly." Ghost said as he held Master by the waist.

"What about my arm?" Master said holding his forearm up in front of his face.

"Hmm, well I can set it now, that way it won't hurt as much later." Ghost grabbed the forearm with his free hand and moved it to its normal position. "Hold it there for now."

Ben felt almost no pain at all, but that didn't help because he knew once he left the ghost world, the nerves would start blaring again.

Up on top, Stargazer stood next to Spot, while Rat Bastard stood behind them facing the rear.

"Do you think they'll be able to understand us?" Rat Bastard asked from behind.

"Arbitrator spoke our language so I hope they do too." Stargazer replied.

"Don't you find that kind of weird that the aliens know English?" Spot commented.

"If we really are in the Andromeda galaxy right now, then no." Stargazer said and walked forward a few paces and raised his opened hands.

"I'm Lord Stargazer, we come in peace!"

Chapter Three

❖---✻ ✪ ✻---❖

Destroyer of Ordis

Janu Barrier Defense Grid Command Center, Andromeda Galaxy

A lively group of reserve Soldiers and technicians watched the broadcast of the Ordis defense campaign. The war started days ago, but the first signs of enemy ships making an aggressive action entered the star system minutes ago commencing the Battle of Janu, an orbital outpost. The central news signal brought up a live transmission by the enemy forces of the Kalar.

A very large stone like giant with a modified space helmet resembling a Roman gladiator, articulately spoke their language. “Inhabitants of Ordis, you have failed to surrender and have been sentenced to death.”

The transmission was replaced with a view of a glowing yellow figure of a man flying through space besides a star cruiser. The cruiser was half the size of a US aircraft carrier, but the brilliance of the figure overshadowed the spaceship as if a small star passed by it in seconds. The camera view changed several times as many sensors tracked the star like figure blaze into an Ordis Battlestar spaceship, coming out the other end as the ship exploded into a nuclear ball of light and heat. The audio was on, but the vacuum of space made it look like a silent color movie clip in high definition.

The Ordis space fleet maneuvered thousands of ships to attack the figure. Small and large armored and energy protected ships warped within weapons range of already destroyed ships near the figure.

Thousands of laser beams burst out of the figure in all directions expanding into arches defying the laws of energy as the beams moved faster than the speed of light. Many of the sensors sending the video transmissions in space blacked out as the beams passed through anything in their way.

Aboard the bridge of the Kalar flagship, Commander Paldar, Chief Executer Bhala, a scientific task force and crew members viewed the battle screen. A three-dimensional computerized representation of Cyer's assault clearly showed his progress and destruction.

The scientific task force comprised of eight experts in warfare and genetics. A narrator spoke as Cyer dashed across the battle screen, the onboard computer matching his movement. "Sir, the battle damage assessment computer cannot keep up with the genowraith." One of the scientists reported.

Commander Paldar turned his head to Bhala. "Did you expect this to happen?"

Clusters of explosions and light followed Cyer's movement on the screen as the viewpoints constantly changed trying to keep up with him. Executer Bhala's stone like face smiled. "I didn't expect it to be this fast. He's already obliterated the fleet and I don't think they had enough time to decide to try to escape."

"Sir, the genowraith's energy and speed has increased after every attack. But there seems to be irregular readings as if the genowraith paused slightly prior to destroying and moving on to new targets." One of the scientists at a bridge console reported.

Executer Bhala walked up to the console, reading the results.

"Why has he stopped his assault?" Another scientist asked.

Commander Paldar turned his chair in Bhala's direction expecting an explanation.

Bhala sighed as he raised his sight back on the screen.

Cyer's golden yellow brilliance showered the planet Ordis. His presence was a mystery to anyone still alive on or around the planet. The space fleet was over a light year away from the planet, now there was a small star like object a thousand miles from the surface and inside the planetary defensive barrier. Cyer's speed was unmatched by any spaceship, friend or foe.

Cyer floated above the northern axis of Ordis with folded arms, but his brilliance hid that fact.

"What's he doing?" One of the scientists asked.

"He's waiting." Bhala sighed again.

"Waiting, waiting for what...? Sir." The scientist was almost belligerent, but caught himself.

"He's waiting for them to attack him."

"What happens if they don't attack him?" Commander Paldar calmly asked.

"He will keep his word and kill them all." Bhala said and started to key in commands on the console.

Cyer looked down at the inhabitants. Ordis was eighteen thousand miles in diameter. He could make out small insects on the deserts and microscopic life at the bottom of ocean beds. The planet was simplistic for his liking and held nothing of importance to him.

However, plasma beams shooting all around him caught his attention. One beam engulfed his body, but as fast as it hit him, it had dissipated. The plasma energy seemed to be drastically weakened because it hit his body, with no visible damage to him. Cyer looked at the origins of the beams. Thousands of anti-planetary ground turrets were trying to kill him.

Cyer put a hand in front of him, palm exposed toward Ordis. A bright light came out along with an immense amount of heat. The beam hit the lower atmosphere causing a nuclear reaction, but continued into the crust of the planet. Clouds, ground and water moved out of the way. A ripple effect of massive tsunamis made of liquid and earth refaced the surface of the planet. What would have been a five hundred mile wide crater turned into a thousand and then half of the planet imploded into ground zero of Cyer's constant energy attack.

The onlookers aboard the Kalar spaceships witnessed the apocalyptic event in horror. Half of the space traveling warriors had seen planet destroyers at work, but none compared to what Cyer was doing in less than a few minutes.

Ordis cracked in half with most of it already vaporized by Cyer's energy attack and nuclear explosions to match. The once richly populated planet was now a rich source of exposed minerals in a very large area of space orbiting a star. Minuet rare patches of intact ground holding super-microorganisms were the only survivors of the extinction of countless of life forms.

Cyer heard the transmission Bhala was sending, but he didn't warp off towards the call. He flew several hundred thousands of miles away from the planet, landing on a far moon which was now chaotically spinning out of control through space.

Cyer was almost seven feet tall, but the rock mountain peak he stood on made him look puny. His skin seemed pale, but most of it was clothed with a shinny yellow skin tight metallic looking suit. His yellowish hair was short and spiky as if hair gel was part of his genetic makeup. His human figure suggested he was a human, but that was far from the truth. There was a genetic influence of some human like form, but the energy which supplied his destructive powers were kept at bay in the inner core of his body. He looked at a moon base, housed with probably the last few survivors of the Ordis race.

He looked through the ground and superstructure of the complex. Ordinians were scrambling to survive the disrupted change in orbit and intermittent quakes. "If you're strong enough, you will live." Cyer said to himself.

The Ordinians weren't about to send out a distress call. That would only attract the attention of the Kalar forces, which meant instant death. They would have to wait it out and hope an opportunity presented itself to send out a message for help once the Kalar forces left the area.

In an instant, Cyer warped towards the Kalar flagship. A bright light surrounded him as he entered the flagship bridge. The bridge crew were frightened by the ease in which Cyer entered the sealed room like a glittering spectral without a need to enter through a docking arm or airlock entry chamber.

The scientists and Bhala were unsurprised, but their expressions quickly changed.

"I did what I promised I would do. But you failed to give me what I wanted." Cyer floated inside the bridge with arms by his side, a few feet in front of the battle screen.

"You're referring to the challenge?" Bhala replied.

"Yes." Cyer's voice was clam, strong and reflected perfect pronunciation.

"There are stronger forces we have yet to fight." Bhala countered.

"No, there are no other forces here worthy of me."

"What are you trying to say?" Commander Paldar interjected.

"When you find someone worthy of killing, let me know." Cyer flew out of the bridge, continuing into outer space and vanished into hyperwarp.

Commander Paldar looked at Bhala. "I hope you can explain this to the Emperor?"

"The Emperor will listen to me... I will take care of this." Bhala's iron pale stony face hid his fear as he left the bridge and prepared to communicate with his master.

Istarie Front, Darkwater Plateau, Heedro System

Lix slid down the snowy slope. The arctic gear was a little cumbersome to her liking, but adequate for her purposes. A squad of

Soldiers followed her into the frigid dark green liquid coming down from the mountain's inners. The lake wasn't frozen and the de-crystallizing properties of the algae kept it that way.

The Soldiers sunk into the greenish water down to their necks. They moved slowly skirting the edge of the lake to the north, with Lix as the guide. She kept an eye on the sky overhead. An inverted tornado loomed a mile above the lake, its swirling red and white vapors threatened destruction on whatever it decided to land on, should it land at all.

The layers of synthetic memory plastic in the clothing regulated temperature and buoyancy. The red long slit on Lix's goggle was the only contrasting color around her head with the environment. Fourteen dimly lit red slits moved swiftly and silently along the surface of the water for almost a quarter of a mile.

Lix came out of the water holding a short staff like object in front of her. The dark clothing changed color to dark white as she moved onto the snow. The dimly lit red slit opened up to reveal her eyes. She ran into the wooded terrain of Darkwater, halting to scan the area for enemy targets and security devices.

The squad behind her formed a cigar shaped perimeter. The Assistant Patrol Leader moved up next to Lix. "Sir, all present." He whispered.

"It's too quiet." Lix looked down at a handheld digital compass. A GPS 3D reading displayed, showing the objective rally point as a small blue triangle and the primary objective in the distance.

"Could they have evacuated the base?"

Lix looked at the Soldier with concern. "Let's move"

The APL stayed where he knelt and let Lix continue towards the objective, counting the squad members as all of them passed by him.

The squad stopped short of the objective inside a dense patch of bushes and trees. The petrified trees were icy white with dark brown slivered pointy leaves, but the darkness of the night made everything seem black with very minuet differences in shades of gray. The reddish light from the tornado was far from them now, but it did provide some illumination for the goggles to work at peak performance.

Lix and the communications specialist, the RTO, laid prone in the middle of the circular defensive perimeter. "Sir, the base seems to be powered down." He whispered.

The APL crawled next to Lix and the RTO. "Sir, Jath's armor needs to recharge and heal. The lake water must have frozen some of the connectors in his leg."

"We will use the time to scan for ground vibrations. Tell Poth to setup the ground radar." Lix replied.

The APL reported back five minutes later. "Sir, Jath's armor is functional and Poth reports no unnatural activity."

"Prepare to move." Lix commanded and rose to a knee, the goggle visor changed color to black.

A minute later, Lix moved up front as point man again and disappeared as she passed the APL. The armor clothing became transparent as all the Soldiers disappeared after passing by the APL and moved into position before assaulting the objective.

The underground base entrance was closed, but the surrounding fence line was vacant of sentries, vehicles, or robots. The exploded electrical mines had left several thousand small three foot craters on the ground outside and in between the triple layer fence line which should have been cloaked but was now visible to the naked eye.

"It looks abandoned." The APL said coming up next to Lix.

"Okay, move by twos, Bravo team stay outside for cover in case we need to evac in a hurry." Lix motioned the Alpha team leader to move his team up.

The goggles allowed the squad to vaguely see each other in short distances, which was enough for Lix to see Alpha team breach the fences and enter the base grounds. She moved in with the last pair as the entire team secured the front entrance and panel. The small hill the entrance occupied created a low silhouette, which almost made it seem like the team was about to go into an outside basement entrance; except the front doors were wide enough to let a concert grand piano in without effort.

The doors opened slowly as the manual override had to be used since power was out. The team moved inside the long corridor two stories down to an elevator and branching hallways.

"Sir, friendly forces have taken the plateau." The RTO reported.

"Understood, maintain silence until we clear the area." Lix said and motioned the team to split up in two.

The Soldiers moved swiftly with very small assault rifles in front of their faces down the two hallways. The base was very large, but the lack of personnel in it made it easy for the team to clear. Their invisibility armor gave them the element of speed and surprise so chances of someone waiting in ambush was highly unlikely.

"Sir, first floor cleared." Alpha team leader reported.

"Assemble at the east wing stairwell. We'll go as a group to the genetics lab computer center."

"Moving."

The team worked their way down four floors and entered a maze of computer terminals and core drives.

The team looked on as half of the eight foot tall silver core drive cylinders were smothering or severely melted.

"It seems they tried to destroy the evidence." The A-Team leader said.

"Let's hope they failed." Lix ran towards an intact terminal on the far end.

"Nath, call up to Hoth and relay message. Need retrieval assistance immediately. Send in units to permanently deactivate self destruct systems." Lix almost tripped as she ran over harden melted plastic, metal and debris on the floor.

The electricity was off, but the translucent lamps were shedding chemically induced light into the room as an emergency measure.

"We need to get power back on." Lix commanded to the team.

"Sir, the fire extinguisher system works on a separate power source and infrastructure. We might be able to divert power." The RTO suggested.

"Something happened to stop the core drives from being destroyed and extinguishing systems from completely working, so before you put anything back online make sure those two are disabled." Lix prepped the terminal that seemed to be in good physical condition.

The team split up around the room, half securing the room, while the other three Soldiers searched for a power conduit. The Soldiers left the room in search of the geothermal generator room. The minutes seemed to take an eternity to pass as Lix waited for good news.

Finally, radio silence was broken. "Sir, systems are disabled and power is coming online in ten seconds."

"Understood." Lix turned on the terminal once half of the room came to life.

Nath and the A-Team leader looked on from behind Lix's shoulders. The screen showed the lab's logo and login information. Lix typed in the information without hesitation, the computer granting complete access to the level ten genetics projects.

Nath and the A-Team leader looked at one another in disbelief, then down at their Captain.

Lix quickly typed in a search. Videos and reports popped up, a small woman with the same skin and hair characteristics of Cyer appeared in a fusion chamber. A brilliant light came out of her, blinding the screen, but voices spoke in the background and the light was filtered to show the woman's figure pulse with energy.

The three kept silent, but Nath jerked backwards as the woman exploded, body chunks and dark liquid spattering on the camera lens ending the experiment.

"Why would they blow up people?" The A-Team leader asked.

"I don't know, but Nath, I need you to take a video of the screen. If I try to download the information, the database will be formatted.

The RTO touched his headset and started the video, keeping his stare, steady on the screen.

Lix looked back and forth between the screen and scientific keyboard. The latest documents and project results came up on separate windows and folders.

"What's a genowraith?" The A-Team leader had wanted to ask since the term popped up from the beginning.

"It's a genetically created super being and there he is." Lix replied and put a video on full screen.

"The destroyer of Ordis." Nath said out loud in awe.

Cyer floated in space with a very large asteroid in front of him. Light energy came out of his hands and the fifty mile wide asteroid instantly shattered into pieces. The video clips and angles changed as well as target types and sizes. The final demonstration was the destruction of a dwarf star. The three looked on in awe, but the last video was more disturbing.

Cyer dressed in a silver yellowish skintight suit, stood inside a space bay from what seemed to be a starship. "Command central has transmitted your next mission, please follow me?" A background male voice said.

Cyer stood like a statue overlooking the closed bay doors.

"Genowraith, you will comply." A different male voice stated.

"Are you sure I will?" Cyer calmly countered.

"Your programming includes obedience to your emperor. You will obey."

Cyer turned his head towards the off screen speaker. His eyes glowed yellow but his dark pupils could be made out. "You creatures believe in power, but have no understanding of creation. No one commands me."

Cyer walked towards a turbo-lift entrance with the video following his back. "And, you should be mindful to watch your tongue." Cyer said and instantly held out his arm and hand behind him. A flash of light blocked out the screen for a second, and the camera view shot up to the ceiling and then back down to a dead man on the floor. The middle of his body was gone with green powdered sediments everywhere. Two figures came into view in disgust as thick blood splatter was additional evidence of the murdered Kalarian scientist by the hand of a genowraith.

"That's all that I can salvage." Lix said in disappointment.

"Isn't that enough?" Nath asked.

"No, I needed all the genetic information to find a weakness. The core cylinders that contained most of that information are gone. Now, we have no idea how to kill this monster." Lix replied.

"So, what now?" The A-Team leader asked.

"You all go back off the grid. I need to hurry and rejoin the campaign before they start to question my whereabouts." Lix stood up and started to quickly walk out of the large room.

"Sir, do you think a fleet of our best ships can stop that genowraith?" Nath asked.

Lix didn't look back at the RTO. "I think the only hope we have is with the queen, or some other miracle."

The reply brought sorrow to Nath's heart. The queen was rumored to be Emperor Korvax's slave, or half dead. Cassandra's able forces had been scattered throughout the galaxy and they were losing the war, star system by star system.

Chapter Four

Legend Has It

The reserve security forces sprinted towards Stargazer's group. A few dozen men and women spread out as they approached, surrounding the three men. "Get on the ground!" Several of the Soldiers commanded in their Arloian language.

Stargazer looked over his shoulder but did so only to assess the situation behind him. "The natives don't understand us."

"Maybe you should have said, take me to your leader!" Rat Bastard barked; Spot chuckling.

"Huh, maybe I'm being too submissive." Stargazer lowered his hands by his side and walked up to the nearest Soldier.

A projectile along with a short beam of light burst out of the Soldier's rifle. Stargazer saw the trigger squeeze and guessed the trajectory. Without hesitation, Stargazer continued to walk as the round hit his left leg. The metallic energized round hit hard, pushing his upper leg back a few inches. "You guys aren't playing around."

Another round was shot once the intended effect had failed to put the intruder down. But this time, Stargazer was in no one's sights, as he flew and ran beside what he thought was a leader in the back of the formation. The round instead of hitting Stargazer continued onward and hit Rat Bastard in his lower back.

"What the hell! That could have killed someone!" Rat Bastard yelled in anger and turned into the Rat.

Half of the guards jumped back in shock, the other half were confused as Stargazer had simultaneously subdued a male guard in their rear with a chokehold.

Stargazer grabbed the rifle and wrenched it with great force from the man, dropping it to the floor. "Don't do it Rat! They might still be friendly!"

Rat Bastard twirled around to face Stargazer and where the shot came from.

"Weapons hold!" A Soldier ordered, but this time it was in English. "Stand down!"

Stargazer looked at the Soldier giving the commands. He was in the middle of the group and had Stargazer known the meaning of the small insignias on their uniforms, he would have gotten a leader instead of a private.

"We're not going to harm you. Arbitrator sent us here to save your galaxy." Stargazer announced, letting go of the Soldier.

Rat Bastard stayed in rat form and was ready to attack at Stargazer's command. Spot turned to him and eased next to him. "It looks like they know who the boss is, you can relax big guy."

The slight pain on his back told him otherwise, but it quickly left him once he realized this was his chance to get to know more than one alien who spoke English.

"Alright Spot, but next time you take the rear." He turned back into human form, as all the Soldiers lowered their weapons and half of them started to go back to their duties.

Stargazer walked towards the leader and waved for Spot and Rat Bastard to come to his location. The shredded fatigues now had an extra burn spot from the bullet, but it was the last thing on his mind. "Why didn't you guys speak our language before I got shot?"

The guard stood the same height as Stargazer, but the armored helmet and boots had much to do with it. "My apologies Sir, but the universal translator didn't initially recognize the ancient language."

"Do you normally trust what strangers say?" Stargazer looked at the man through his helmet. The man had a rugged prehistoric frame with thick brown hair fibers covering most of his face and body.

The lieutenant raised his helmet visor, revealing what Stargazer already saw. He resembled a cross with chimpanzee eyes and forehead; and a human male nose, mouth, cheeks and chin.

Spot came up to the two men. "Where are we?"

"You are... we are aboard the Vorgoling system space station. I am waiting for my commander and the historian for us to be able to answer all your questions. But in the meantime, I have questions of my own." The lieutenant's mouth moved but it didn't reflect what the speakers on his helmet said. A tiny echo of the real language could be heard in the background as the translator did its job, but the echoed noise was there mainly because the men were standing close to each other.

"Excuse me Sir. But my name is Lord Rat Bastard. May I ask who you are?" Rat stuck out both hands and grabbed the lieutenant's unoccupied off hand, shaking it rapidly but with care.

"Lord Rat Bastard, it's my pleasure to meet you." The lieutenant's stiff posture showed a little bit of confusion. "I'm Lt. Ostarnie, Assistant Security Officer for this station. I'm assuming you are not from this sector of the galaxy?"

"No, we're from the Milky Way Galaxy." Stargazer replied.

"We're real aliens." Rat Bastard smiled.

Lt. Ostarnie had a blank, emotionless apelike face. "Are there fake aliens in your galaxy?"

"It all depends on which government is in charge at the time." Spot grinned as he gazed at the details of the bay and what seemed like a small group of Soldiers coming their way.

The metallic alloy on the floor and ceiling was primarily bright gray with very thin ten meter long black straight lines as texture. The walls were off white, with large embedded lights all throughout the ceiling. The ceiling was at least sixty meters high, and sectioned off with the bay itself covering a rectangular area roughly four hundred meters long. Spot was very impressed, knowing they were probably in a small section of the space station.

"It all depends on perspective, but back to the why we're here. I would like to know why you're so accommodating since I subdued one of your men and ignored your warnings and commands." Stargazer placed his hands behind his lower back as a sign of calmness and confidence.

"The station computer indicated you were a priority VIP. I don't know why, which is also why my commander and the historian were alerted." Lt. Ostarnie turned to face the small approaching group of people in similar spacesuits.

The group was standing on a large circular platform with thin railings at waist level, moving rapidly in front of them. The railings collapsed into the four inch thick platform once it stopped in front of the four men, and landed gently on the metallic floor.

The helmet visors were open on all the aliens, exposing the white hair of the commander and red haired historian. The historian was smaller and a female, but the chimp-like appearance was minor compared to the males, which light makeup helped to cover. The chest plate design also made it easy to identify the genders, but Stargazer ignored the importance even though female Soldiers in combat were not a routine practice in his native United States of America.

"Welcome aboard this station, I'm Commander Exleter and this is Major Krodis."

"Thank you Commander, Major. I'm Lord Stargazer."

"I apologize for interrupting my Lord, but according to the computer recordings, I must say that it's critical that all of you come with us to a secure debriefing room." Major Krodis excitedly responded by quickly standing into Stargazer's personal space.

The commander grabbed Krodis' arm and pulled her away. "Excuse her zeal Lord Stargazer, but we're in the middle of a war and the only reason I'm not ordering my men to imprison you is because the computer and Major Krodis believe you and your men are the Burik'dir?"

"The what?" Spot replied.

Krodis put her hands in front of her as if praying or giving a lecture to a small group of students. "Legend has it that the Burik'dir are five saviors from the planet called Earth. The origins of King Alexmarks; Queen Cassandra's father. Many people have been waiting for your arrival in the midst of our greatest despair."

"But I only count three saviors." Commander Exleter's tone was cynical as he looked at the would-be saviors and then at Krodis.

Krodis looked around in anticipation for someone to answer the question, or get a glimpse of two more strangers.

"There are five of us; Lord Ghost and Master are hiding because Lord Master was injured during the trip here." Stargazer relieved her anxiety. "But since we're skeptical or intrigued to some degree or another, we'll be willing to go to your debriefing room, but would ask for medical assistance for Lord Master first."

The Commander turned his head towards one of the Soldiers in the background. Two Soldiers quickly reported next to him. "These two specialists will attend to the injured Master."

"Thank you very much commander." Stargazer said and turned in the direction of where Ghost and Master had disappeared.

Ghost and Master reappeared in the middle of the assembly. Master let out a grunt and slight whimper as he held his forearm.

Stargazer looked at the two Soldiers who were surprised by the unnatural appearance. "Lord Master needs your help."

One of the Soldiers gave a fleeting look at Stargazer before following the other Solider in a quick jog.

"One of the saviors is a boy?" Exleter asked, astonished.

"He's a little man genius and is willing to fight for you, so please don't get on his bad side." Stargazer warned.

Master was sat down on the floor by the medics. He eyed the silver ace bandage with mixed painful emotions. "This isn't a sprain. You guys know this, right?"

"Lord Master, this is necessary to immobilize the arm."

"What I need is a cast for a few hours so the bones will mend." Master said as the Soldiers finished wrapping the arm. A small coin size digital electrode was placed on top of the bandage. One of the medics touched the quartz screen on the electrode and the bandage harden like steel.

"What the… cool." Master's eyes widen with joyful interest. One of the medics held a small lens like object in her hand and scanned his arm. The other medic touched the digital coin and the bandage softened so they could adjust the arm into the perfect position.

"Ahh, when will the pain subside?" Master asked, wanting to know if he was going to get a highly advanced alien aspirin.

"It should be going away about now." The medic replied while touching digital numbers and settings on the electrode.

"Awesome." Master scrutinized the silver fabric and electrode with great intensity, ignoring the aliens or other neat gadgets around him. The medics helped him up and gave him instructions on caring for the cast.

Ghost had left Master, walking towards Stargazer, while Spot and Rat Bastard talked to Soldiers near them. Major Krodis was also busy talking to someone in her helmet making arrangements for the escort and integration of the Burik'dir into a new era of change.

Stargazer casually walked up to meet Ghost halfway. "I was hoping you could read my thoughts to let you know everything was fine."

"I don't know why, but it's very easy for me to read your thoughts, even from far away. Normally I can read people's minds for several hours and after that it is very sporadic. Sometimes, I can't read any minds at all, but I could always read my mom's thoughts no matter what was going on or how far. I could also mentally communicate with her sometimes. I think it's because she gave birth to me." Ghost looked at Stargazer. "She died a long time ago, but now you seem to be the only one I can read all of the time."

"So you're saying I'm like your mom?"

"Don't worry Steve. You're not my new mother." Ghost eased his sarcastic thoughts.

"Good to know. Besides I'm sure I'm not pretty enough to be your mom." Stargazer smiled.

"You can be my mommy if you want." Rat Bastard stepped in between them with a wide grin.

Stargazer looked up at the man. "I'll put you in time out if you ease drop like that again."

"You know that rats can hear better than dogs and cats. Maybe you and mom should be talking softer." Rat Bastard addressed Ghost first, then turned back around, smiled and moved away from them.

The two men looked at the big guy walk down the bay. Spot blissfully slapped Rat Bastard on the back for a job well done having also overheard the conversation.

'I like this group.' Stargazer thought.

"Yes, we sure have a good team. Do you think that's why we were put together?" Ghost whispered.

'We don't know what's going on and I don't trust people on face value, let alone aliens from another galaxy; if we really are in another galaxy. We need more information and not from one or a few people. I need you and Master to find out what you can from computer systems or documents. Hell, even ease dropping on conversations will work. If things are advanced like in Star Trek episodes, their computers should have the answers to confirm what is going on and who we can trust. But don't let anyone know what you two are doing. The rest of us will get information the old fashion way and talk our way into whatever crazy thing is next.' Stargazer glanced at Ghost.

"I'm on it." Ghost nodded and flew to where Master was being treated, whispering into Master's ear.

The Soldiers looking in the same direction paused their duties in wonder, having never seen someone fly without the use of a flight device or gadget. Stargazer noticed the reaction through their visors and body language, and erectly flew next to Major Krodis.

"I think we need to go to the debriefing room right now." Stargazer said while Spot grabbed Rat Bastard away from his new audience.

Krodis' blinking eyes and awe were honest. "Yes, we really do."

Commander Exleter motioned them to stand on the platform and kept unexpectedly quiet.

Ten figures jetted across the bay on the platform. "I assume your people have never seen a person defy gravity like we have?" Stargazer continued the conversation.

"No, Lord Stargazer, we have, but only recently. I will explain in detail in the debriefing room. I have heard of such innate powers, but only in the legends of books."

"Queen Leavan can't fly?" Master asked.

"You mean Queen Cassandra."

"Isn't her full name Cassandra Leavan?"

Krodis smiled. "I think you don't understand the naming dynamics. Leavan is the station which the Queen holds as ruler of many races within the entire galaxy. Since many races have two titles assigned to their origins and authoritarian status, the Queen's authority is Queen. Leavan is the origin of her power and species which is accepted by all the races."

"So to sum it up, Queen Cassandra of the house or station of Leavan would be correct." Master replied.

"Yes, that's perfectly stated." Krodis' impressed tone said it all for her growing admiration of the humans.

"So Queen Cassandra can or can't fly?" Stargazer refocused the conversation.

"I really don't know. I assume she can if she wanted to, but I have never met her in person or know of any instance when she flew like you did. But she doesn't need to fly since she can appear where ever she wishes."

The platform stopped in front of the lift doors. "Where's the Queen at this time?" Spot asked.

Ghost kept quiet, seeing many things in the five aliens' minds, but it was visions more than anything else. The foreign language was a mystery to him and it seemed like he was viewing clips in a mixture of Greek,

Asian, Russian and babble he couldn't compare with any coherence. The information he and Master would be expected to gather would be much harder than he thought, but hopefully the computer would translate in his spying activities, whenever that would begin.

"That's another thing we need to talk about in the room." Major Krodis said as all of them entered the large multidirectional elevator.

"Well, since we seem to be compartmented at the moment. Could you tell us why we only see one type race in this space station if it's supposed to be for many races?" Master asked.

"Not all races interact efficiently with one another, so our people are tasked to sustain this station, to include security. There are other races here, which you will see once we enter the upper levels and sections, but this is a unique station and in the process of evacuating." The commander answered.

"Are we in danger of being attacked?" Stargazer asked.

"Not at the moment, but Kalar forces are moving in our direction." The elevator stopped at the intended destination and the conversation changed to a quick introduction and tour of the level.

The group walked down several hallways and into a large conference room. The level seemed to be deserted of people except for a few technicians working on the ventilation and electrical systems in the passages.

Stargazer scanned the area as a habitual precaution against foul play, but only saw advanced construction material of a space station and people moving about with a purpose. His guard tempered as he sat in what seemed to be center stage for a briefing. The room seated several hundred people, resembling a large university tier seating classroom with no students. The three man security team that followed the group standing at the entrance.

Once the entire group was seated, Major Krodis started the briefing. "Station computer, please record entire session and present ancient historical file Burik'dir."

"Affirmative." A male voice replied through the surround sound speakers. The lights dimmed and a display of written text in Greek came up on a theater sized screen. The video backed off the book and a young woman dressed in an elegant blue silk dress sat on a glass chair. Her medium golden blonde hair frizzled with static electricity as she turned towards the camera.

"Welcome. I'm Queen Cassandra and these writings I hold in my hand is what many would call a holy book back where my father was born. There will be many people who do not or cannot believe that our destiny has been chosen for us. Destiny and time is complex, but what you, the viewer of this video need to understand is that destiny is set in stone because my father made it that way. How we get there is what, might change and also what I call life and death; free will, if you prefer. I'm not going to lecture you on what might or will happen, but I will tell you that this text must be protected from alteration or misinterpretation. The Burik'dir will save the galaxy and this book is for them and whomever it concerns."

Cassandra's eyes were crystal blue with a hazel brown inner ring and had the perfect skin of a young adult. Her smile was mesmerizing as the video faded into darkness.

"As you can see, this book was created for you." Krodis placed a very thin eight inch tablet in front of Stargazer.

The tablet displayed the book contents as Stargazer tried to make sense of how to work the technology.

"There are tablets underneath the table for you to use."

"Is there a translator on this thing?" Stargazer asked.

"You don't know the language?" Krodis' eyes narrowed.

"It's written in Greek. I can understand it, but my friends here probably need it translated into English." Master replied.

"Computer, please translate the language text into En-glish."

"Affirmative." The screen highlighted into a dark color and text changed into English.

The group read through the book, which at first was like reading a science fiction story about the Argonian Empire and Galactic Guardians. The story got personal as vivid descriptions of each of them ended the last chapter.

"How old is this book?" Rat Bastard asked.

"King Alexmarks wrote it almost seven hundred Earth years ago." Krodis automatically converted to the correct chronological terminology.

"How old is Queen Cassandra?" Ghost asked while viewing her video on mute.

Stargazer turned his gaze at Ghost, then at the tablet and smiled.

"The Queen is six hundred forty-one years of age." Commander Exleter answered.

"That's some fountain of youth." Stargazer continued to smile.

Ghost half smirked. "So where's Cassandra now?"

Krodis looked at the commander. "Queen, Cassandra is believed to be imprisoned by Korvax Bac'dir. He is leading the Kalar in this war and winning at the moment." Commander Exleter replied and stood up to take Krodis' post in front of the group.

"Computer, display campaign highlights until present time."

Commander Exleter explained how the Kalar forces from a neighboring galaxy, known to the Earthlings as Pegasus Dwarf or Andromeda 6, attacked the capital world of Arlos. "The surprise attack divided the Andromen Empire's forces, which is being exploited as we speak. Friendly forces had momentarily stopped the invasion, but the neighboring forces were not able to retake the Arlos system. In addition, we the Vorgs, joined the Queen's able forces twenty Earth days ago. But yesterday, a Kalar doomsday weapon caused the generals to divert all forces to the Pasik sector of space. This is the doomsday weapon." The commander pointed at the screen as the broadcast of Cyer's destruction of Ordis was played for the group.

"So the generals diverted all forces to find and kill this thing, instead of rescuing the queen?" Ghost asked after the broadcast ended.

"And this is why this station is so barren?" Stargazer added.

"Not everyone was in agreement, but they thought it would be useless to commit on two major objectives." Exleter replied as he sat down in front of the group. "I don't believe in the legends, but if you really can do something... I'm willing to hear how you can help."

"I don't have any answers right now commander, but I think we need to do more research before we go off to save the day." Stargazer replied.

Exleter looked at the group in thought. "The Kalar forces are two

Earth days from the station. Unless, the Andromen armada has stopped their advance."

"Are the starships traveling faster than the speed of light?" Master asked.

"Yes, the fastest ships travel eight times the speed of light."

"Is it possible for us to spend some time here to analyze a way to help you?" Stargazer asked.

"Major Krodis will stay by your side. The guards posted outside are there for security and your assistance, so if you need anything they can escort you to the right locations, like the mess area, or a room for sleeping. At the moment I need to get back to the command center to finalize the evacuation. So please excuse me."

"Thank you, commander."

Major Krodis sat in Exleter's unoccupied seat while the commander left the auditorium.

"Major Krodis, I would like to know more about Queen Cassandra and the capital." Stargazer placed the tablet on his lap.

Major Krodis started to explain as Ghost disappeared and then Master. She stopped talking with a concerned stare at empty chairs.

"Don't worry, they're going to look around. No one will be bothered or hurt. Please continue." Stargazer said.

"You don't trust us?"

"You are as alien to us, as we are to you."

"There have been false saviors in the past, but I can feel in my heart that you are real. I will show you that you can trust me, as I have faith in you." Krodis said and continued to tell the three men about the queen and Arlos system.

Ghost and Master flew through the station, Master telling Ghost where to go, pausing in areas of interest to them both. They finally stopped at a computer console in the empty auxiliary command center.

Master sat in front of the console, while Ghost made them tangible, being able to interact with the physical world.

"Computer, enable keyboard functions in English." Master said.

"Identification required, please provide access name."

The computer console screen displayed above the keyboard. 'Audio authentication' was colored in green. 'Access Name' was colored in yellow.

"Master."

'Access denied.'

"Lord Master."

'Access denied.'

"Rumpelstiltskin." Master puffed.

'Access denied.'

"This will take forever. Especially, since I can't read these peoples' minds to get a password." Ghost stated.

"I don't think it would help since the audio doesn't match. But the computer accepted our audio, so…" Master exhaled slowly.

"So what?" Ghost countered.

"Computer, access name is Benjamin Dempsey."

'Access granted.'

"What kind of lame security system is that?" Ghost asked.

"No one knows my name except you guys, and our real names aren't mentioned in the ancient legends book, but if Cassandra's father wrote it, he must have known our names. It's the perfect security system if you think about it. Someone could probably duplicate our voices, but not knowing our real names would have made it fool proof." Master said while the keyboards and all displays converted into English and allowed access to all locked files.

"Wow." Ghost looked over Master's shoulder. "It's the schematics to the station, names of all the crew. It's military and star systems information for everything, friendly and enemy."

"That's what I'm talking about." Master said with a wide grin, typing in commands and touching the screen with lightning fast robot reflexes.

"How did you know to touch the screen?" Ghost asked while coming to the realization himself on how the advanced interfaced worked.

"I'm a..."

"Genius, yes we all know." Ghost's peeved facial expression was unseen as both were invisible to the naked eye and Master's back was to him.

Master scrolled and viewed through thousands of schematics, military historical data and planetary and star systems information.

Ghost was interested in the information, but soon bored not being able to keep up with the youngster.

"Why would all this information be in a computer database, in a space station on the edge of the galaxy?" Ghost asked.

Master stopped his computer surfing. "Huh, I'll have to get back with you on that one, but if it helps, there seems to be a data feed through other computers from outer space at different times. Not sure if the information is transferred from other ships as they visit the station or distant radio signals from planets."

The console screen turned blue for a second and the station security system lights came on. "Intruder alert, intruder alert, intruder alert." The computer announced through the station intercoms.

"What did you do?" Ghost scolded.

"It's not me; the bay energy fields were illegally disrupted. And that's what did it." Master pointed at the three main screens on the far wall. Framed windows of camera views were open revealing the presence of dozens twenty meter long and three meter wide dark green snake-like creatures. Blue electrical streaks crackled inside their wide opened oval mouths as they slithered across the bay floor attacking people and small machinery.

Master rapidly touched the console, opening up a schematic of the station with every level. "Computer, override station systems control to this console and open all internal comms channels."

"What are you doing?" Ghost was about to lift Master out of the seat.

"All personal, enemy creatures have entered the bays. Secure for quarters, until the Burik'dir can repel the intrusion." Master said over the loud speakers in English and was automatically repeated in Arloian.

A window of a camera shot of the conference room opened on the right side of the main screen. "Stargazer, I'm patching in what I see to the conference room. I need you guys to go kill those things while I try to contain them in sections of the station." Master quickly announced into the conference room.

The group looked behind Major Krodis at the multiple screens as a backdrop. Stargazer jumped out of seat and stood in front of Krodis.

Krodis turned back around from the screens in complete surprise to see Stargazer inches from her face in a fraction of a second.

"Is there a way to communicate without the use of a helmet?" Stargazer firmly grabbed her arm.

"It's an implant in the ears and throat which would allow such a capability, but it will take too long to put one in you."

"Okay, it's a race to the bays. You're coming with me." Stargazer hugged Krodis and flew out of the room as Spot and Rat Bastard cleared the way by opening doors. "Master, open the lift doors and shut down all the elevators!"

"Go to the command center and protect it?" Spot commanded the guards as they flew by them.

The auxiliary command center screens were full of hundreds of video camera views and maps of all personnel in the station. Master started to give commands to personnel as to where to go, opening and closing automatic doors and systems. "Sector four loading dock, retreat right now into blue rooms 12A thru 13B."

The security Soldiers stood their ground firing at seven creatures in the bay, while technicians ran for their lives. The fully automatic weapon response was ineffective as only one creature laid motionless from hundreds of plasma impacts. "Fall back now, so I can take care of the worms!" Master screamed.

"Take it easy." Ghost said.

"Do as Master said, now!" Commander Exleter instructed in their earpieces.

The Soldiers ran back with one creature almost gobbling a strangler before Master closed the thick doors behind him.

"Thank you. Finally!" Master said as he overrode safeties to the outer force field generators and turned them off. Fourteen creatures and numerous loose crates and machinery in sector four bay blew out into space with extreme velocity.

Master touched another icon and one of the hallways into the bay also caught a creature slamming the corners, leaving black tar like blood and skin in its wake.

Spot entered the all too familiar sector 3 bay except this time it was littered with dead body parts, machinery half eaten by forty or so creatures, scattered all around the concentrations of people or doorways.

Rat Bastard instantly turned into the Rat and screeched in the direction of two worms within ten meters from their entry location. The piercing sound vibrations took Stargazer and Spot by surprise, but more so Major Krodis who fell to the floor with both hands on her helmet where her ears would normally be positioned.

Spot and Stargazer paused for a moment to gain control of their bearings, seeing the two long creatures hit an invisible wave of destruction. Their exterior shells of a body torn off; revealing the skeleton of blue static charges and black organ segments. The sonic vibrations threw the creatures backward fifty meters before they stopped being shredded into black splatter. The wave continued to the opposite side of the bay annoying several creatures within the arc of the attack.

All of the creatures in the bay stopped moving and all turned their mouths toward Rat Bastard.

"That's right, come and get it!" Rat Bastard yelled getting ready to huff and puff once again.

Spot helped Krodis up while Stargaze got in front of Rat Bastard.

"Go to that door, we can funnel them there." Stargazer pointed at Green entrance 3, leading into one of several mess areas.

Master contained seven creatures within the hallways and rooms near the bays, but two had made it to the turbo lifts. "I'll take care of them, you continue kicking ass." Ghost said and flew off toward the two intruders.

"Okay." Master replied out of impulse being busy trying to figure out where the worms were coming from.

Worm Infested Ship Bay

Stargazer led the way, followed by Spot carrying Krodis and Rat Bastard on his heels.

A worm lay between them and the ten meter wide sliding metallic doors. A laser beam passed Stargazer by inches, hitting the worm's outer mouth. The worm turned into the laser taking in the laser beam as if attracted to the energy.

Stargazer glazed back at Spot then flew as fast as he could into the worm. The worm's flesh was more like very hard plastic scales to him, instead of hide or bone. He didn't stop to take notice as the blue energy stung his entire body as he made a large hole through the worm. The impact slowed him down, landing on his feet past the creature. His body tingled, with an almost numbing effect, lasting but seconds.

Spot and Rat Bastard stood defending the entrance of the doorway with Krodis running inside the corridor.

Tar-like ooze covered Stargazer's skin, which also started to burn away the remains of his torn trousers. He flew next and in between his two friends. The worms moved like sidewinders looking for vengeance. "Wait until they get closer before you take them out with that scream of yours."

"I can only do it one or two more times, so you might want to have a backup plan." Rat half growled.

"What? Is there anything else we should know now?" Stargazer quickly asked.

"Yeah, In-coming! Screeeeee!!!" Rat Bastard's cone directed sonic wave obliterated a dozen worms and stunned the other two dozen.

"Fall back into the corridor." Stargazer flew backwards into the very wide corridor, with Krodis and a few Soldiers at the other end.

Rat Bastard flew next to the Soldiers, while Spot stood by Stargazer's side at the entrance.

Rat Bastard looked at Krodis and grabbed her arm forcing her into the small mess hall. The Soldiers followed them not sure what Rat Bastard was doing. "I'm sorry guys, but you can manage on your own!"

Spot and Stargazer looked back in shock as the door closed in front of Rat Bastard. "He really is a bastard." Spot said, bewildered.

Stargazer peered through the two foot thick metallic alloy doors with interest and disbelief. "He locked the doors too." Stargazer smiled, seeing ten people in the mess area. "He's protecting the crew so we don't let any worms inside."

"Okay, any ideas?" Spot asked as he gauged how long it would be before the worms would be on top of them.

"They seem to like your light show, so can you get them to follow you so I can spear through groups at a time." Stargazer replied.

"Huh, okay naked man, here I go." Spot laughed and flew up thirty meters shooting all the worms with laser beams from his fingers.

Spot flew in a two hundred meter circular pattern as wide as the walls of the bay allowed, laser beams burning small few inch trenches on the bay floor when he missed a worm's hungry mouth.

Stargazer was partially covered with the black ooze now; the floor he stood on was sizzling from the acid like properties. *"The worms seem to be ignoring me, this stuff is camouflaging me, I think?"*

Many of the creatures coiled up and erected themselves close to thirty meters high. Spot almost flew into the path of a few worms, but he compensated and flew a little higher. "Anytime now!" Spot yelled.

Stargazer flew down the bay to get some distance away from the horde of worms slithering in a circle. He focused on a path and flew as fast as he could against the direction of travel countering the circular pattern Spot was taking them. The impact and effects of the first few worms felt as before, but as Stargazer flew in the large circle the velocity slowed greatly. He adjusted by trying to open his eyes as fast as possible after exiting a worm and speed up.

Spot flew lower seeing that Stargazer was killing all of the worms.

The increase in speed slingshot Stargazer out of the circle and he missed the last living worm. He flew out into the far wall of the bay leaving a long black streak of blood on it for fifty meters before he could stop.

The uninjured worm struck at Spot with viper like speed. The mouth grabbed a hold of Spot's lower body, feet first. The blue energy didn't disintegrate Spot's body, but it did paralyze him for the moment.

Spot looked down at the black edge of the mouth, thousands of shark like teeth held tight on his waist. The teeth didn't pierce his skin, but the blue energy crackled louder the more he tried to free himself. He grabbed the mouth with both hands on opposite ends trying to open it so he could slip out. The effort was futile as his legs were completely numb now.

"Let go of him!" Rat Bastard came out of nowhere and lunged onto the worm's body near the mouth. He flew in as a rat, but when he made contact with the worm, he turned into his large human form. He dug his fingers inside the worm's outer scales and bear hugged the monster with cross stretched arms and legs.

The worm thrashed about like a wild bull in a rodeo. Rat Bastard quickly squeezed harder, his arms and feet dug into the body a few feet as the worm slammed him on the bay floor, spitting Spot out many meters away. The worm lifted back up, but Rat Bastard's relentless hug, tighten.

Black clumps of blood gushed out of the worm's mouth as if something inside its body had ruptured. Rat Bastard and the worm's head landed on the floor hard with a very loud slap sound echoing to the other side of the bay.

Stargazer flew to Spot's side. "You okay?"

"Why didn't you tell me it can paralyze you?"

"What are you talking about, I'm fine?"

Rat Bastard stood up now covered in black tar-like ooze. "Oh, that tingles." He looked at Stargazer and Spot in the distance, then looked down at his black clothes. "Oh no, that burns! It burns!" Rat Bastard turned into the rat and shook himself like a dog gone wild after existing water.

Black ooze sprayed everywhere creating a mist in the air. "You see, it burns and paralyzes." Spot's clothes were wet, but not from the black ooze, but more from a bluish residue of energy or plasma from the inside of the worm.

"It burns!" Rat Bastard screamed again having ooze still on his body and flew at top speed into space beyond the bay entrance force fields.

The two men looked at Rat Bastard fly past the energy force field barrier and float outside in the vacuum of space as if relieved from a terrifying plague or itch which wouldn't go away.

"I guess rats can survive anywhere." Spot said.

"Rats survived the Ice Age, why not the space age." Stargazer smiled, but his face turned to concern as he saw a transparent shadow of a ship in Rat's background. Stargazer peered closer, as if trying to see details instead of going for distance with his extraordinary vision.

Rat Bastard flew back inside toward Stargazer and Spot at the same time turning into human form. "I think I'll do what Bastard did and get this stuff off of me." Spot commented.

"No! there's an invisible spaceship outside, that's where the monster worms are coming from."

"A cloaked ship? Like the Romulans?" Spot looked back at Stargazer and then at empty space with interest.

"Fall back to the corridor again. Rat Bastard this isn't over, come over here now!" Stargazer flew back to the corridor, but kept his head facing and examining the cloaked ship.

The three flew quickly to the corridor entrance several hundred meters from the bay space entrance. "Are there more of those fire worms?" Rat Bastard asked.

"Go tell Major Krodis to tell Master that there's a cloaked spaceship outside. I hope the station has weapons, otherwise we will have to board that thing very soon." Stargazer instructed, as Rat Bastard flew next to an intercom near the doors.

"Why don't we board it now?" Spot asked.

"If they can travel through space or have force fields like in Star Trek, then we might be outside in space unable to board and be in the way of friendly fire by the station."

"Huh, that makes sense." Spot faintly said, feeling very tired, with his strength slowly returning. "How big is the ship?"

"It's big enough to take up the entire view of the bay entrance."

Master heard the conversation over the intercom and diverted weapons to the outside of Section 3 Bay.

"Did you hear that Master?" Rat Bastard asked.

"Yes, but the ship's computer won't fire without a target lock so close to the bay and for some reason most of the weapons are offline, probably because the armada stripped most of the station's firepower before they left. But I got an idea." Master replied, Stargazer and Spot hearing from a distance through the intercom.

Ghost flew directly and swiftly to the first worm which was closest to the command control center having burned through the lift door at that level. He flew next to it and placed his hand inside the beast. A strong current of energy paralyzed his hand, but he was able to quickly withdraw his hand. A surge of pain raced up his arm as he stayed next to the monster, matching its speed and direction of travel.

The pain felt like the worse charley horse ever on his arm. The worm was slithering rapidly down the hallway and would soon hit the command center entrance. He wasn't sure if it could instantly get through the doors, but the four security guards in the hallway were his main concern. He thought quickly and concentrated on his transmutation command instead of the annoying painful numbness of his arm.

The worm slid forward down the hall, but stopped several feet in front of the guards who were firing their plasma rifles to no end. The crackling energy sound the creature made had also stopped, which was also drowned out by gunfire.

A ten meter section of the worm turned into light green jelly as if it had melted away in a microwave oven, while the rest of the body remained dark green, black and hard.

"We killed it!" One of the guards yelled with joy over the radio and helmet speakers.

Ghost looked at the guards and smiled. "Yeah, you're the man." He whispered to himself and flew off to his next target.

It wasn't long before he came up on the second loose worm which was about to enter the engineering sector. His transmutation command quickly killed the worm and kept the enemy attack from disabling the station's main power supply.

Back in the auxiliary bridge, Master brought up an inventory of items in and near the bays. His eyes lit up with delight as the inventory revealed what he wanted, but was yet disturbing to his teenage view of life. "Computer, activate cargo item 120K-9034. Set for remote detonate at my command."

"Activated." The computer's tone was emotionless and deep.

Three worms appeared in space and entered the sector 3 bay entrance. Stargazer scanned the entire area trying to see what was going on in other sections of the station.

Master turned off sector 1 bay force fields and a large portion of cargo crates the size of semi-trucks blasted outside into space.

"What now boss man." Spot asked, readying himself.

"We wait for more worms to enter and take them out in large numbers. It will help you guys conserve your energy."

"What's that!" Spot pointed at the debris blown out into space from sector 1 bay underneath them.

Stargazer looked at the debris and smiled. "Spot, shoot the debris from here... Quickly!"

Spot was slightly confused, but did as his military training taught him. "White laser beams came out of his hand, passing the entrance force fields and showering the debris."

Master touched the intercom icon on his console. "All personnel, brace for impact!" Then touched the cargo icon.

Stargazer quickly looked around for something to hold on to, just in case. A brilliant flash of light came into the bay as Spot and Rat Bastard turned away from the nuclear explosion outside the station. Stargazer ignored the flash and grabbed Spot's wrist, yanking him towards Rat Bastard. "Fly against the vacuum!"

Stargazer stuck out his free hand to get a hold of the big guy as the blast of radiation hit the force field, bringing it down. Rat Bastard's shirt ripped as Stargazer's held on to it; the atmosphere escaping the bay taking anything loose along with it. "Hold o..." Stargazer shouted, but the lack of air cut the message short. The three men flew against the air current for a moment until the force fields were restored. The gravity was also weakened as the three men looked on at the enemy spaceship, now marked with extensive damage to its rectangular superstructure and quite visible.

"Yeah that ship is too big for this bay." Spot said but no one heard him as air was still being dumped into the bay.

Stargazer tapped Spot and Rat Bastard on their shoulders. "Follow me." He said and instructed with his hands by pointing to them and back at himself.

Stargazer flew towards the enemy ship, but before they reached the bay force fields, the enemy ship blew up into a ball of energy and light. It was smaller than the initial twenty megaton explosion and the station's force fields held strong. He stopped in mid air with Spot and Rat Bastard by his side. He scanned the area for life pods or survivors, but none came into view.

The air was now shallow near the vents in the ceiling. "I don't see any survivors." Stargazer said.

"Could they have killed themselves to prevent capture?" Rat Bastard asked.

Stargazer and Spot looked at him, amazed. "That's a very good question." Spot smiled.

Rat Bastard smiled back, but his face quickly changed into a sunken look. "But you don't have an answer, do you?"

"Sorry big guy. Answers are something we all want but aren't getting." Stargazer replied and flew off to find the few worms Master had trapped in the station. The worms were to his relief, motionless as if they ran out of batteries.

"All personnel, decontamination procedures have been initiated. Do not touch traces or go into a sector that has a dead Bether." Master announced and brought up a view screen of Commander Exleter and the bridge crew in the command center.

"Commander, I apologize for the takeover, but you have full control of the station at this time." Master said to the entire audience.

"It's so kind of you Lord Master, but I want you and your companions to meet me in the conference room in an hour." Commander Exleter replied with an irritated face and turned off the camera.

"Eye eye Capitan. And you're welcome." Master replied to a closed window and hundreds of camera windows of the station. "You and Black Beard would make great friends." Master said as he opened the locked door and made his way to the conference room.

Master rallied everyone back inside the conference room with the new tablet he had taken personal possession of. Major Krodis was able to supply the heroes with fitting clothes. The Vorgoling uniforms were of various colors. Stargazer and Master wore navy blue skin tight space suits. They were not the padded armor type, but they were space worthy and helmets were part of the ensemble. Spot and Rat Bastard wore black suits, while Ghost's was pearl white.

Master was the last one to enter the conference room with the new attire. "You guys don't believe in long showers I take it."

Gus looked at the young man and smiled. "Were we supposed to shower?"

"I know you took one Rat. You sing like a parrot." Master stood next to Stargazer who had saved him a seat.

Rat Bastard laughed. "Good one, I'm make sure to sing louder next time."

Stargazer smiled. "I heard you pissed off Commander Exleter."

"I thought it was you guys, repainting the walls. But, I guess I did. What's the occasion?" Master replied motioning at the saved seat.

"I want you next to me when I tell the Commander my plan to save the universe."

"You have a plan?" Master pointed at him and sat, amused.

"Ghost told me you examined all of the military and star system information on the computer."

Major Krodis sat in front of the group, listening to the conversation as well as the other members, all quiet and intrigued.

"Do you think you can mastermind a victory for the armada and rescue the queen?"

"So you think I'm like Captain Kirk?" Master replied turning his chair to face Stargazer.

"More like the Doctor, considering we have probably already traveled through time." Rat Bastard casually said.

Stargazer turned his gaze on Rat Bastard in admiration, but answered Master. "You're a genius who destroyed a cloaked enemy spaceship and have us as assets that the armada doesn't have at this time. Cassandra picked all of us for a reason and well, I'm asking a lot from you, but can you do it?"

Master turned to look at Major Krodis. Her eyes showed wonder, not of confusion, but of witnessing history in the making. Master smiled, "I will need complete access to strategic space battle history, current space assets, how subspace communications works, timelines in the armada plan of attack, engine technology and anything you have on planet destroyers."

"We will also need your fastest spaceship, and I want to know if it's possible to broadcast a message to all star systems in the galaxy..." Stargazer looked at Krodis. "Something that won't take years to receive."

"Through subspace communication buoys and wormhole repeaters, messages can be sent across the galaxy in days." Krodis replied. "As for a ship, the fastest and probably the only one within many parsecs is the transport, but I don't know if it's travel worthy, since the Bethers attacked the bay."

"Bethers are those fire worms, right?" Rat Bastard asked having been briefly informed of the creatures during his time before returning to the conference room.

"Yes, Lord Rat Bastard. They're robots more than anything else. They disrupt and absorb energy, but also have numerous biological diseases in and outside of their bodies."

"That explains a lot." Spot said.

"Anyways, back to the subject. We will need to get that transporter working, along with a working battle center inside. Do you think we can get that done within the next twelve hours?" Stargazer asked.

"I don't know Lord Stargazer since I'm not an expert in the fields you need. I do know who to assemble for that; but..."

"But you need Commander Exleter's approval." Stargazer stated for her.

"That's correct."

"Understood, in the meantime prepare to gather and execute what we asked. I will get the approval." Stargazer said and turned towards Ghost.

Ghost nodded in approval and started to work on his tablet with great zeal.

The time passed quickly as they kept busy with their research and strategy, while the station personnel cleaned up the mess of dead Vorgs, worms and continued the final evacuation procedures.

Commander Exleter entered the room alone and less irritated by what Ghost could tell. His prideful walk and straight face said otherwise as he stood next to Major Krodis who was at the position of attention. Stargazer stood up out of respect, as did the rest of the group.

"Commander, before you say anything, I want to let you know that we have a plan to save the universe, but we need your help."

"Is that right? And how do you plan on doing that?" Exleter crossed his arms.

"The five of us will announce our legendary arrival to your galaxy and challenge Emperor Korvax and whatever forces he has. We will travel to the armada, help them win a victory, make our way to Arlos, have the armada attack Kalar forces, while we rescue the queen. By this time, all friendly forces will have united and assembled in Arlos, where we will defeat Korvax and his band of henchmen."

"And you think that the Destroyer of Ordis won't get in the way?"

"We will figure out a way to kill or neutralize him, long enough for us to rescue the queen."

"And you think you can do what I fear the generals and tacticians will not be able to do with the armada that is out numbered four to one?"

"We have our own secret weapon." Stargazer said. "And the element of the unknown." Master added.

"What are you talking about?"

"We have my brain, and a PR campaign this galaxy has yet to see." Master replied.

"You will place the future of the galaxy on a boy?" Exleter looked deep into Stargazer's crystal brown eyes.

"No, we will all place the future of this galaxy and mine in the hands of Lord Master."

"Do you think the enemy monsters and invisible spaceship was destroyed by accident, brute force, or a genius?" Rat Bastard interjected.

Exleter looked at Rat Bastard, then at Master. "No, you all saved the station."

"Then trust Stargazer and this real master of war, so that many lives can continue to live." Rat Bastard softly replied, pointing to the boy.

Ghost smiled as Spot's thoughts leaked into his head. *'He's a smart bastard too, go figure.'*

"Lords, this station and its people are at your total disposal."

Stargazer turned toward Major Krodis, and then back at Commander Exleter. "Here's a list of what we need as quickly as possible. The longer it takes us to travel to the armada, the lower the chance of us getting enough firepower to attack Arlos."

Exleter took the list and called for the department heads to report to him immediately.

Master finally got his chance to eat, with Rat Bastard socializing with anyone he could in the mess area. Spot also tagged along, all three lords inviting many questions about Earth.

Stargazer assisted in the repairs to the transport, learning much about space travel in the process.

The time finally came when Stargazer sat inside the transport with a fully functional battle table. The cockpit was linked to the battle table console and monitors which mirrored a starship bridge. The communication implants were placed in each of them except for Stargazer and Spot who used external ear pieces and audio transmitters attached to the inside of their throats. All commands Stargazer gave were automatically heard and executed in the cockpit and everywhere else in the transport.

"Commander Exleter, my helmsman tells me we are ready to depart." Stargazer said on an open communication channel.

"Lord Stargazer, we wish you the best and will spread the word as you directed." Exleter replied.

"Thank you commander… Helmsman, take us out and head towards the armada at maximum speed." Stargazer smiled.

Ghost also smiled as he saw Stargazer's delight in imitating a captain of a starship.

Master diverted the communication broadcast to all channels and amplified the output towards the Arlos star system. "We are ready when you are."

Stargazer sat in the middle of the oval battle table, with his friends on both sides. The section of the room was bright, but the table was glassy black with a stellar map as a background. Stargazer looked at the main screen which was also the source of the camera view he was showing the audience.

"Inhabitants of Andromeda, I am Lord Stargazer leader of the Burik'dir. I and Lords Master, Rat Bastard, Ghost and Spot are superhumans from the planet Earth in the Milky Way Galaxy. We have come to destroy the Kalar forces along with Korvax, and just in case some of you doubt our powers, I have included a video which you can examine on your own time."

Master smiled, touched an icon on one of the table's six consoles; displaying the scene of Spot shooting laser beams from his hand out into space causing the nuclear explosion which destroyed the Kalar infiltration cruiser, coming to an end as the three men flew and floated in mid air close to the bay entrance.

"The sneak attack has failed and the Vorgoling Station is safe and well. All Kalar forces, you will surrender and retreat to your home worlds immediately or face a far worse punishment than Ordis. As for you Korvax, you and I will meet very soon."

The broadcast ended in blackness, Major Krodis and the Vorg crewmembers eyed each other with mixed emotions. Master looked at Major Krodis. "You disapprove?"

"Lord Spot didn't destroy the cruiser."

"Sure he did and now the Kalar think we have our own planet destroyer like the Destroyer of Ordis." Stargazer countered.

"So what are you going to do about the Destroyer of Ordis when he decides to fight you, Lord Spot?" Krodis asked.

Spot turned to Stargazer. "Yeah, what am I going to do?"

"He will fight me since I'm the leader and probably assume I'm more powerful. Hopefully, he won't be with the armada and we can get closer to Arlos before we do meet him. In the meantime, Master and I will think of something."

"Well, he's right about being more powerful." Rat Bastard turned towards Spot.

Spot smirked. "Everyone will fear or love me when I'm done."

"That's the spirit. You'll need it when a thousand spaceships hunt you down once they get your scent." Ghost laughed.

"Yeah, then he and Ghost will disappear and leave us up the creek." Rat Bastard laughed along.

"Why are you laughing?" Master asked, confused.

"Because that's what we do." Stargazer joined the laughter.

The Vorg crewmembers sat in awe as the Burik'dir joked about fighting against forces capable of wiping out star systems in a single day.

Queen Cassandra's Thorn Room, Planet Arlos

Stargazer's broadcast projected above the entrance to the majestic room, once filled with hundreds of dignitaries and parliament workers. Now, it was a command center full of Kalar Soldiers. Their stone like bodies weighed on the polished conglomerate limestone floor marking their presence with many scuffs and scratches from their metallic-like boot soles.

Their skins were of various textures from light to dark rock and minerals. They were not bulky as one would think of when describing a rock, but mirrored a medium stature of a muscular human male. Each person had one primary type of mineral, recognizable by the skin not covered by military attire. The battle armored uniforms were all the same flat onyx color, making them seem like they were mimicking a colony of black Army ants. The room paused their war gaming as Stargazer spoke and the demonstration by Spot was displayed on a thirty by fifty foot projected hologram above the entrance.

On the throne sat Emperor Korvax. His pure gold chair was imported, allowing for his ten foot stature to be accommodated. He wasn't wearing battle armor and his alarsite skin was rare for a Kalar. The yellowish brown aluminum texture complemented his white diamond like robe. His eyes were also very unique, almost rectangular in shape and glowed topaz blue. Different gems were implanted on his fingers, taking the place of eight would be rings. His quartz boots were trimmed with dime sized sapphires around the soles. There were no genitalia on the elemental Kalar race. A belt made of a silver alloy, boots and diamond robe was his only clothing by any standard of modern Earth-like civilizations.

He eyed the video and without any commands to his subjects, the image paused and zoomed in on Stargazer; then moved slowly towards the rest of the group as if he were memorizing their facial features.

"My Emperor?" Three mildly shorter Kalar knights knelt in front of Korvax awaiting instructions. They worn glossy black armored plates covering every part of their anatomy without restricting their movement. Their helmets were lightly spiked at the top with only their ruby red eyes exposed to the elements, leaving a smooth look throughout the head. Each had a unique weapon on their back, one a Great Sword design, another a crystal halberd and the last one had a bastard sword and short sword made of pure black diamonds.

"If Commander Paldar fails you will find these Earthlings and kill them." Korvax's deep base voice carried out to the entrance of the throne room.

"As you command." The three Realgar Knights simultaneously replied and left the room without delay; everyone quickly getting out of the way; returning to their duties in tracking the war.

Siglar Moon Base, Lakros Star System, 987 light years from Arlos

The massive dome covered twenty miles of livable space, with its citizens scrambling to prepare for the brewing storm. The war between the Kalar and Andromen Empires affected them greatly since they were a high source of minerals and chemicals for many races in the star sector. However, the warring ships had not made it to the star system, and what mattered most at the moment was the condition of the atmosphere, which was kicking up the worst storm in decades. The storm would buy them more time to prepare and hide any valuables. The inhabitants of the moon base were a mixture of all sorts of races and professions, mainly miners and engineers. The prosperity from the resource output made for a very sophisticated and state of the art type of lifestyle in space, the dome being one of many engineering masterpieces.

A teenager looked up at the standard I-MAX screen above one of the many plaza centers. Stargazer's broadcast was loud and clear, being received with mixed feelings. People left the eateries and stores, with still many continuing as if the broadcast was a paid advertisement. The young girl was messaging on her wrist phone at the time, but saw darkness at the corner of her eye.

She turned and jumped back as a black robed person stood inches from her side. Her legs froze, and her heart would've as well, but she needed it to continue living.

"Don't be afraid, I won't harm you." The young man's alluring voice calmed her as he looked at the screen which repeated the broadcast as reporters commented on the event.

"Who are you?" The girl's curiosity caught the best of her as she saw Cyer's handsome alien face.

"I'm a traveler and would like to talk with you, if that's alright with you?"

"I think it's okay." She sat back down on a short wall ledge next to a grassy garden area.

"What do you think about these Earthlings and the Kalar?" Cyer said as he sat next to her with is head turned to her, hood covering most of it.

The girl thought for a moment. "The Earthlings must be very brave and powerful to fight the Kalar all by themselves."

"And you're not afraid of them?"

"I'm an orphaned girl, what good would it do to fear so many people who may or may not kill me?" Her pink eyes blinked slowly as she scrutinized Cyer's face.

"What if you're raped or enslaved instead of being killed?" Cyer scanned the girl's body language and bio-chemical levels.

"My parents, grandparents, uncles and aunts all died fighting in the last several wars. There will always be good people fighting for me."

"So you want to go fight in a war when you grow up?"

"Shouldn't we all if there are bad people around?"

"What if I told you I was bad?"

The girl slowly reached out with her hand. "If you were bad, you would have killed all of us already."

"What makes you think I can or won't later?"

"You're the Destroyer of Ordis." She boldly replied.

"And you don't fear me?"

"I wish I could do what you do; then I wouldn't fear anyone."

"That would be easy since I was created without fear."

"So you are an android or something like that?"

"I'm a biogenetic hybrid of the most powerful beings in the universe; there is no one like me."

"Did it hurt very much when they raised you?" The teenager's eyes widen, understanding erroneous basic genetic grafting and splicing methods.

"No, I was born as I am now."

"I guess you wouldn't want to be my friend then?"

"I don't have any friends, but why would you ask me that?"

"Because you are so powerful and intelligent, how could I ever be there when you need me, if you ever do need anything from anyone?"

"Just because I don't feel pain or fear, doesn't mean I wasn't programmed with emotions."

"Really? So will you be my friend?" Her face brighten with joy.

"It makes me, happy, when I disintegrate self exalted beings."

Pananthra's smile straighten, but she touched his exposed hand. "It's okay; I sometimes like it when bad people get what's coming to them."

"And what do you consider as bad people." Cyer scanned the girl internally, down to the genetic level.

"Oh, I guess it would be people who care only about themselves, people who like to hurt others because they get some weird pleasure in seeing someone suffer. People who are very prideful and think they are better than everyone, but they're not." She paused for a second. "I guess those people who want to enslave people, making up stupid reasons to try to justify their own injustice."

"That's a very short list." Cyer smiled for the very first time in his seventh month of life.

"My grandmother told me before she died. It's easy to find bad in people, but it's better to see what is good in those that are truly good. She said they just need a nudge in the right direction sometimes." The girl held Cyer's hand with confidence.

"What's your name?" Cyer let her touch him.

"Pananthra, and yours?"

"Cyer."

Pananthra smiled. "Cyer; I like it."

Cyer looked around the large center and pointed. "Do you see that family dressed in yellow and brown garments, with the two children?"

Pananthra looked into the crowd and after some coaching, spotted the family. "Yes, I see them now."

"Would you like to be part of their family?"

"What are you talking about? How?"

"We go and ask them if they would like to adopt you."

"Why would they want to adopt me, they already have two small kids?"

"Are you going to continue to ask me questions or answer me?" Cyer's tone became stern.

Pananthra looked at the husband and wife talking and smiling as they ate their lunch. "Yes, I guess I would."

Cyer stood up and walked toward the family, holding onto Pananthra's hand. The mother looked up at the very tall man and almost choked on her food as Cyer entered their personal space. "I have a gift for both of you. This girl is very intelligent and understands how to live a life that is destined to end in approximately three centuries." Cyer's body glowed yellow for a second with the black robe falling to the floor, ignoring his physical body.

The husband and wife jumped up from the table. The wife grabbed one of the children, and Pananthra grabbed the other seeing the fear in their eyes, being too far from the parents.

Cyer spoke loudly as if his vocal cords had turned into a megaphone and walked away a few meters letting go of Pananthra. "Hear me people of Siglar. I am Cyer, the Destroyer of Ordis!" Cyer flew up ten feet into the air with an aura of yellow to white light around him; slowly rotating once for all the people to see.

"This orphan girl, Pananthra, is being adopted by this family. Pananthra has saved all of your lives, and all of you will bless her and her new family for the rest of their natural lives. Let it be known, that anyone who harms this girl or her family will answer to me and die. In like manner, Siglar will also be protected by me. Teach your offspring to remember this day. You are all witnesses and I will never forget your DNAs, all seventy-four thousand three hundred twenty-three inhabitants! So I suggest you inform all of the people in this base!" Cyer floated down to the couple.

"Do not fear the girl. She is good, so you will love her. Do you understand?"

"We will do as you say." The husband replied with relief, but yet concern.

The wife nodded, looking back at Pananthra gently holding their daughter. "Yes, we will be a family."

Cyer flew in front of Pananthra. "I told you all you had to do was ask."

"That was more of a command than a request?" Pananthra half frowned.

"Everyone here will make sure you are cared for."

"Does this mean you will stay here?"

"No, I have other things to do in space. But, now you know I am your friend." Cyer flew up silently and rapidly a hundred meters and instantly vanished as he warped out of the dome and into deep space.

Pananthra stared at the doom until her new mother softly gripped her shoulders. The girl looked at her new family and wept with joy.

The void of space was interrupted by thirty Kalar vessels many light years from Siglar. The flagship confidently raced through space, uncloaked with shields up.

The automatic alarm from the sensors jolted everyone into action. The battle technicians started their protocols trying to identify what set the alarm off.

"How many vessels?" The captain instinctively asked.

"Sir…" Before the technician could reply, Cyer entered the bridge as a very bright white stream of energy, forming into his physical body.

"I am Cyer, Destroyer of Ordis. I assume you command this group of vessels?" Cyer body glowed slightly, so that he could be recognized.

"Have you come to fight with us?" The captain asked, confused.

"No, I have come to tell you to order all Kalar vessels to turn away from your current trajectory and declare Siglar Moon Base off limits for the next three centuries." Cyer floated in front of the main screen.

"We have been ordered to occupy the base and extract resources for the empire."

"The base has been placed under my protection; you will meet the terms immediately."

Three security guards moved close to the captain ready for battle. "You answer to the Emperor and the orders we have, come from him."

"You Kalar think that since the Emperor had a hand in my creation, that I must obey his orders. I agreed to fight for him, is true; but because of this agreement, I did not immediately destroy your vessels… Do you comply?"

"The Emperor will have your head and we will not comply." The Captain lashed out with contempt.

Two of the guards fired their plasma rifles center mass on Cyer's chest. The energy dispersed throughout his body as if he were an unquenchable lighting rod.

"Your ship will be last." Cyer lit up the entire bridge with a flash of light and energy.

Several of the bridge consoles shorted out; burnt beyond repair. The Kalars' eyes were used to intense light, but all were temporarily blind. The crews' visions came back to find Cyer nowhere in the room.

The main screen was black, but two small screens at the navigator's console were operational. "Sir, the ships around us are exploding."

The Captain rushed to the console only to see the second to last ship blow up in a nuclear ball of light while in warp. "Evasive action. Communications officer, send out a message to the Emperor about Cyer's treachery!"

"Sir, our communications array has been disabled." The officer replied as Cyer once again returned to the bridge.

Cyer entered at the back of the bridge this time and lased everyone except one of the battle techs. Eleven Kalar lay dead with partial holes in their chests except the captain who was decapitated. No blood was present, but there was residue of charred powdery sediments everywhere.

The slender tech looked around in fear, but quickly regained his cool.

"You're wondering why you're still alive." Cyer flew and stood in front of him.

"Yes." He stood at ease now accepting his impending death.

Cyer stepped next to the console. With dexterous fingers, he re-engaged the computer and internal comms. Energy pulsed through his fingers as he interfaced with the computer. "You are Captain of this ship now. You will take the ship and return to your galaxy. The Kalar cannot win against the Burik'dir or Queen Cassandra. You are the future of the Kalar. Do you understand?"

"We may not be able to make it back to our galaxy alive."

"You will die if you stay in this galaxy; take the challenge for the voyage back. Or are you not a Kalar?" Cyer turned his face away from the console and looked straight into the tech's emerald gem eyes.

"All hands. This is the Destroyer of Ordis. You will follow your new Captain's orders and return home or face oblivion as prisoners or refugees in this galaxy. Your Emperor is doomed; your new hope is with you and your new captain." Cyer looked at the tech. "Captain." Cyer's body glowed yellow as he flew out of the bridge as quickly as he entered.

The Captain looked down at the navigation console. The ship was already on course back to his home planet, ETA: fourteen or so Earth years.

Chapter Five

❖---✳ ⚙ ✳---❖

Watch and Learn, Me Capitan

Master talked in his sleep with great enthusiasm as Rat Bastard read up on the Andromen Empire. "You cannot defeat me… take that… pulse generators… swing back…"

"I hope he's winning." Spot said as he reclined by the table, relaxing.

"The little guy always does that." Rat Bastard replied.

"Well he has every right to." Stargazer added, reviewing the simulations of Master's attack plan.

"So it's good?" Rat turned his attention to Stargazer across the table.

"It's fantastic." Stargazer looked around the table, Ghost was sleeping in a passenger seat, and eight Vorg crew members were also sleeping as if in hibernation. "Hopefully we will be in time to save the armada."

"The pilot said that the armada might hold off their attack because of the transmission, but since they're in communications silence, we won't know until the ship gets closer." Spot explained.

"Let's go over the plan once Ghost wakes up. In the meantime, do you two have any words of wisdom?" Stargazer asked.

"How are we going to fight ships that go faster than light when you can't go past Mach 3?" Rat Bastard asked.

"We haven't tried flying in space and Einstein said that an object can't travel faster than the speed of light, but I think that the force field around the ships allows them as energy to travel faster than light. If that's true, Spot or I might be able to travel faster than light. This will help us in battle so we can keep up with the spaceships."

"What do the rest of us do?"

"You protect Master for the most part, but according to the plan you will not be needed in the initial attack."

"I have to admit that I don't have the combat experience you guys do."

Stargazer smiled. "My combat experience is getting shot at three times. But I'm sure you'll be fine."

"I was in a deuce and a half when machine gun fire cut through seven guys all around me. The tarp was down, so it wasn't hard for me to jump out of the truck and kill the platoon who ambushed us. I was the only survivor." Spot paused in recollection.

"We might be bulletproof, but we need to take care of our emotions and minds. It's going to get really ugly, here and back home." Stargazer looked at Spot.

"Do you think the visions are real?" Spot wanted to doubt.

"I don't know, but if it's a possibility of a future we haven't experienced yet, then I'm going to try to stop it." Stargazer replied.

"But how can the sky be green over the Capitol?" Rat Bastard asked.

"Maybe it's World War III?" Spot suggested.

"Aliens, mutants, people just being people, it doesn't matter how, all I'm concerned with is stopping the bad guys. But for now, you two need to get some rest. We won't get much once we get closer to Arlos" Stargazer replied and moved towards the cockpit.

Spot watched Stargazer leave the compartment, then turned to Rat Bastard. "Whatever you do, don't pull your punches anymore."

"What are you talking about?" Rat Bastard tried to act surprised.

"You can tunnel through hard ground, and I'm sure you can screech a lot more than two times."

"So you think I can yell anytime I want?"

"Yes, and if you're scared of killing people or living creatures, don't be. The things we're going to fight won't care if you're nice or not. They will try to kill you or capture you to experiment and torture you."

"I don't like killing people?" Rat Bastard sadly replied.

"You try not to, and you mourn for both the good and bad people. Many of the Soldiers and civilians fighting in wars are only following orders and what they believe to be right. The leaders who push them in that direction are usually the ones to blame, but it's not about blame or who started it. We need to be better than that and end the conflict by fighting if that's our only way."

"I won't let you down." Rat Bastard sighed.

"That's good to know." Spot half smiled while imitating Stargazer's concern and lay back in his seat, closing his eyes.

A slight grin at the corner of Ghost's mouth went unnoticed as he overheard the conversation.

The day's travel came to an end as the passengers of the transport entered sector 3390 Tier'dir. It was an open sector of empty space with the exception of a phenomenon known as a dark matter vortex.

Stargazer and the rest of the group squeezed inside the cockpit behind the pilot. "Shouldn't we see some sign of a friendly ship?"

Captain Sorin looked at his instruments. "Slowing down so we don't run into a cloaked ship by accident."

"What are the chances of that?" Rat Bastard asked.

"Extremely, extremely rare, but if it isn't zero, I'm not going to chance it." Sorin quickly replied.

"Send out a short range signal, so we can contact and board the Kolisco." Master instructed.

"You heard him Lieutenant." Sorin gave the okay for the communications officer to open a channel in possible hostile territory.

"Sir, we're being hailed." The Lieutenant replied.

"Tell them we're in a hurry and need to board the flagship. If they refuse, let me know." Stargazer commanded and left the cockpit.

The group followed him except for Ghost, who stood next to the captain and console.

Stargazer walked through the ship with Major Krodis and the rest of the team. "So what's the range of this implant again?"

"About four parsecs, without any large mass in between. But…" She said while fitting her helmet on.

"But?" Stargazer paused, his walk and continued after glancing at the major.

"The dark matter vortex will limit any communications to this side of space. And if you're inside it, the implants won't work."

"Good thing Master thought of all this." Stargazer smiled as he waited patiently in front of the transport's main entry way, looking out into space.

Everyone in the transport heard Sorin's report. "Kolisco has decloaked and we're entering their telemetry beacon.

Stargazer scanned the area and spotted the uncloaked ship, as well as several other cloaked ships. He looked deep into the interior and found the exact spot in the engineering section he expected to find. He quickly panned onto other ships while the transport entered the small landing bay of the starship.

The transport door opened shortly afterwards and Stargazer led the way down the ramp into a squad of security guards.

"Lord Stargazer or whoever you are, I don't know what you think you can do, but Admiral Novis has instructed me to assist you in any way we can." A human-like Soldier greeted them, except his skin was light blue and coated with a thin layer of glossy plastic like material.

"Master will need eighty fusion grenades with short range detonators." Stargazer replied, Master, Ghost and Spot stepping forward ready to go where the weaponry was.

The Lieutenant Commander looked at the boy in his navy blue Vorgoling spacesuit. "Follow me, my Lords."

"We're in a hurry Lt Cdr, double time, please." Master instructed, breaking out of a brisk walk into a jog.

Stargazer and Rat Bastard made their way to the bridge, finding an eager crew and captain wanting to follow their instructions. "Lord Master will need to sit in the Captain's chair, while I and Rat Bastard will be here in these chairs."

"You're not going to fight the Kalar like the Destroyer of Ordis?" The science officer asked.

Stargazer looked at the almost human like female whose skin was light peach. Her hair was dark blue and he could tell it wasn't a chemical dye, but if she had been on Earth it would have passed for a fad. "I would tell you the entire battle plan, but due to operational security, its better you don't know at this time how we'll defeat the Kalar."

"Don't worry Ma'am, Master will have everything under control." Rat Bastard interjected.

"In the meantime, I need the communications and weapons officers." Stargazer waited to be introduced and gave them instructions as to what they would be doing.

Rat Bastard walked up in front of the captain. "Everyone else will be performing your normal duties, except for you Captain. You will need to stay behind Lord Master while he does his thing."

"Am I supposed to say anything?" The Captain replied.

"No, you just need to look calm, no matter what you see and hear." Rat Bastard said, then turned into the Rat.

The Captain flinched and moved backwards a few inches, with a bug eyed face.

"You see, you can't do that while Master does his thing. Otherwise, people will be paying attention to you instead of Lord Master."

"I guess everything will be fine as long as there's no more transforming into animals without any warning." The Captain recovered to his calm self.

Stargazer sat in the navigator's seat to the left and looked out into space through the dark matter void.

"Master, where are you guys?" Rat Bastard called returning to his human self.

"I'm here." Master entered the bridge followed by a security team. He stood for a few seconds looking around the bridge. The circular bridge was very well organized and roomy compared to the cockpit on the transport and auxiliary control center on the space port. One large screen in the center displayed open space in high definition. He eyed the Captain's chair, with shock absorbers underneath, black padding all around and state of the art arm consoles. "Nice…"

"Yes, we're ready." Ghost replied to Stargazer's mental question.

"Okay, here goes nothing. Comms, tell the armada to move back half a trillion miles… There are three scout ships moving slowly through the void."

"What? How?" The science officer and a few others whispered.

"On our way." Ghost said over the communication console.

Master sat in the Captain's chair, owning it with pleasure. "Please focus your camera on me, and do not show Lord Stargazer or Rat Bastard."

Stargazer typed instructions on the console, which were shown on the main screen for Master and everyone to read. A digital representation of the Kalar ships appeared on the screen.

Half the bridge crew looked on in astonishment, wondering how the cloaked Kalar ships were being tracked, especially since they were on the other side or in the dark matter vortex.

"Okay, let's take this nice and easy, starting from the left and closest ships first." Stargazer said out loud as if speaking to himself.

"Let me know when the first ten are nearing the end of the vortex." Master commanded.

"First one in place, and in green." Stargazer said, with the closest scout ship icon turning green.

"Nice." Master replied.

"Yeah, just hope they don't start moving in erratic directions." Stargazer scanned feverishly back and forth tracking all the ships he could see.

The Andromen armada moved quickly into position as the twentieth grenade was emplaced.

"It's time to start this thing. Communications officer, please broadcast open frequency." Master combed his hair with his spread fingers before the start of the show.

"Yes, Sir." The officer replied.

"No… It's yes Master." Master looked at the officer, smiling.

"My apologies, Master."

"Attention rock people, I'm Master. And today I will be giving you your first lesson in war. As you can tell by your ship scanners, we are probably outnumbered five to one. However, what you fail to calculate is that I am in charge of this armada. In my world, there is a weapon which is feared among all alien races who tried to invade our magnificent planet Earth. It's called the Tardis Beam. You think you have the advantage of starships, but because you have ship engines you are already defeated. I will demonstrate by instructing my weapon's officer to scan the area in sector 33010 with the beam." Master looked at Stargazer off screen and pointed at him.

Ghost pushed the short-range detonator while Spot flew by the ship. The grenade exploded inside the engine capacitors, creating a chain reaction, amplifying the already extremely lethal grenade's damage, a hundred fold.

A Kalar scout ship exploded, breaking in half and decloaking while speeding through space short of the speed of light.

"As you can tell, we have not lifted a finger. Well, except my weapons officer. So the question of the day is do I need to continue to destroy all of your ships before you surrender to me?"

The bridge was quiet as Stargazer displayed the movement of ships trying to spread out.

"Which of you boulders is in charge? Are you afraid of me or something?"

Commander Paldar appeared on the screen. "We will not surrender because a small ship has been destroyed. And we are not afraid of you."

"Oh, you should be." Master turned towards the crew members around the room. "And why am I talking to a rock man with pebbles for a brain?"

"I…" The life support tech tried to answer.

"Don't answer that. I already know." Master turned back to the screen.

'Send out a mass detonation' Stargazer typed on the screen.'

Ghost saw what Stargazer had in mind and instructed Spot to continue to the flagship while the already emplaced grenades would be detonated.

"Since you don't want to take a hint. Surrender now and this won't happen to you." Master pointed at the weapons officer and thirty-two ships exploded from within.

The Captain's tension left him as he managed to crack a smile.

"Commander of rock people, decloak all your ships and surrender before I litter this entire area with an unnatural number of ship debris!" Master said.

"Where's Stargazer?" Commander Paldar replied.

"He is on his way to Arlos if you must know. But why does that matter? You really don't understand the gravity of your situation or the empire for that matter. I have just commanded you to surrender, but you seem to really be too egoistical for the welfare of other people's lives." Master pointed once again and three more ships exploded from within, one being totally disintegrated with a nuclear reaction from the engines.

"We will not surrender without a fight." Commander Paldar replied, commanding his ships to rush the armada.

"Once again, you have not understood that this will not be a fight, but a massacre. Your ship will now be destroyed." Master said, Ghost seeing the entire conversation as Stargazer heard and saw it.

The Kalar flagship's engines exploded while in the vortex causing the ship to implode leaving no survivors.

"Attention, armada, target the Kalar ships and fire long-range missiles." Master commanded as the communications officer transmitted Stargazer's tracks to the armada.

Hundreds of missiles made their way to the intended locations, half missing their targets; but it was clear that the Kalar were not expecting to be effectively engaged while cloaked at maximum weapon's range.

"Any Kalar leadership hearing my voice, fighting will only get you killed and you won't take any of us with you. Do you surrender?" Master continued to sell the alternative.

"Master, it's highly unlikely any Kalar will surrender." The Captain replied.

Master turned his head with a tilt, looking at the Captain. "Watch and learn, me capitan."

Master stood up. "Hear me Kalar, your honor will stay intact. There is no shame in being defeated by me, or the other Burik'dir. We will not enslave you or harm you once you have surrendered. However, you must surrender or you will face death in a most humiliating way, because I will not allow any of you to abuse your power on others anymore. Your legacy in dying here today will be with dishonor and misguided pride to be told and known throughout the universe. Now, which of you noble warriors will concede and live to fight another day?"

"This is Commander Ur. I order all ships to decloak and deactivate weapons." The Kalar starship decloaked and stopped in space.

"You see; a diamond in the rough... Your surrender is accepted Commander Ur. We'll initiate boarding procedures once everyone has complied, and advise all Kalar ships to maintain positions while your ship's weapon systems are disabled and you are taken to the nearest able star base for processing." Master glanced back at the Captain, as the communiqué ended.

"Wonderfully done." Stargazer smiled and half bowed at Master.

"Sir, Admiral Novis is hailing us." The comms officer reported.

"Yes, where is our fearless leader? I thought he or she would be here on the flagship." Master said, sitting back in the captain's chair.

"I'm on the real flagship; which doesn't matter anymore since you have saved us a very costly battle." Admiral Novis answered; his pray mantis looking head displayed on the screen.

Master turned towards the communications officer with a death stare. "Admiral, that was a rhetorical question. We knew where you were the entire time." Master turned back around to face the screen and smiled.

Stargazer stood next to Master and the Captain. "It's good to see the admiral has an efficient armada and tactical prudence. But we need to quickly disable the Kalar ships and move on to our next objective."

"You are correct Lord Stargazer and I would be very interested to see what that next objective will be, not to mention honored to meet the Burik'dir." Novis' armored spacesuit was lean with silver plating, a trademark of the queen's Imperial space fleet. His prey mantis dark green features were strikingly identical to an Earth insect, except that it was super sized.

"Once the Kalar ships are accounted for, we will meet." Stargazer replied.

The Andromen ships met no resistance in disabling key weapon systems and cloaking capabilities. The overwhelming numbers of prisoners required special attention by half the armada to process and presented a major problem.

Once the Kalar forces were processed, Stargazer and the group flew into the flagship conference room by passing the hull.

The computer sounded the alarm, but it was turned off at the admiral's command. The large oval table accommodated fifteen seats, all magnetized to the floor. Spot looked at the center seat which was moved away from the table much more than the other chairs.

Admiral Novis entered with an entourage of Soldiers. His body was long with six limbs and four wings. The specially designed spacesuit tucked in the wings on his back. The long arms and legs were characteristic of giant basketball players. He extended his four arms and greeted the humans with firm handshakes; then had his people scatter to their normally designated seats.

Stargazer examined every detail of this incredible insect-like alien. The admiral's spacesuit covered his exoskeleton made of chitin, which seemed to be able to withstand a space environment for a good half hour. However, like most other living beings, the admiral's lungs would not be able to work without a supply of air. The admiral, like the rest of the crew carried a personal helmet by his side, a combat ready procedure while in space.

"Admiral, I apologize for the shortness of the situation, but we need to talk to all the ship captains and second in commands as soon as possible." Stargazer sat facing him.

"It will be some time before we get all of them to a secure conference call, unless you need them in person, which will take longer." Novis replied.

"A conference call will work." Master chimed in.

"Commander." Novis motioned to his battle commander.

"It should take us about 15 minutes, Sir."

"While we're waiting, we would like to tell you what our plan is before the conference." Stargazer assured the admiral, motioning to Master with a nod.

"Admiral, I have plotted a path to the outskirts of the Tritany 10 system. As you're aware, it's a system of low population with massive resources. According to your intelligence, it's also the least protected at this point. Perhaps because the Kalar believed that this armada would've been destroyed or be used for a direct attack against a larger military target. The intent is to get the Kalar to divert their forces from the Dortin and Jifu sectors of space to attempt to attack us. We'll lure those forces into a kill zone, where we'll conduct hit and run tactics until we get to sector Hansis 2. Once there, we should have destroyed all of the forces and have to focus on the Kalar Supreme Guard forces which will probably be moved to intercept us. The armada's firepower was diminished greatly by having to devote ships to prisoner transport and security; but this plan to compensate for that loss will work properly as long as the captains understand to hit and run and not try to gain a full victory by pressing the attack on stragglers." Master explained as a 3D star map displayed above the table.

The admiral raised a hand in thought. A moment passed in silence, "Even with two armadas at full strength, we don't have the power to take control of Arlos and we don't know where Queen Cassandra is at the moment."

"Admiral, things have been set in motion and there will be enough firepower when the time is right. In addition, the armada itself doesn't have to be at full power, we just need the enemy to think so." Stargazer politely retorted.

"The legend of the Burik'dir is taught in the academy as an elective for many; but for officers, it's required. The Queen thought it was important enough to keep it in the curriculum since its conception. I don't dispute the legitimacy of the Burik'dir, but as for your legitimacy, I can only speculate. You are asking me to put the lives of trillions in your care, and the only assurance I have is your unorthodox combat skills and a Vorg crew under your command." Novis glanced at MAJ Krodis and then back at Stargazer.

"Actually, you have more than that; you have our willingness to help you in the face of death, and our word which so far is true."

Novis' semi-ocular mandible slightly tightened. "I guess we can start the conference now."

"Admiral, all captains are standing by." The communications officer reported.

Stargazer and Master looked at each other in unison. "That was a very fast fifteen minutes." Master commented.

"I just wanted to make sure I didn't get blindsided, and my captains need to see that I approve of the plan first before they travel to this spot in space." Novis pointed at the 3D plot of the Tritany 10 system. "May the living stay alive."

The conference occurred without a hitch and the armada quickly started its movement to Tritany 10.

Crew Quarters A112, Andromen Flagship

"I hope the Captains don't mess this up." Master drank his new favorite protein mix.

"Everyone seemed to have liked your plan." Rat Bastard replied as he lay in his assigned bed cubical; the soles of his feet barely pressing on the outer edge of the one foot tall transparent steel railing.

"Three hundred twenty-seven ships, that's a lot of chances for one to spook the enemy or send out a treacherous message."

Rat Bastard turned his head, his brows tightening. "Why don't you have any faith in people?"

"I have faith in some people. Just not everyone. Do you know how many people have died due to wars and crimes, because of people making mistakes or just being evil?" Master propped his feet on a small table extending out of the wall.

"I'm sure you're going to tell me." Rat Bastard crossed his arms behind his head amidst his pillow.

"More than I'm willing to count."

"Wow, that's a lot. But I think you're forgetting something."

"What are you talking about? I don't forget anything." Master relooked at the plan on his tablet.

"The good guys always win if you have faith."

"Sorry to break it to you, but in real life not all good guys win."

"Hmm… as long as there's one victory, the good guys always win one way or another."

"I really don't know why I put up with these philosophical discussions." Master sighed.

"Aaah.." Rat Bastard lumbered out of bed, the railing automatically detracting. "It's because I'm a good listener and very smart."

"If you're so smart, why didn't you come up with this plan to fight the Kalar?"

Rat Bastard moved across the room towards the door. "It's all in my master plan, to let you do the strategy. While you're reading that metal clipboard, I am going to enjoy some alien female company."

"Where're you going?" Master's picked his head away from the tablet, showing an annoyed posture being temporarily distracted by Rat Bastard's remarks.

Rat Bastard turned his head as he walked out of the room smiling. "I'm going to walk around the ship and find out what they think of us. If you're not going to have faith in people, I guess I'll have to do it for you."

Master stared at the closed plastic looking sliding door for a long while. "I have faith... But we need a miracle." Master looked back down at Cyer's image and the computed statistical energy output of a blue star.

Crew Quarters A114, Andromen Flagship

Stargazer opened his eyes from a long restful nap. His gaze went out through the starship and into a wide view of millions of stars. He jumped from one light source to another as was habitual for him as a child. Earth was his home, but the universe was his visual playground.

"Do you think we'll make a difference?" Stargazer softly asked.

"If we save the queen and stop Korvax, yeah." Ghost instantly replied.

"No, I mean."

"On Earth?.. I *don't* know." Ghost interrupted.

"Can I ever complete my sentences?" Stargazer turned his head, Ghost sitting in front of a computer screen reading historical records.

"Sorry Star, but since we're in the future and everyone's telling us the Earth's past and future are at stake, then yes, I think we'll make a difference... and I'll stop ending your sentences."

Stargazer sat up on the bunk. "I thought I was one of a very few people with powers. Now it seems that there was a revolution of super people on Earth and we missed it?"

"I think we might be more use here and honestly, our future is not fully written, so how do we know that we didn't start that revolution." Ghost turned off the screen and stretched his arms.

"Whatever happens, I need you to promise me, no one will be left behind."

Ghost looked at Stargazer's eyes. His thoughts were very clear, maybe too much. "So you think I have a thing for Queen Cassandra?"

Stargazer smiled. "If she has the same strong feelings for you, I don't blame you if you want to stay with her. But seeing how things have hit the fan lately; you should look at what's best for Earth… but it's your call and I'll honor it."

"Thank you Steve." Ghost wondered how he would have slapped himself, not less than a week ago he thought Cassandra was some pushy female and now he was falling in love with her, if he hadn't already.

"No thanks necessary. Hopefully the woman I want to be with will be waiting for me when we get back."

Ghost didn't say a word and thought about how screwy romance and fate could be when you least expect it.

Lower Deck L8 A, Andromen Flagship

Spot walked into one of several manufacturing decks. The repair and customizing material modules were constantly calibrating or producing needed equipment and ship parts. The supervisor on duty walked up to Spot while the rest of the workers momentarily glanced at them as if the Captain of the ship had walked onto the deck.

"Lord Spot, we were not expecting to see any of the Burik'dir here, but it's a pleasure, welcome, I'm Ensign Gran." The middle aged man stood proud as he saluted him.

"Call me Abaddon." Spot returned a perfect salute.

"Yes, my Lord, but may I ask what that means?"

"On Earth it means the destroyer."

The Ensign smiled, "So it will mean the same here. He extended his hand toward the twenty modules the size of large dump trucks, "Please let me show you our department."

Spot smiled back seeing they didn't fear his name, knowing he was an ally and would bring much destruction on the Kalar.

"The modules here receive raw parts and materials from the floor above us. We repair or synthesis improvements into the matrix of template jobs for all things from personal hygiene items, clothing, body armor, weapons, up to hull material for the ship." The Ensign walked around the modules explaining the details of their important work.

Spot listened intently to all the words and scrutinized the modules and people running them as if inspecting troops for battle.

The Ensign completed his tour with assembling the twenty five workers in the very large room. "Lord Abaddon, told me he has some questions for you and if you have any for him please ask."

Spot walked in front of most of the workers, as a few where in the back of the crowd. "You know my name, but I would like to know each of your names, where you call home and what you plan to do after the empire is saved."

"I'm Chief Petty Officer Dolas Hem, my home is Liwar Prime, and I hope to start my own manufacturing company someday." The smiling and tall light blue skinned woman was the first to reply.

Spot couldn't believe how handsome and beautiful all of the people he had met in this galaxy were. *'What kind of vitamins do these people take?'* He thought to himself having never seen any overweight, underweight, wrinkled or malformed humanoids.

The last worker gave his speel and added a question. "Lord Abaddon, do you really think we will win and see our families again?"

Spot looked at him calmly and stepped back as if wanting to take a group photo. "I think we have a very good chance of winning, now that my friends are here, but you're probably wondering if I can kill this Destroyer of Ordis. Time will tell, but I would ask something from you guys. What's the smallest and most powerful energy storage pack or source you guys can create?"

The Ensign looked at Hem to answer the question. "Lord Abaddon, that's easy. We can make a fission pack capable of storing two-trillion kilowatts and creating two-million kilowatts per second."

"And how big is that?"

"A pack, about 3 feet square by 2 feet deep."

"If you can make things like this, why haven't you used nuclear weapons strong enough to defeat the Kalar?"

The Ensign stepped in, "Nuclear weapons are used by other races, but they are crude and Queen Cassandra outlawed impure nuclear weapons. The plasma cannons on warships like this one do not leave radioactivity like an old style nuclear weapon."

"I don't think the Destroyer of Ordis or the Kalar care about that." Spot interjected.

The Ensign's face stopped in time as in deep thought while his jaw slightly dropped. "We must be the ones to stand for what's right and our future generations."

"So we do, and that's why I must ask you make ten packs for me, and if possible make them quickly portable for fast loading onto any ship I get on. Thank you all for your warm hospitality. I will not let you down, I promise." But the group asked for him to continue speaking.

Spot stayed with them for a moment talking about Earth, the ship and their specific jobs but work had to continue, so he strolled off the floor to find out as much as possible about the people he was fighting for. He walked peacefully; something he was not really able to fully do back on Earth as politics, gossip and false ideology got in the way of doing what was right in a time of war.

The voyage was uneventful for several days, but the emptiness of space were once again filled with distress calls from the planetary system in Tritany 10.

Master tapped the armrest slowly to the beat of an imaginary sonata. "Okay, you can start jamming now." He almost boringly commanded.

"Affirmative, Master." The communications specialist replied.

"It seems like your plan is working." Rat Bastard whispered as he stood next to Master.

"Of course it is." Master, mumbled.

"So why are you so excited?" Rat raised his voice.

Master exhaled in frustration and looked at the three specialists, "Is there anything?"

The long range scanner specialist picked his head up in response. "No, Master. We see no changes to the energy parameters you indicated."

"Take it easy. Chances are he'll show when we get near Arlos." Rat Bastard tried to comfort the teenager.

"He'll show up when he finds out where we are."

"But he knew where we were going to be a few days ago and never came. I mean if I were him I would be thinking why come to us when all he has to do is wait for us near Arlos?"

Master looked up at Rat Bastard's face. "Sometimes, your logic baffles me."

"My mom used to say that all the time." Rat walked away from Master, kneeling beside the life support specialist. "Hi there, I was thinking once your shift is over, if you wanted to have lunch with me."

The female specialist smiled; Master squinting his eyes and rolling them in disbelief. "Oh, brother."

The Kalar forces were overwhelmed by Spot, Ghost and Stargazer's surprise attack in the rear defensive perimeter of the weak garrison bases. The deactivation of automatic weapon systems left an open door for Andromen starships to force a surrender. The battle lasted less than an hour, before the entire system was under Andromen control.

Stargazer and the group quickly reunited in the flagship bridge, looking at the next step in their plan.

Rat Bastard eyed Stargazer's torn and burnt spacesuit. "Too bad they don't make indestructible clothes."

"If they did, there'll be a lot of stores out of business." Stargazer smiled.

"Hmm, I guess there would be." Rat smiled back.

"Captain Olac, we're ready when you are." Master announced. The main screen changed the view to Captain Olac. Her short black hair defined a slender beautiful young face.

"We're in position Lord Master." Olac's mild tone sent chills down Rat Bastard's back.

Ghost smiled seeing the big guy's one tracked mind of being the center of attention for the opposite sex.

"Excellent. Lead the way Captain." Master replied.

Twenty starships warped toward deep space with the flagship in the center.

"Okay, I'm going to change. You guys seem to have a handle on all of this." Stargazer walked toward one of three exit doors.

"Lord Stargazer exiting the bridge." An automated voice announced as the double doors opened.

The Andromen crew paused, turning their heads, to see Stargazer leave.

Ghost walked up behind the science officer. "What's going on?"

The science officer kept his attention on the multiple screens and readouts on the console. "Lord Ghost, there's unusual activity around Hansis 2. There are indications that warships are being ordered to rally in that system."

"Master, we might need to re-think our plan." Ghost spoke loudly.

"Continue monitoring and you two find out everything there is about that sector." Ghost commanded the other two science officers assigned to monitor for the Destroyer of Ordis."

"What's up?" Rat Bastard and the other two walked up to Ghost.

"It seems they're not going to send any forces this way." Ghost stated as a fact.

Rat Bastard and Spot turned towards Master in the trail end of the trio.

"Oh my God. How could I have not seen this?" Master raised his hands to the ceiling with wide eyes. "You two continue with your original orders." Master quickly lowered his hands, pointed a finger at the science officers and slightly frowned.

"Computer, bring up Hansis 2 information on the main screen!" Master quickly got back into the Captain's chair.

"As you can see. The sector has three-star systems with twenty six planets. They will try to suck us into this area." Master moved his hand and finger as if touching the screen from ten meters away. A yellow arrow, line and box appeared in a zoom of a very large planet, labeled Utro-mes. The Kalar even though they have the power to radiate the entire population of the planet, do want the resources without having to worry about hazardous wastes in the atmosphere, oceans and land."

"You're the man." Rat Bastard interrupted, seeing that Master had anticipated the Kalar maneuver.

"Yes, well, as I was saying." Master paused with an annoyed smirk. "The Kalar have been trying to take over the planet's inhabitants since they arrived there. The Utro people, known as Su, have been able to defeat many assaults; however, the Kalar have air supremacy and will take the planet over time. It's possible they're diverting forces to reinforce the sector, but more than likely they're trying to get us to attempt a rescue of the planet."

"What makes you think that? There's so much space out there, why don't they think we can't just bypass them?" Spot interrupted.

"You're thinking in one dimension my friend. Hansis 2 is key because it's close enough to a direct path to Arlos. If we bypass the sector, we'll have the enemy in our rear. If we just destroy the space forces and leave the ground troops there, a Kalar force just needs to come in and use the planet as a base with no opposition. So, yes we will go destroy the space forces and destroy the ground forces. And use the planet as a launching point. What the Kalar don't know is we have the ability to infiltrate without warning."

"We can only do so much and destroying the ground forces will take a very long time." Rat Bastard said.

"We're not the main force. We're the distraction." Master said.

"The short term advantage is time. If the Vorgolings are sticking to the timeline, we should have two extra fleets to occupy the sector when we're done and assemble for the final attack on Arlos."

"So I assume you have a detailed plan on taking the planet?" Spot asked.

"Of course. Rat will be with you, but you'll lead the rebellion as the a great warrior. Stargazer and Ghost will take care of the space forces."

"And what will you be doing?" Rat Bastard asked.

"Keeping us all alive." Master said as an absolute.

Chapter Six

General Mihod

A bleak speck of light filtered through the hydroponic lantern screen. The air was rich aboard the star destroyer, but tense with word of failure by the Kalar attack forces in the Pasik sector of space. Lt. Mar strolled between the protein booster tanks. LED readouts on the edges indicating full reserve capacity attained. Green goggles covered her bright blue eyes. A thin chrome headset kept her long white hair from swinging in front of her face. Her silky dark green skin would have fooled many people into categorizing her as a Martian, but was in fact one of a million Dyskar Soldiers fighting for the Kalar. The alliance evolved out of a slave pact which currently kept the race off the extinction list. The science officer made her final round of inspections and sat at the hydrogenic control center console.

"Bridge, Lt. Mar, all systems ready for departure." Mar touched an intercom icon on her screen.

"Acknowledged." The bridge stations officer replied.

Lt. Mar nonchalantly looked across the fifty meter long field. Several technicians routinely fed nutrients to junction boxes, or washed tubes to maintain efficiency. Mar's gaze slowly moved down to the computer console. Dexterous fingers searched for supply routes and energy output data within twenty parsecs of Arlos. The information was uploaded once the departure order was given. It was her first opportunity to link to nearby relays and find the indicators she hoped would be available. Failure was not an option and time was running out.

Data filled the screen, automatically scrolling down as fast as Mar could speed read. She raised her eyes now and then to make sure a technician or Kalar Soldier didn't get too close while she viewed the information not normally associated with the ship's operational status as it headed to Arlos.

Mar whispered a smile. "Found you." She entered new data and resumed her routine duties.

The ship entered Arlos spaceport a few days later. The ship off loaded its cargo as scheduled and left the next day minus one crew member. As far as everyone was concerned a Lt. Mar never existed in the ship's database and an Ensign got an unexpected promotion with a change of orders assigned to the botany section.

Three space ports away, a very elegantly dressed woman passed customs and Kalar screening with a flash of her identify bracelet. Her purple robe was decorated with silver and onyx gems and a hood covered most of her green skinned face.

"Commander, you are aware that we cannot allow you on board

this vessel without a guard escort?" The lead Kalar Soldier at the entrance stated without fear.

Lix looked at the Soldier's chest instead of his eyes. "I am aware, as my instructions were to be escorted and meet with General Mihod."

The Kalar elite guard stood silent for a moment waiting to see if the Special Agent was really what she was supposed to be. "Your identity bracelet once again."

Lix calmly raised her wrist, showing no impatience or anxiety, but she did raise her piercing blue eyes at his.

White hair strands were exposed from under her purple hood covering a crystal crown. She kept a straight mouth as she tilted her head ever so slightly at the captain.

The guard noticed the tilt and then looked at his scanner on his own wrist. It read: "Special Envoy, top priority, security level access full. Inform central once envoy reaches final destination."

"Your escort will be with you the entire time, even to relieve yourself." The guard didn't show any emotions, but Lix knew he didn't like her or at least what she represented. Her race were slaves to the Kalar and he considered her a traitor as a race for not fighting back to the death.

Three Soldiers carrying rifles walked up to her once the Captain motioned them near. "Escort Commander X to see General Mihod. The general will give you further instructions at that time."

"Yes, Sir." The ranking elite guard motioned Lix to follow. "Commander, follow me." Lix and the new entourage walked into the boarding arm to a shuttle bound for Siris Mark, the second planet in the Arlos system.

The planetary defense system around Siris Mark was in turmoil as computers crashed or were being patched up. Hundreds of military supply and engineering ships worked overtime trying to prepare for an expected battle with the remaining Andromen forces.

General Mihod was short in stature for a Kalar, but his boisterous commands were loud and strong. The lunar base above Siris Mark was a strategic location for the overseeing of the re-establishment of the defensive grid. "Colonel Paxx, why are those freighters parked out in space?"

"Sir, we're waiting for Judar to beacon them in as the fortifications are refitted."

Mihod grinded his rock hard mouth. "You tell Judar to get moving, or I'll have you and them mining quartz for the rest of both your lives."

"Yes Sir." The colonel quickly bowed and ran off to his logistics section, knowing the general was a very hard-nosed person who meant his threats and always followed through.

Mihod eyed him as he left, but the appearance of the purple figure with an escort of elite imperial guards made all of the dozen people around him talking and moving about him unimportant. Mihod raised his hand to a clerk wanting to give him a document, indicating not to be disturbed.

The elite guard in charge stopped a few paces in front of the general. Four of the general's body guards moved in surrounding the entourage as a standard procedure when possible harm was near the general, in particular weaponry or possible hostile intentions. The elite guards ignored the bodyguards' actions and focused on Commander X as their prime assignment.

"General, we have been instructed to report to you, once Commander X has been safely escorted to you." The elite guard slightly bowed out of respect, but not as a requirement for imperial guards, who only bowed to the Emperor and Realgar Knights.

"Thank you Lieutenant. You can return to your Captain. My bodyguards will ensure the Commander is not allowed to wander from her duties." Mihod's voice was tempered with tact.

The elite imperial guards left Lix and General Mihod with Kalar workers running around frantically coordinating the defensive effort. General Mihod looked at one of his bodyguards and then at Colonel Paxx who seemed to be standing by to give a report. "Take charge for a moment, Colonel. I trust you will have everything under control."

"Yes, Sir."

Mihod walked out of the center and into a complex of other rooms and hallways. Lix without a word followed him, as did the four bodyguards.

Kalar Soldiers and workers moved out of the way as the general made his presence known. One of the hallways was exposed to outer space with very large transparent gold windows. All six people easily fitted side by side in the hallway, but the bodyguards kept behind and in front of Lix, her purple robe dragging faintly along the floor. The area was silent for the most part with the only noticeable noise coming from the Soldiers' footsteps.

The view was magnificent as the hallway made a circular pattern around what seemed to be a park in the middle a barren moon surface similar to Earth's moon. The dome covering the park was no more than 75 meters in diameter and very large compared to other areas of the base.

The group passed an air locked door into the park. A fresh breeze of rose scented air passed through Lix's nostrils. The annoying metal on metal footsteps disappeared as they walked on plush dark green grass.

Mihod looked at his guards and they dispersed out, standing by the two entry ways into the park.

"The Soldiers were very efficient in destroying the defensive systems on the planet and here on this base, but as you can tell, they bypassed unimportant areas like this one. Well, not important to the empire, but I suppose it was important to someone else." Mihod casually said as if telling a story to a child on a family stroll with Lix by his side.

Lix walked towards a large stone bench next to a light brown tree, full of bright yellow leaves, almost in the center of the park. She sat on the smooth surface, feeling the coolness of the rock with her fingers.

"The Andromenians fashioned that bench out of the very moon we're standing on. Our people would have taken this same piece of sediment and made jewelry to show off the status of our slaves." Mihod sat next to her. His short seven foot stature made it seem like he was a father and Lix was a teenage girl next to him.

"Good to see you again General." Lix tried to change his mood and subject.

"I'm sorry for our people's actions. If only there had been a better way."

"I'm sorry for you and those like you. If we win or lose, you will live in a place where you won't be free of evil or prejudices." Lix stated as she saw it.

Mihod turned his head down toward her. "Perhaps."

"I know you didn't expect me to be here, but I have reason to believe that the Queen is somewhere on the planet." Lix got to the point.

Mihod's sapphire skin moved slightly as if smiling. "And I thought you were here to say goodbye for the last time."

"As long as we are both living, you will always be a friend, and I don't say goodbye to my friends." Lix looked out across the grass and distant five other large trees.

"Yes, the Queen is on the southern region of the polar ice cap, in a complex specially made to contain her unusual powers. I thought about what could be done, but she is surrounded by a large amount of imperial guards and anyone approaching without the Emperor's clearance will be killed on sight."

"Do you have clearance?"

"I had for a brief moment, having to see what resources they needed, but once the supplies were delivered, I and everyone else who visited were told to forget about the location and never speak of it again. We never saw the queen, but I'm sure she's there, since there are very few secrets I am not in the fold of."

"I must try to get in there. What's the closest I could get without arousing suspicion?"

"I was told you were one of the best in situations like this but the closest is many miles away. Not even you can do it without being seen."

"I'll run the entire way in a stealth suit, if I have to." Lix sighed.

"What about the Burik'dir? Aren't they supposed to be able to defeat the empire and bring peace to the galaxy?"

"I don't know if they're real, or if they can defeat Cyer. They might as well be on the other side of creation seeing that the entire Kalar empire is gunning for them." Lix said the extent of her knowledge of the situation.

"Ever since Lord Stargazer sent out the broadcast, Cyer has disappeared and is said to be rouge, plus the Realgar Knights were sent to kill all of the Burik'dir."

Lix's eyes stared into Mihod's ruby eyes looking to confirm the truth. "Why would Cyer be going rogue?"

"I warned them that the genowraiths would not be controllable. Cyer has his own mind and great power we have yet understood. The Emperor thought that no matter the situation, the genowraith would want to destroy any opposition which meant the Andromen and anyone who would not allow such a creature to exist."

"So, Korvax thought he would let the monster loose and deal with him once he got the Queen's powers." Lix summarized.

"Sort of. I believe that the ancient legends King Alexmarks wrote about caused the Emperor to see Earth and anyone from the Milky Way Galaxy as a threat to life itself. The genowraith confirms this, because the genetic makeup of the strongest beings from the Milky Way Galaxy are part of the genowraith program. All inside of Cyer."

"So the Emperor is not doing all this because he wants power?"

Mihod stayed fixed on Lix's green face. "Who isn't influenced by power every now and then?"

"Hmm... well me." Lix smiled.

"Maybe that's why I liked you ever since we met in the banquet hall decades ago."

"You know it was my job to learn about you and many other dignitaries at the banquet?" Lix stopped smiling.

"Do you know what I love about spies, especially female ones, something the Kalar don't have?"

"What's that?"

"They think that everyone can't see they're spies. I did make general for a reason." Mihod smiled, the sapphire crystals of his skin seemed to crack and reassemble instantly as it moved.

"You are the most noble general and person I have ever met."

Mihod looked straight at the greenery. "Thank you, that means a lot to me."

The two sat silent for a while. "I know you have much to do and I don't want you to be linked as a traitor, so if I can get a passage back to Arlos, I will return on my own without anyone's knowledge." Lix stated.

"Once we leave this paradise, don't speak of anything. I'm old school and everything is monitored except this area of course. So you must know that the Kalar armada was decimated and the Burik'dir have suffered no losses. If they're who they say they are, then it might behoove you to prepare things here so when they do get near, the queen's rescue can be better facilitated."

"I'll take your wisdom to heart. Take care of yourself my friend." Lix said and stood up.

"Don't get up Rashell. Let us sit a little longer, in case this is our last meeting." Mihod pleaded.

Lix looked at the general with gratitude. This was the first time anyone had ever used her real name in years and coming from a person she thought didn't know, comforted her. The general was true to his word and if he knew her real name, he hadn't revealed it to anyone; otherwise she would already be dead.

"It's a good thing no one can read your mind, unlike other beings in the galaxy." Lix softly said and sat back down.

"Thank goodness… people would think I have no sense of humor."

Lix almost burst out into laughter as she put her hand on her mouth; giggling escaping.

Mihod however, laughed a heavy laugh. "Stop that, or I'll tell a joke!"

Hansis 2, Outer Orbital Defense Grid

The Realgar Knights existed a star destroyer, each piloting small long-range fighters. Telemetry placed the three fighters in the middle of the system above Hansis 2. Kalar chatter indicated heavy maneuvers on the planet's surface, but no recent major contact had occurred on the main continent. One of the knights peeled off formation and descended to the surface, while the other two flew to opposite ends of the orbital defensive grid of satellites.

Kalar spacecrafts littered the system, the ships around the planet providing intelligence and coordinating unit actions for ground and air assets. The rest of the space fleet was focused towards outer space hearing reports of an oncoming Andromen armada.

Long-range scouts disappeared from the direction of last known

Andromen spacecrafts. But there was no advance into the Hansis system.

"Admiral, the Realgar Knights are not responding." The second in command reported.

"Let them be. Just keep feeding them intel so they know what's happening. In the meantime, send out more scouts to see if we can locate the armada."

The second in command looked at the communications officer making sure the instructions were sent out to the ships assigned to deploy scout ships. "They should already have been here by now." He stated while standing next to the seated Admiral.

"They're waiting just out of range, trying to bait us to go to them."

"We outnumber them, why don't we take the bait?"

"Because time is on our side and being on the defense is our advantage. Let them come to us." Admiral Glac confidently stood his ground.

Andromen Flagship, outside of Hansis sector

"It seems you were right Master." Spot said while the entire bridge crew looked at the main screen of the Hansis system.

"Captains, just keep picking off any ships that approach, as we discussed. Stargazer's group will depart shortly." Master said manipulating the armrest console on his chair.

Stargazer stood in front of Ghost. "Are you sure you can do this?"

"If I couldn't I would have told you."

Stargazer looked around at his friends, all wearing body armor, Spot carrying a large backpack. "Alright, let's all hold hands."

Rat Bastard turned into the Rat and grabbed Stargazer's hand, while Ghost on the other side held Stargazer and Spot's hands.

They all turned semi-transparent and flew out of the bridge with Stargazer as point.

Rat Bastard looked back as the spacecraft was not cloaked but instantly disappeared when Stargazer warped towards Hansis 2. "Wow! Why didn't you guys ever tell me how this roadrunner flying thing was like?"

"Yeah, I forgot you never went faster than light with us before." Stargazer replied.

"Is this how you feel all the time Ghost?" Rat asked.

"Try not to talk to him Rat, he needs to concentrate and keep us invisible."

"Oh, sorry about that." Rat said, and everyone kept quiet for some time.

"Stargazer, do you know where you're going?" Rat had to ask, seeing nothing but empty space with stars in the distance.

Stargazer smiled and looked at Rat Bastard. "If you keep asking questions and distract me enough, we might collide with the planet."

"Oh, sorry I won't say another word, until we get there… Whenever we get there."

Stargazer laughed and turned back to the front focusing on the planet and hundreds of moving objects in the area his path took him.

"Believe me big guy; you'll know when we get there."

Less than forty minutes later, the sixteenth planetoid came into view for a few seconds as they happen to pass by it several hundred thousand miles away. The Hansis star, Yimos, was yellowish hot white and small but was definitely a reference point for the group to notice, even though Stargazer was actually flying toward the upper right of the star. "We're going to slow down once I get ten million miles from the planet. They will have mines and sensor buoys at that distance. If for some reason we separate, stick to the plan and find allies and win the war, Ghost and I will find you in time."

"Roger." Spot replied.

"Let's kick some butt." Rat Bastard grinned with his sharp rat teeth blaring.

Stargazer navigated the group through a maze of buoys, two space stations and sixty Kalar starships. Hansis 2 was a blue planet, similar to Earth except it was a little larger and had more ocean with what seemed to the group as one major piece of land not yet separated into many continents.

"Woww..." Rat spoke for the group.

"Yeah, this planet's a keeper." Ghost spoke for the first time since they left."

The group almost halted before hitting the atmosphere as gravity was making it harder for Ghost to keep everyone invisible and intangible. "It's okay Star, get us down on the ground quickly. I can rest down there before we continue."

"Roger." Stargazer turned on the afterburner having not to worry about air resistance and landed on the side of a mountain near the equator.

"That was a rush." Rat Bastard said having never flown past Mach one in an atmosphere. "But I thought there would be sonic booms or something."

"Stick with me and you'll hear plenty of those." Spot assured him as they stood on a mountain ledge in the middle of a rainforest.

Ghost almost collapsed on moss covered hard rock as they all turned tangible. The one-hundred percent humidity and heat hit their faces while they removed their helmets. The temperature control of their spacesuits was working so Stargazer made Ghost keep his helmet on so he could rest in the coolness of the internal environment. The air was a little richer than Earth's atmosphere, which only meant the planet was not polluted by hundreds of years of hazardous wastes and unnaturally made gases.

Stargazer looked across the vast jungle. Spot stood next to him as Rat Bastard turned to human form and sat next to Ghost. "I don't understand how you of all people could have picked this spot to land on." Spot's sarcastic statement ran deep.

"It's not my fault the planet is ninety-five percent jungles." Stargazer scanned seeing nothing but a barrier of green all around him, except straight up where the Kalar forces loomed in orbit.

"You could have picked a place on a coast or next to a desert, or a city."

"I couldn't find any cities not burning." Stargazer sadly replied.

"Oh… this will do then." Spot soberly sat on the wide ledge next to Rat Bastard.

"I'm going to the top of the peak and see if I can spot anything made of metal or plastic." Stargazer said as he flew up towards the peak.

"I could use a steak about now." Rat Bastard muttered.

"Didn't you eat before we left?" Spot eyed him.

"Yeah, but I like to eat when I'm bored."

"You're sitting on an alien planet waiting to fight thousands of Kalar who want nothing better than to say they killed a Burik'dir, and you're bored?"

Rat Bastard looked at Spot then out at the mountainous canopies of tree tops. "All I see is probably a thousand things, maybe wanting to bite or eat us."

Spot smiled. "Yeah, so do I, but I'm sure you'll protect me." Spot scooted backward and laid back to take a nap.

"You bet I'll protect you and Ghost." Rat Bastard placed a hand on Ghost's shoulder and moved the sleeping man into a flat position. "Relax my friends. I'll protect you." Rat turned into the rat and perched himself silent and still so he would hear any approaching danger.

Stargazer returned after a few minutes with Rat motioning him to be quiet. "It looks like there's several hundred miles of jungle in all directions, but I did see sections of construction material of a village a hundred miles to the east. It's going to be dark soon, but we'll wait a few hours before we check it out." Stargazer whispered.

"Okay boss… but I hope they don't snore, because it might attract some prey of bird or other predators."

"They have body armor, what does that matter?"

"It will wake them up." Rat Bastard frowned as if mad at Stargazer for being so insensitive. "If only everyone were as smart as I am."

Stargazer stood silent in shame, but smiled as Rat Bastard soon curled up into a large furry black ball and slept.

The hours passed as Stargazer scanned the sky and animals in the area which came out of the foliage. The creatures were similar to Earth rainforest animals, but a little larger in many respects. The black bats in the area were four feet tall with a massive wingspan. As long as they stayed low they would not be bothered, Stargazer thought, so he focused most of his scanning on the ships above for future reference.

Ghost and the others woke up refreshed. The night stars above were a little consolation to Ghost who couldn't see in the dark. But his reading of Stargazer's mind made it seem like he had a special mobile camera seeing everything like daylight.

The group turned intangible and invisible once again and flew towards the suspected village. They arrived in no time to find a complex of wooden buildings underneath the tree canopy. The villagers were very tall, resembling ten foot trolls, except they had knowledge of engineering, crafts and much more indicated by the complexity of the buildings, water collection, waste disposal system and electricity which they seemed to not be using at the time.

Stargazer floated above two guards in front of the largest structure in the almost eight hundred meter complex. The universal translator was working, but no one was talking. "Ghost turn tangible, but stay invisible. Everyone else be quiet." Stargazer instructed.

Ghost did as instructed, seeing Stargazer's plan. "The Burik'dir have arrived to your village. Lower your weapons and take us to your leader." Stargazer loudly said floating above the guards.

The startled guards looked all around them with spears at the ready. "Show yourself!" One yelled.

Stargazer floated down and in front of the two guards who spread themselves out a little to give each other room to fight. Ghost let go of him, knowing his next move.

The darkness of the night and overhead cover would have made anyone think how could the guards see, but they had no problem seeing Stargazer materialize in front of them as he floated two feet in the air. "I am Lord Stargazer. Do not be afraid."

Both guards screamed a terrifying high-pitched siren like alarm training their weapons at Stargazer.

The village came to life in an instant as if everyone in their dwellings slept with combat gear and weapons by their side.

Ghost and the other two were intangible now, as Spot said. "What now?"

"Star says to let it play out, they can't hurt him and maybe we can get some answers."

Fifty or more warriors came from all directions and surrounded Stargazer even from high vantage points in the trees. The howling and roars to include a lighting of fires in the square made it seem like a festival more than an intruder response. "Who are you?"

"I am Lord Stargazer, one of the Burik'dir. I have come to save your people from the Kalar and Emperor Korvax."

"He's with the Kalar!" A warrior in the crowd yelled.

"The hell with this." Spot said and separated from Ghost.

A huge amount of light came out of Spot's hands and head area which was not covered by his suit, illuminating the entire village and scaring hundreds of surrounding animals a mile out. "We are the Burik'dir, you will lower your weapons and hear us. The Kalar is the enemy and we are here to help you fight them!"

Spot floated ten feet above the square and turned as he spoke. "I am Abaddon and Lord Stargazer below me is the leader of the Burik'dir, you will pay your respects to him and listen to him."

"If you are the Burik'dir, you cannot bleed!" A very hulky looking warrior with a few feathers more on his leather headgear than others, yelled.

Stargazer saw the release of his spear with all the weight the warrior could muster behind it come straight at his chest. Stargazer stood firm and used his flight to compensate for the impact as the surprisingly very hard diamond tip warhead entered the body armor, but bounced off of his chest, the wood splintering into pieces; Stargazer catching the warhead in the palm of his hand before it ricocheted into the crowd to the side. "You are correct. I don't bleed, now are you going to put down your weapons so we can talk?" Stargazer dropped the warhead to the ground.

The warrior stood amazed staring at Stargazer, Spot and the ruined spear. The villagers lowered their weapons one by one, many bowing to the ground or kneeling as Spot maintained the area lit up.

"You might want to turn into a person." Ghost suggested to Rat.

"Yeah, I don't want to scare them, like boss man just did."

Spot floated down next to Stargazer who was now standing on

grassy ground. "That was easier than I thought." Spot said.

"You have that deity touch. Too bad they don't know I can kick your ass." Stargazer smiled as he walked up to what seemed to be the chief who was making his way to them from the large building they were in front of.

"Can you really?" Spot replied dimming his light to the area of the square alone.

Ghost and Rat Bastard appeared on the ground next to Spot. "Do not be afraid. This is Lord Ghost and Lord Rat Bastard." Stargazer loudly said.

"I am Chief Ehor, forgive us, we are at your service. Lord Stargazer."

"No Chief, it is an honor to be here. We came to give you freedom from the Kalar. You owe us nothing, but we would like to know if there's an army or armies of warriors that are willing to fight the invaders."

"Lords, it would be better if we spoke inside and not out here where the Kalar can see our gathering in this light."

Stargazer looked at Spot as he stopped illuminating the square which was replaced by eight lit torches.

"What tribe or race is this?" Ghost asked as they were escorted inside the large town hall type of building. The interwoven vines and carved wood indicated a high level of expertise in wood crafting.

"We are Su. Our race has lived in the jungles of Tisle for over five centuries." Chief Ehor and an entourage of Su people crowded around the group as they came to a very large circular room with benches made of smooth oak facing the center.

Rat Bastard and Spot looked with interest at the artwork on the walls and the fact that the inside of this room was lit by glowing gems or Kem lights on the ceiling, twenty feet above. Stargazer scanned the people, clothing and weapons as much as he could, but noticed that much of the clothing they wore had plant properties which made it difficult for him to penetrate. However, he was able to see the bone structure of the slender troll like people with smooth brown tanned skin.

"I assume your people have not lived in this village for a very long time and are hiding?" Stargazer asked as he and the others sat in the center of the room with over two hundred people as an audience all around.

"Our people are many, we lived mostly above out in the sun, but the Kalar came and destroyed our cities, so our great chief commanded everyone to return to where our ancestors lived and organize to fight the Kalar until they are forced off of the planet… We have hoped that the Great Queen would come and save us." The chief stated while the large audience silently listened.

"The Andromen starships are near. We came to find people like you, but we also need to find a supply of explosives we can use to destroy the Kalar space forces around the planet." Ghost said, seeing the thoughts of many of the warrior and priest class Su.

"We left behind almost all of our technology for war in the cities. But there are some who have not retreated to the jungles and are fighting the Kalar. The Kalar cannot easily find us here in the jungle with no technology to track us. Here we have the advantage."

"It's important we get to the other Su, quickly." Stargazer stated.

"They're many months travel from here and we don't know if

they're still alive."

"Where are they Ghost?" Stargazer looked at him, hoping he would know how to get to the Su still using modern weapons.

"About twelve hundred miles that way." Ghost pointed.

Gasps of air could be heard as some of the audience realized that Ghost located the tribe which the Chief was talking about.

"We must leave at once, so we can get to them before sunrise." Stargazer stood. "Thank you Chief Ehor."

Awes and mumbling erupted. "How are they going to get there in hours without the Kalar seeing them?"

"Where's your ship?" Chief Ehor asked.

"We are more than ships, thank you all, may you soon see peace once again." Stargazer floated up a few feet with the rest flying next to him and holding hands.

They turned ghostly and flew straight up through the ceiling and jungle.

Some people cheered, while others jumped up in shock. Some fell to the ground in reverence, and the chief stood staring at the ceiling and then at a far wall; a colorful but small illustration of five ghostly figures rising out of a star, representing the miracle that had just occurred.

Stargazer wasted no time as Ghost directed the way to the northeast. It wasn't long before he could make out a coastline and the terrain dispersing into less dense jungle. Several hundred miles out, Stargazer slowed down. "I don't see anything, except a Kalar military garrison to the north."

"They're not going to be out in the open." Spot stated.

"Head towards that mountain. You will see gulches on the west side; you can get into their bunker from there." Ghost directed them, only knowing the ground passage they would have used had they been on foot.

"So why don't we attack the Kalar garrison and get the explosives you need from them?" Rat Bastard asked not once having every thought about questioning Master's plan.

"Cuz, they don't use grenades, and the explosives they do use are too big and not user friendly." Stargazer replied.

"Didn't you read the plan?" Spot asked.

"Sorry, I only read the parts that talked about me so I would know what to do." Rat replied.

Ghost smiled as footnotes and college study habits flooded Rat's thoughts. "It's okay big guy, Master knew to put everything you needed in the footnotes."

"You guys are the best." Rat proudly smiled.

The group hovered above a gulch, the blackness and depth of the natural feature was awesome to behold in the day, but at night it was an explorer's nightmare.

Stargazer scanned the area and found what he hoped was an entrance. The group flew down into the pitch blackness as the stars were but a distant small slit of sky above. "Good thing you guys aren't claustrophobic." Stargazer said as he landed on hard leveled ground at the bottom of the two hundred meter deep crevice with no more than six feet of space between the side walls.

"Why did we stop here?" Stargazer asked Ghost.

"Spot." Ghost replied as he materialized everyone and they all came back to reality.

"I see tracks, maybe half a day old." Spot answered.

"Really?" Stargazer looked at the moss covered paved stone. "Dam plant slim."

"Do you hear that?" Spot asked as if everyone had super hearing.

"Barely." Rat Bastard replied. "Wow, that's very good Spot."

"A beeping sound." Ghost said.

"You hear it too?" Rat looked in Ghost's direction.

"No, I hear your minds."

"I wish I could do that." Rat sighed.

"Don't we all." Spot smiled and led the way.

Fifty meters down the winding path was a metal door, which Stargazer could see with small sections of it being exposed from rubbed off moss. "Okay, it's time to ignore the keypad and doors."

They quickly held hands and Ghost took them through the man sized entrance and into a network of interlocking chambers and doors. "Well, I'm glad we didn't try to fight our way through here. They have many automated kill zones through these hallways." Stargazer said, being able to see a large section of the fortified underground complex.

"These walls are very dense which is making things hard on me so try to go through less dense areas." Ghost suggested.

"Not a problem." Stargazer spotted a command center or at least that's what he thought it looked like. They flew quickly through a thin wall along the earth and traveled through the rock itself until they got to the ceiling of a large hanger type room.

"The assembly line is up and running." Stargazer commented as the group saw heavy machinery and construction occurring on armored vehicles and rocket launchers.

"So do we just steal the grenades or go through the take me to your leader speech?" Spot asked.

"Haven't we scared enough people?" Rat replied.

"Yeah, maybe we should have brought one of the Su people with us." Ghost said what Stargazer was thinking.

"Yeah..." Rat Bastard started to say.

"Don't say it Rat, and no one is going to mention this to Master, right?" Stargazer demanded an answer.

"Not me." Spot and Ghost replied.

"The little guy's ego is big enough. I agree." Rat Bastard concluded.

"Okay Spot, you see that double door down the hall?" Stargazer asked as the group entered a large hallway one level below the factory line.

"Yep, I see all the rifles and machineguns that will pour into there." Spot replied as they flew above a crowded maze of Su people wearing body armor, carrying weapons and moving about as if the place were a busy ER.

'This time will be different. You will appear coming out of the main screen and before that, we will post a message on the screen announcing our arrival." Stargazer had it all thought out.

"That's a good idea." Spot admitted.

"Yeah, just make sure we write it in gibberish so they understand

English." Ghost stated.

Stargazer stopped the group above the entrance of the command center, a large square room the size of an average supermarket. The Su people were large, so the space was cramped with many tables, seats and a few sectioned off cubicles dictating the narrow passageways for people to walk back and forth.

"Good one Ghost, but if the access to the computer on the Vorgoling Spaceport worked there, it should work here too."

"Normally I would say you have a better chance of winning a lottery without ever entering it, than what you're suggesting. But things in this galaxy are so freaking screwy it just might work." Ghost replied.

"If all fails, we go with having the guards shoot at Star." Rat Bastard giggled as Ghost and Spot smiled.

Stargazer also smiled as he spotted an unoccupied computer and keyboard.

"The rest of you will have to stay above Stargazer and be quiet, because we will have to become tangible for us to affect the keyboard." Ghost instructed as he moved his hand on Stargazer's shoulder without losing contact with his body.

"Okay, here goes nothing." Ghost said as Stargazer stood in front of the keyboard.

"Computer, full access, Steve Messer." Stargazer whispered and typed in.

"Access granted. Lord Stargazer, logged in." A female voice replied.

"Computer, display text on main screen in Earth English and Su language."

The main screen changed the display to a blank gray background with bright green text. "Greetings Su people. The Burik'dir have heard your need for help. Lord Stargazer, Abaddon, Ghost and Rat Bastard will appear soon in this very room. Do not be alarmed, we mean you no harm and wish to speak to you on how to destroy the Kalar who have invaded your world. If you understand, please stop everything that you are doing."

Stargazer grabbed Ghost's hand and flew the group in front of the main screen, the size of miniature theater screen.

The sudden halt of all activity except for guards already inside the room dispersing out looking for people out of place or possible infiltrators.

"I think it would be better if we all appeared at the same time. Hopefully one of us will be recognized from the universal broadcast we sent out a while ago." Spot said.

"Sounds good to me." Stargazer agreed and asked Ghost to turn them visible.

All four men appeared in mid air in front of the main screen as they all stopped holding hands and slowly looked around the room.

"I am Lord Stargazer, who is your chief?"

Many of the Su started to howl and raise their hands in praise. Spot and Rat Bastard could hear people in the back say: we're saved, it's a miracle, praise the Great Queen, or I can't believe they're here.

Stargazer floated down in front of what seemed like the chief, as his colorful feather colors were similar to Chief Ehor, except the feathers were painted on the armored plated shoulders and collar. "Chief... It's good to meet you."

"My people welcome you." The Chief turned towards the four men with an Andromen bow.

"How much time do we have?" Spot asked Ghost.

"Maybe twelve hours." Ghost hoped.

Chapter Seven

❖---✳ ✿ ✳---❖

Halix the Realgar Knight

Kalar Headquarters Hansis 2 Ground Forces Command

A steady stream of reports populated the battle screen with a very large number of Su infantry and tank forces moving through the eastern barrier straits. "Tell Task Force Muse to engage the armor units and prepare the particle bombs. I don't want any of the savages to escape into the jungle this time." General Dithrow ordered.

Dawn hit the long, narrow strait of desert terrain as Su tanks and multi-missile launchers raced across to the base of the plateau. Kalar heavy gunships flew in to intercept the advance. "Red and Blue squadrons, focus on the launchers. My squadron will attack the rear." the wing commander instructed.

"Commander we have incoming high at one o'clock." A report arrived as many co-pilots struggled to see their instruments which showed a bird sized object swooping down on the lead aircraft.

"What? Is it Andromen?" The commander asked, knowing the Su

had no air assets or if they did, the unknown boggy would have been spotted a long time ago.

"No Commander..." communications stopped as lasers ripped through cockpits, wings, engines and weaponry.

Two dozen aircrafts exploded or started to break apart as they dived towards their doom. Thirty gunships banked or climbed performing evasive measures trying to locate and engage the enemy.

The black Vorgoling spacesuit did Spot a little justice helping with the surprise attack as he flew very quickly above the gunship task force shooting at anything moving still under its own power.

Two gunships opened up with their missiles and plasma cannons. The attempt was well made, but Spot was quicker and had no desire to see if he was invulnerable to Kalar munitions.

"General! Task Force Muse is under attack and receiving heavy loses." One of the battle captains reported.

"What? Find out how. Move Second Division to the edge of the plateau so they can engage the enemy directly."

"Sir, the Su artillery is targeting the edge."

"Call in the starships to destroy the artillery." General Dithrow said as if he was committing a shameful act for getting help from the space fleet.

"General. The starships above are being engaged as well." A lieutenant reported.

General Dithrow looked at the rock man, and then at the battle screen. Tell Second Division to pull back and let them move on top of the plateau. Prepare the fusion launchers.

High above in orbit, Stargazer and Ghost flew together carrying a hundred fission grenades, similar to the ones used on the Kalar forces in the dark matter vortex.

Starships and particle beam satellites started to explode from the inside, many losing propulsion and energy; leaving them at the mercy of Hansis 2's gravity if they didn't get outside assistance to move them out of a rapidly decaying orbit.

Stargazer, every now and then looked down at the ground campaign. Spot was holding his own by destroying an entire wing of Kalar gunships. "We better move faster." Ghost said as they had only placed and detonated two dozen grenades, with spaceships still within range of the Kalar ground forces to try to give them support.

"We're okay, we have time. Let's place these grenades and return for more. By then, they would have moved more ships into orbit." Stargazer replied as they entered the warp accelerators of a star cruiser.

"So far so good." Ghost stated.

"Yeah, keep thinking positively." Stargazer grinned.

Spot landed on the top of a Su munitions truck. His helmet was on, but everyone knew he was in charge. "Tell your men to get out of the trucks!"

The platoon leader relayed the command to his Soldiers. Spot saw the all clear from one of the Su on the ground and flew underneath one of five trucks. The truck bolted into the sky like a rocket. The Su warriors could see the black dot of a truck disappear in the distant sky like a mortar round had just been launched.

Spit flew around the truck while its momentum kept it hurtling through the air and opened the large bay doors. Hundreds of artillery rounds quickly left their mounting brackets as Spot grabbed the truck and pushed against it so the warheads separated from the moving chassis. The large troll sized warheads fluttered around the sky almost instantly stabilizing into an almost straight down trajectory.

The Kalar forces on the far end of the plateau moved slowly as if they were not expecting to be attacked so early in the battle. Spot turned on the afterburner and four sonic booms turned many heads. Laser beams hit a convey of vehicles as the hundreds of warheads carpeted a grid square of total destruction to the northeast of Spot's strafing run. Dust and sound shattering debris laid waste to Spot's return path at tree top level back to the Su trucks.

The spacesuit was tough and could withstand the heat and cold, but not the air resistance of hypersonic travel. Spot looked down at his tattered chest and missing tips of his boots, "Now I know what Stargazer feels like." Spot swooped down underneath another munitions truck and repeat the same tactic.

The Kalar reacted differently on the fourth truck. Missiles and anti-aircraft plasma fire caught the truck in mid flight. The warheads burst into a gigantic ball of fire, creating a momentary shift of wind for several miles in all directions.

Spot's spacesuit had gaping holes exposing his slightly blacken skin, but he maintained his flight plan and made sure he targeted the missile launchers and gun positions with his laser attacks.

Kalar Soldiers shot at him with every hand held or mounted weapon available to no avail. Horror struck their minds as Spot's trail of sonic destruction left them towards the Su frontlines. A full on retreat was announced, ignoring high command's orders to hold the plateau.

Rat Bastard perched himself on top of a command assault vehicle. A Centurion's upper body stood outside of an open cupola. "The Kalar are retreating." The Su leader said, looking through digital binoculars.

"Is that normal, because this is only a small part of the land?" Rat Bastard asked with his tail slowly swaying back and forth.

"I do not know Kalar strategies, but we Su would retreat to draw in the enemy and surround them if we had the numbers." The commander's mid tone's voice said with elegance as the universal translator relayed the information into Rat's implanted receiver.

"What's that?" Rat replied, seeing a single missile launch its way toward Spot's fifth truck maneuver.

The commander looked at the missile intently. "It looks like a straggler." Intense light stopped his reply as the miniature nuclear explosion blinded him and many Soldiers who were looking in the same direction. "Seek cover!" The commander yelled as he felt his way inside the armored vehicle.

People scrambled in many directions, especially onto the ground. The areal detonation pushed mainly air, as the shockwave uprooted nearby trees and standing Soldiers were whooshed away into an unwanted horizontal nightmare. Rat Bastard flew in the way of a transport before it crushed a few Soldiers laying in the prone. He stabilized the light armored transport into a canted angle on the ground so the return of air would have less of a chance in picking it up again. The sound of shockwave wasn't too bad since the Su were several miles away, and the expected heat and radiation was minimal, the explosion being more like a neutron bomb.

Rat Bastard looked in the direction of Spot as the hurricane-like shockwave returned to add to the magnitude of devastated jungle. The sky was clear as if the explosion never originated from that location. The return shockwave passed by with less force as the Su initiated their battle drills attempting to reassemble and assess damages. Without delay, Rat Bastard flew off towards Spot's last known location.

Rat Bastard scanned the ground for miles noticing Kalar units in defiladed positions as if waiting for something before moving out on the attack.

A missile was launched at Rat Bastard. Anger filled his heart as his friend's words came back to haunt him, seeing the missile's white exhaust pointing at him. Rat Bastard flew down and towards the Kalar forces, ignoring the missile. The expected missile explosion bypassed him as it sped off past him. "I thought so." Rat said to himself as he flew up to a Kalar missile launcher. The missile exploding at its minimum arming range.

The small half a kiloton nuclear explosion detonated in the vicinity of the last explosion. Plasma blasts and metallic projectiles hit Rat Bastard's skin. His black fur kept its texture and only angered him some more as the pricks on his skin started out as minor, but now they were very annoying and stinging like stepping into a bed of fire ants. He braced himself by digging deep into the ground with his claws and screeched as loud as he could in a waving motion. The cone of destruction vibrated wide and long in unison with the nuclear shockwave ripping through fourteen vehicles and a hundred Kalar Soldiers. The earth between Rat

Bastard and the enemy was overturned as if an imaginary train had a bulldozer plow ramming everything into submission. Rage burned still as Rat Bastard flew on to new targets down the line.

The sunlight mixed with shadows of a spiked helmet. The dark visor reflected a partial scene of vegetation. Warm metal rubbed at Spot's wrists and arms as the figures of Su warriors placed a foil blanket on top of him. "I'm not dead, what are you guys doing?" Spot sat up with a mild headache.

The four warriors jumped back in surprise, then raised their weapons in victory.

"Abaddon lives!"

Spot brushed aside the blanket, revealing his nakedness. "Ah man, I lost my suit."

"Private, bring it here!" The Su scout leader said. "Don't worry Lord Abaddon, we have gear better than that Vorgoling garment."

"Really?" Spot looked at the Scout leader's charcoal dark green armor, which seemed to change brightness as it was exposed to the light. "Is it like yours?"

"Better" The scout leader said, looking away from Spot and at the running private as he leaped up to the middle canopy of the large tree limb they were on.

"Here it is Sir." The private held up a light purple and white skin tight tunic with padding.

"You're joking, right?" Spot looked at the scout leader then at the tunic.

"It's the last piece of sniper gear available in the entire jungle."

"What? Why didn't you say that from the beginning?" Spot jumped up and put the suit on with a smile. "I assume it changes color with the environment."

"Yes, it does, and it fuses with the genetic code of your body."

The suit covered Spot's entire body except his head. The padding made him look like a hockey player without a team. Spot looked at his arms and body as he turned into a transparent liquid without losing his form. "Cool."

"The suit is supposed to change color, but not like that." The scout leader said with his men surrounding them.

"That's me doing it. It's so much easier to do with the suit." Spot felt relaxed as the suit obeyed his ability to blend with his surroundings.

"Sir, Lord Rat Bastard has repelled the Kalar." A Su warrior leaped up to the limb.

"Thank you Scoutmaster. I need to join him to prepare for a counterattack." Spot said, feeling a lot better now that his body had time to regenerate from the nuclear attack; flying up through the foliage.

Rat Bastard flew around to different high points on the battlefield, scanning for Kalar activity and any sign of Spot.

Spot came upon the scene with admiration. Several dozen very large trenches scattered the area Rat Bastard was surveying about. He flew and floated above Rat Bastard in his new disguise.

Rat Bastard looked around with alarm as he saw a bloody uniform on the ground. He sniffed the air in confusion as the scent of Spot and alien blood mingled.

"Did you drop your keys Big Guy?" Spot asked making himself seen, with his suit turning glossy black.

Rat Bastard looked up, startled. "You're okay!" He flew at Spot with lightning speed and hugged him with his small rat arms.

"Good to see you too Big Guy. But I don't understand what happened." Spot replied separating himself from Rat Bastard's firm grip.

"You don't remember the tactical nuke going off?" Rat Bastard's eyebrows narrowed.

"Oh was that what knocked me out?" Spot's impressed himself.

"Don't you ever do that again?" Rat Bastard growled.

"I have no control over nukes being shot at me." Spot said and looked in the direction of the Kalar to the west.

"Well, you know what I mean." Rat Bastard also looked towards the west.

"How come they didn't throw a nuke your way?" Spot asked, seeing more destruction than what he had accomplished with his attacks.

"I don't think they wanted to blow up a nuke with me next to them." Rat Bastard said as he flew slowly towards the west. "Come on Spot, we should get closer to them."

Spot looked at the black rat fly away from him. "I think you get smarter as a rat."

"No, I just want to bite something."

Ghost felt a burst of anxiety which caused him to turn visible. "What happened?" Stargazer asked as they dramatically slowed down, flying silently in a high orbit.

"Something happened down there." Ghost replied.

Stargazer looked down where he last knew Spot and Rat Bastard to be. The effects of the first tactical nuclear explosion were clearly visible to him, but he wasn't able to find the signature properties of Spot and only found Rat Bastard on a rampage.

"Is everything alright?"

"No, I can't find Spot?"

Ghost looked down and across the horizon. The stars and alien world was wondrous to see, but at the moment it felt so big and made him feel so puny in a world far from home.

Stargazer focused back on his course as a space station rapidly approached. Both men phased through the thick hull and into an unoccupied room. 'So should I find out if they need help?' Stargazer thought.

"I don't know? I sense something weird." Ghost replied as he locked the electronic door and looked out into space through Stargazer's eyes.

"Huh? Like what?"

"There." Ghost pointed hoping Stargazer would look in the direction he indicated.

Stargazer peered through the hull and into deep space. He scanned a large section of space seeing nothing. He kept scanning a few degrees at a time, "Can you be more specific about what I'm supposed to be looking for?"

The space station violently separated into pieces as a fusion explosion tore into all areas of the superstructure. Stargazer rode the blast out with the intact debris. Ghost phased and flew through the least path of resistance. 'What the hell?' Stargazer mentally yelled.

'I told you it was weird.' Ghost calmly replied.

Heat and light overwhelmed the immediate vicinity as a small spaceship the size of a modern fighter loomed in position several miles away from the dispersing sections of the station. A Kalar stood outside on the craft's cockpit. He held a halberd out to the side, covered in glossy black armor. 'Isn't he a Kalar soldier?'

'I don't think he cares about his own people.' Ghost's mental concern was easily felt.

'I'll take this guy, but be ready to cover me.' Stargazer diverted his flight path towards the alien.

The Realgar Knight flew off of the cockpit with lightning speed meeting Stargazer half way. He swung at Stargazer with ninja-like precision. Stargazer instinctively dodged to the side, but the unexpected technique and agility of the knight left an opening as the halberd's edge slashed into his shoulder.

A second of pain stung as the wound almost instantly clogged with his superhuman blood. Stargazer flew away from the knight trying to get some distance to rethink his actions.

The knight pursued him continuing the attack flying at Stargazer with great maneuverability. Stargazer dove down towards the space station debris. He kicked in the afterburners moving through large and small projectiles of station structures, furnishings and dead Kalar bodies. With hands to his front he plowed swiftly through miles of space. Glimpsing back, he saw the knight fall back not being able to ignore the debris which hit him with great force.

The knight sliced his way into the debris area, but greatly slowed down looking in all directions for Stargazer. His diamond crafted halberd hummed at high frequencies as it separated everything in its wake.

Stargazer looped up and around flying as fast as he could into the knight's back. The impact with the knight was different than anything Stargazer had imagined. The crystal skin didn't cave in like the metallic or organic matter which he had been used to flying through. Instead, the knight's body twisted from the impact, Stargazer feeling a slight cracking of the knight's upper back. He followed through with his move through and vanished out of sight once again. Stargazer looked through the debris seeing the knight was injured as if nursing a severe backache.

Before Stargazer could make another pass, the knight flew out of the debris near his spacecraft. The craft automatically maintained a controlled orbit, turning its front towards him.

'It looks like a trap.' Ghost said into Stargazer's mind.

'He wants me to just come out in the open.'

'That's called a trap to me.'

'Then trap it is.' Stargazer smiled, flying a very wide arc, around and below the spacecraft.

The fighter tilted down as it detected Stargazer's approach, but before it could employ its weapons, Stargazer flew from end to end of the ship like an armor piercing round punching through a watermelon. A plasma explosion erupted from the center of the craft while the knight charged Stargazer's, now known position.

The knight swung his halberd trying to cleave Stargazer in half. The attempt failed from the start, as Stargazer focused all his attention at grabbing the halberd by the staff end midway before the swing could be fully performed. Both men held the weapon twirling in space hundreds of times. The knight kicked at Stargazer hitting him all over his lower body. Stargazer felt the gem armor with interest as his superhuman strength was being matched by the Kalar Soldier. The kicks were doing nothing to him and chances were that his own martial arts skills would also be useless against the knight.

Stargazer gripped the solid diamond shaft as hard as he could, as did the knight. It vibrated in his hands as if it wanted to repel his grasp. The knight placed both his feet on Stargazer's chest and used his body as leverage to lift the weapon away from him. Stargazer swung his legs around locking them around the staff end. The two twirled aimlessly through space, but Stargazer quickly flew to stabilize their path without spinning.

The knight kicked at his head with no effect, except to annoy Stargazer's concentration to scan the area. Stargazer found what he was looking for and flew towards the target as hard and fast as he could. The knight didn't counter the motion focusing on trying to wrestle the weapon away from Stargazer's unyielding attachment.

The knight looked behind him, too late to see a large metallic container instantly get humongous. Just before hitting the debris,

Stargazer let go of the weapon with his legs and straighten up like a missile. The flat side of the halberd's blade hit the container with extreme drag as the two men and the rest of the weapon penetrated through the container as if it were made of weak cardboard. The knight's grip failed for a second as Stargazer took command of the weapon and swung it with all his agility and might at the knight.

The wide end of the blade hit its mark and embedded itself half way into the knight's neck. Stargazer couldn't hear the Kalar scream, but he saw him utter something in agony before finally dying.

Stargazer placed his feet on the knight's head and chest, pulling at the weapon, dislodging it from the Kalar's body. He held the weapon up close in front of his face as it disintegrated into small ant sized diamonds and slowly scattered. 'Cool', Stargazer thought.

'We have company. Master and the lead ships are moving into orbit.' Ghost reported.

'I wonder how many more of these guys there are?'

'Hopefully, he was the only one.' Ghost replied as he flew in Stargazer's direction.

'Yeah, I don't buy that. Stay alert, he actually hurt me.' Stargazer felt his healed shoulder and six inch gash on his spacesuit armor.

Spot and Rat Bastard confidently soared over retreating Kalar vehicles and foot Soldiers. But their victory was shorted lived as the Soldiers suddenly stopped in the distance.

"What now?" Rat Bastard raised his voice being at a good fifty meter interval from Spot.

"It seems they have a champion." Spot flew towards a small space fighter which ejected a Realgar knight at low altitude. The knight reached up from behind and unsheathed a bastard and long sword. He flew at Spot creating two sonic booms.

"Watch out for the swords!" Spot yelled as he too bolted into supersonic speeds.

Rat Bastard flew out in a wide arc at tree top level, disappearing behind the foliage and contour of the land.

Spot traveled towards the knight then changed direction down at the ground. The angle of attack was very steep causing the knight to slow down greatly so as not to fly into the ground. Or at least that's what Spot hoped for.

The knight did slow down, but only to below Mach 1 as he swooped down like an eagle swinging his swords with deadly elegance.

Spot tapped the ground with his feet, slid forward on the hard sand and rolled to the side, dodging two back to back swings, but his stomach caught the tip of the long sword. The pain was real as he shot a laser blast at the knight.

The knight quickly moved his hand in front of the beam with the flat end of the Bastard sword near the hilt on the fuller, taking most of the energy. He almost instantly stopped mid air and flew back at Spot.

Spot placed a hand on his stomach and flew away from the knight towards the edge of the jungle.

The knight's speed rivaled Spot's as he overtook Spot before reaching the trees.

Spot twirled around knowing he would have to face the Kalar champion and take his chances, or else be struck in the back by both swords.

The knight was upon Spot as a sonic vibration of destruction came from above the trees and blasted all around the knight. Rat Bastard's screech took the knight be surprise as he flew to the ground in disarray, but managed to hold on to both swords without injuring himself.

Rat Bastard continued the attack by flying in front of the knight and screeching again. A huge cloud of sand lifted, leaving a triangular shape sand storm. The knight was knelt on the ground with his Bastard sword deeply buried into the ground using it as an anchor to keep from being pushed back. He instantly withdrew the sword and charged at Rat Bastard with his flight abilities.

Rat Bastard dodged to the side as his tail was cut off by the knight's weapon.

The knight turned and swung around towards Rat Bastard, then looked towards Spot's last location. The dust was thick, but he could see through it as Spot materialized in front of him.

Spot's new camouflage suit and ability allowed him to get near the knight before being noticed. An extreme flash of light lit up the area for a hundred miles. Everyone was blinded by Spot's light attack, even people with their eyes closed or looking away thinking it was another nuclear explosion. The knight was blind but not totally disorientated as he sensed Spot on his right and turned in his direction taking a battle stance.

Spot raised both hands and shot out a laser beam at the knight's closest hand. The beam burned into the armor and sedimentary flesh.

The knight quickly placed the fuller part of his long sword in front to protect against the laser, but the attack had done its work as the knight dropped the Bastard Sword to the ground. The weapon heavily landed on the sand almost sinking out of sight seeming to weigh tons.

Spot flew in with lightning speed and grabbed the knight's wrist and pushed his back against the knight's front. Another laser blast from his hands on the knight's wrist made the knight release the long sword, but the knight knew Spot's exact location now.

The knight extended his free hand out away from him and called for his weapon. The Bastard Sword telekinetically sprang to life as the handle felt the knight's regenerated grip.

Rat Bastard instantly flew in and bit this forearm, then transformed to human form and held the arm in a bear hug. The knight couldn't maneuver the sword as Rat Bastard squeezed his wrist while Spot held the other wrist. Spot flew down on top of the knight forcing the three to the ground.

Without delay, Spot placed one of his hands on top of the knight's face and blasted his left eye with a tight beam of light. The laser did its work quickly, burning deep past the helmet's armor and into the Kalar's brain.

The knight stopped fighting back, dropping the Bastard sword on the ground for the last time. Spot turned to face the knight still clinging to his wrist. He placed his free hand back on his stomach feeling the armor had covered his wound like a bandage. Spot let go of the knight and looked down at his stomach. "Man, I love this suit."

Rat Bastard mashed his teeth. "He cut my tail off!"

"Will it grow back?"

Rat Bastard's made a goofy face with mouth open and checks puffed up. "Well, yeah."

"So what's the problem?" Spot narrowed his eyes.

"Well... it hurts, and I don't like the idea of my tail pieces being left all over creation."

Spot looked concerned. "Look at it this way. One day there will be someone or maybe even a whole nation of people wanting to find your tail as part of an archeological find of the century."

Rat Bastard let go of the knight' wrist, looking down at the two swords which had disintegrated into millions of small black diamonds. "You really think that will happen?"

Spot looked at Rat Bastard smile and puff up his chest. "Nah, not really, they'll probably want to eat it to get some god like powers."

"Wow, that's even better." Rat Bastard's eyes gleamed with joy, looking at his tail lying far off in the distance ignoring the diamonds. "Let me go bury it before the animals get to it."

Spot watched on in disbelief.

"Sir, we're being hailed by the Kalar." The communications specialist reported.

"You mean there's still Kalar in space?" Master replied.

"It's a small fighter in orbit near Lord Stargazer."

"Bring it up."

A new window on the main screen opened up on the top right corner. "I am Halix, Knight of the Realgar. You all will die soon."

The transmission ended abruptly as a missile made its way at Stargazer. The light and energy emitted by the exploding warhead briefly blurred and distorted the main screen.

Master almost jumped out of his seat and turned towards the science officer. "Damage assessment."

"Working on it."

"We're okay." Ghost calmed the boy. "But Star is pissed."

"Oh, thanks." Master turned his head toward the navigator. "Fall back and give them room to fight."

The nuclear explosion cleared the area of debris for several hundred miles. It didn't explode on top of Stargazer or Ghost, but it was close enough to give Stargazer a quick tan.

Stargazer focused his scan on Halix, seeing the Realgar Knight flying through space like his last opponent. 'I don't think you can grab that sword away from him.' Ghost commented seeing what Stargazer saw in his mind.

'You think you can weaken it or something?'

'He needs to be closer and since you guys are speed demons, that might not work well for you.' Ghost stated as he flew invisible and intangible behind Stargazer.

'The other guy hit me dead on, so I might be able to take a light swing without major damage. Maybe you can do something then.'

'There's nothing light about that Great sword. So try your best and I will see if I can transform it.' Ghost encouraged him and flew up to get a good vantage point once the two men made contact.

Stargazer tracked Halix move quickly through space but slower than he or the other knight in the past. 'He's a cool one.' Stargazer thought as he flew backwards to see a response.

Halix didn't alter his approach and held his Great sword behind him as if dragging it at the ready for a killing blow.

Stargazer bolted forward in a constant loop like a twister directed at the knight. Halix swung the sword as if it were a foil with fantastic swiftness, but Stargazer was ready and flew away and maneuvered his limbs from getting hit.

Halix kept his distance as not to get into a wrestling match.

'Now' Stargazer thought hoping Ghost understood his plan.

Ghost concentrated on the Great sword and attacked it with his transformation power. Halix stopped his pursuit of Stargazer and held his sword in front of his face. The sword started to disintegrate in the center of the blade.

Stargazer warped away from Halix and reversed his path back at the knight. Halix's attention on his sword was long enough for Stargazer to fly through the sword, dispersing the weaken diamond particles along a large area of space.

Halix twisted around towards Stargazer with a broken sword, down to the hilt, the rest dispersed like dust in a very strong wind. He instantly placed the hilt on his back and flew at Stargazer. This time he sped up and tackled Stargazer from behind.

Stargazer flew straight down towards the planet's surface as Halix swung his arm around Stargazer's neck in a choke hold. Extreme heat enveloped the two men as they soared through the planet's exosphere and into the thermosphere. Stargazer's armor glowed yellowish red while the knight's armor stayed black.

Halix's strength was incredible forcing Stargazer to use both hands to lessen the pressure around his neck. The two men plummeted deep into the atmosphere, causing several sonic booms upon entering the dense air and reducing their speed. Stargazer flipped before hitting the side of a mountain, but Halix countered and rocked with him as both men tumbled through trees and entrenched themselves into the earth.

Stargazer was loose from Halix's grasp, but laid on his back as Halix jumped on top of him punching Stargazer in the face. He felt his cheekbones crack and reform to normal several times, the pain was sharp for a fraction of a second, but pain was pain and it hurt. Stargazer kneed Halix's back, pushing him off of him. In an instant, Stargazer engaged Halix with all of his martial arts knowledge going for killing blows at the throat, knee cap and trying to pin an arm to break it.

With all the strength both men could muster, nothing worked to break or injure one another. They broke contact and stood several feet from each other foliage surrounding them with a deep trench next to them.

"You can't beat me, so how are you going to beat the others?" Stargazer asked, thinking they were in a stalemate.

"I will cut you up into little pieces, now that my sword has regenerated." Halix reached back and the Great sword materialized.

Stargazer's eyes widen as he saw diamond particles come off of

Halix's back and recreate the sword. Without a second thought, he blasted off into high orbit producing eight sonic booms before Halix caught up with him.

'Spot is coming to help you.' Ghost assured him.

'Good to know.' Stargazer turned around to face Halix swing away. The sword's blade nicked him on the side of his waist, cutting into his armor but not his skin.

Halix wielded the sword one handed as easily as if it were a dagger, but that ability was negated by Stargazer's astoundingly fast reflexes.

The two danced around, Halix trying to make contact and Stargazer dodging like crazy.

Stargazer couldn't dodge everything though and soon, a full contact blow hit him in the forearm. The sword sunk in two inches, but gave him the opportunity to move in and grapple with Halix. His arm ached for a second like a bad bruise, but quickly healed as he placed both hands on top of the sword hand keeping Halix from manipulating against him.

Halix quickly used his free hand to pry Stargazer's fingers off.

'Any day now.' Stargazer told Ghost.

Spot burst in next to the two men and shot a laser beam at Halix's head. The beam hit dead center, but didn't penetrate his armor like it did with the other knight.

'I think you made him angry.' Stargazer thought as Halix twirled like a crocodile in a frenzy.

The Great sword disintegrated and reassembled itself in Halix's free hand. Halix flew at Spot while Spot retreated flying towards the Andromen starships.

Stargazer didn't follow closely but measured his distance to Halix. 'Ghost, I need you to transform the sword again.'

'You make it sound like it's easy to do.' Ghost replied.

'No, but this is harder.' Stargazer mentally laid out his plan.

Ghost grumbled but maintained his proximity to Halix and Stargazer. 'Okay, go for it.'

Spot sped towards the flagship, but slowed down and turned to face Halix.

"Lord Master, we have incoming." The science officer said with alarm.

"Yes, I can see that." Master replied, looking at the battle screen with icons of Spot, Halix and Stargazer on the move.

"No my Lord, there's an unidentified object approaching from quadrant 34." The officer replied, putting up the track of a super fast energy source almost on top of them.

"Battle stations, get everyone into spacesuits!" Master commanded recognizing the phenomena. "Hey guys, the Destroyer of Ordis is here." Master warned over his arm console.

Spot frowned. "Crap..." A flash of light erupted out of both his hands, illuminating thousands of miles all around.

Halix flew into the light without pause and swung at Spot's head. Spot raised his forearm as the blade once again broke off upon impact. Ghost materialized behind Halix and touched the knight from behind. Stargazer instantly warped in next to Ghost and the three dematerialized into Ghost's environment.

Stargazer quickly put a choke hold on Halix from behind as Ghost stayed behind his leader. Ghost controlled their movement and flew towards Halix's broken sword's point. The intact blade twirled through space being overtaken by the three men. Halix attempted to use his flight power to maneuver, but the only thing working was his strength. Stargazer held strong as the three foot section of broken sword moved inside of Halix's chest. Ghost and Stargazer synchronized their pull away as Halix rematerialized with his own section of diamond blade in his chest.

Halix screamed in pain, grabbing the protruding crystal blade. Stargazer and Ghost looked on as Halix pulled the foreign object out of his chest and turned in the direction of the now invisible men. 'We have a problem.' Ghost said.

Cyer flew behind Halix as if teleporting from almost nowhere. 'This fight is over. Return to your emperor and prepare for the Andromen counterattack.' Cyer mentally said with all hearing his words in their minds.

Halix turned around and spoke. "This is not over."

'You mistake my command as a request. Fly away now, or die.' Cyer replied not moving his lips, a glowing aura of yellow light shown around him.

The Great Sword reassembled almost instantly in Halix's hand.

Cyer extended his hand out in front of him just as fast as Halix twitched. A bolt of energy engulfed Halix and continued to travel into outer space. The Realgar knight was nowhere to be seen as he evaporated in the intense anti-matter attack.

'Holy Sh...' Ghost caught himself hoping Cyer couldn't hear his thoughts.

Cyer instantly moved in front of Stargazer. Stargazer separated himself from Ghost, becoming visible.

'Are you here to stop us?' Stargazer asked with curiosity, instead of fear and scanned his DNA.

Cyer smiled. 'You and your friends are not able to harm me, but I find it very interesting that your abilities are part of mine.'

Stargazer floated at ease. 'So because you have my vision, you are sparing us?'

'No, your vision is limited, unlike mine. Do not concern yourself about me. I will not stop you from saving the queen.'

Stargazer thought deeply. 'I understand, I think.'

'Until we meet again.' Cyer commented without emotion and warped out of the area.

'What the hell was that about?' Ghost asked.

'I don't know if it's luck, a time traveling related thing or we aren't worthy enough to fight him.' Stargazer replied and slowly started to head for the fleet.

'Why didn't you ask him to help us?' Ghost asked, holding on to Stargazer's wrist.

'Having not to fight him is enough help for me.'

Ghost pictured Cyer destroying Arlos and the emperor along with it. 'Never mind, you might be right.'

Chapter Eight

Siris Mark Ice Cap

Hansis 2 inhabitants cheered for the victory, but mourned for the dead and devastation caused by the Kalar. Andromen settlement units landed on the planet to assist is recovery, while the fleet secured the system, receiving a constant flow of allies from all sectors of space. Master assembled the group in the flagship after their assistance on the planet and in space for security was not needed.

"Commander Exleter did a fantastic job." Spot commented as the entire group, Admiral Novak and the tribal leader of Hansis 2 waited in the conference room.

Stargazer and MAJ Krodis went over their report and last minute coordination on the next step in Master's plan.

"We owe much to the commander and many more who have and endured thus far." Admiral Novis acknowledged all the effort and sacrifice by millions of beings, in particular the Vorg's assembly of allies to their location.

"Admiral, we have accounted for 637 cruiser class and above ships ready for departure." An ensign reported.

Novis looked at Stargazer. "Lords, are we ready?"

"Yes, we are admiral." Stargazer stood in front of the center screen. All ship bridges received a secure feed of the briefing.

"As you know, the Kalar are at a disadvantage at this time with their primary forces being used to attack and invade 800 sectors of space, and being defeated here and in the dark matter vortex. The Realgar knights known to be the last three of the emperor's champions are dead and the Destroyer of Ordis is at this point neutral. It's not known if the Kalar will destroy Arlos before we take the sector back, so time is against us. I and the rest of the Burik'dir will leave shortly to infiltrate the Arlos defenses and locate Queen Cassandra. Admiral Novis will lead the main attack to divert Emperor Korvax to focus on the fleet. The fleet is outnumbered and I'm sorry to say that we will not be able to find the queen and neutralize the Kalar forces at the same time. Admiral?" Stargazer turned it over to Novis as the rest of the group to include MAJ Krodis got up to leave the room.

"The future is in our hands again and we thank you ahead of time." Novis stated and waited for the five ghosts to leave. Stargazer led the group to the shuttle bay as MAJ Krodis went over the checklist.

"Relax, major." Stargazer slowed his pace and turned to her.

"But we're getting mixed reports, I'm not sure if it's a trap or worst, it could be wrong information that will mislead us and waste valuable time."

"I thought your sources were reliable?" Spot asked from behind.

"They're not my sources, but yes they have been reliable to this point, except that they were wrong about the Destroyer of Ordis, or Cyer as some sources indicate."

"No, they're right. Cyer's extremely powerful and dangerous. I think his allegiance is what they got wrong. But aside from that, I trust your intel will get us close to the queen. So, please relax." Stargazer stepped into a multidirectional elevator.

The entire group stood silent in the elevator for a while. "Do you think we can beat Korvax?" Rat Bastard asked.

"You mean if we have to face him… I don't know." Stargazer replied.

"Emperor Korvax is said to be able to control matter with telekinesis and it rivals the queen."

"I don't see him being stronger than Cyer." Ghost commented.

"It's not always about strength; it's about teamwork and a winning attitude to never give up." Master stated.

"Having a cool name helps too." Spot smiled.

Stargazer turned his head. "I'll call you Ra or Set if that sounds better?"

"I'll think about it." Spot crossed his arms.

"Ra, sounds very formidable." Krodis smiled thinking of a type of roar or battle cry.

"It represents the Sun god, which is the star of our star system." Master explained as they walked out of the elevator now at the shuttle bay level.

The group entered the bay, Ghost lagging behind and stopping in front of their new spacecraft. He looked at the silky black metal reminding him of old extraterrestrial television shows. The saucer like frame along with the loading arm caused him to take in the reality of the past several weeks. He looked out into space as the bay doors were open with force fields activated.

"What's wrong Ghost?" Spot asked noticing him fall back.

"I'm just enjoying the little things in life."

Spot looked at Ghost's view with a small frown. "I guess you rather stand there looking at the stars, then save your girlfriend." Spot turned back around and entered the stealth ship.

Ghost looked at the stars as he walked up the ramp. "Hold on, we're coming."

The orange sky on a clear day was beautiful but the strong whistling gale current dashed between the low skyscrapers. Roads were barren of people with the only vehicular movement visible being cargo caterpillars. The train-like containers attached themselves to the magnetic rails along all major highways. The automated cargo system never stopped and only slowed down during cyclone season. The city was constructed without protruding signs, traffic lights, mailboxes or cables. An extensive underground network made life in the city of Oscith practical to a point, so the ability to live above ground during select months of the year gave people a sense of freedom. The tallest skyscrapers were no more than seven stories high. Dense alloy windows and walls made them seem more like fortified bunkers above ground instead of commercial and residential properties.

Lix looked out past the edge of the city over the icy hard rock gray horizon. She could feel slight vibrations of the ten by ten inch Kevlar window. The almost invisible wind current pushed small particles of chipped ice and rock across the city blocks at over a hundred miles per hour. Lix turned away from the window and walked back to her seat. The office room had computer monitors and diagrams across three walls. A table in the center surrounded by three very comfortable reclining wheeled black chairs showed heavy wear and tear. One large slinging door was the only entrance into the room. The room seemed to be a communication center for the company's business, but it was more than that as Lix sat quietly staring at the back of an Andromen female.

"Rasue told me I should stay positive and be brave in the face of evil." Dye slowly swiveled around on her chair and rolled it up to the table. "Does this classify as one of those times?"

"If they come in and arrest you, yes. But don't worry, there's no reason for them to do that." Lix assured her.

Dye looked at Lix's dark blue robe and black material padding underneath. "I don't understand why you want information on the ice cap."

"I believe the queen is being held somewhere in there."

Dye's blue eyes widen with confusion. "Why would they hold her so close to Arlos?"

"Who would look for her in the ice cap with people living near it?"

"But we aren't near it and if you plan on going across the sea on foot, it's suicide."

"Well for right now we need to find a specific location before I go anywhere."

Dye waved her fingers over the table, as images of the monitors displayed on it. "I can tell you that if we start looking for imagery of a base, the Kalar security forces will find out."

"Yes, which is why I need data from visual spotters of the orbit above indicating a trajectory of ships above and into the cap." Lix scooted her chair next to Dye's.

"My mom told me you were one of the best." Dye turned her human like face towards her. Dye's long ebony black hair dangled loosely over the table top.

"I'm sorry for not visiting you for so long…" Lix sat back against the back support.

"I didn't understand until I was fourteen. Maybe one day when you're not doing your cloak and dagger stuff, we can talk on a regular basis."

"Maybe one day…"

Dye browsed through data as she spoke. "Your name isn't really Myra, is it?"

"I have many names, but its better you don't know any other for now." Lix replied, monitoring the data Dye was scanning.

"Maybe one day." Dye stopped and smiled.

"I promise." Lix smiled back.

Dye moved some files around. "Here are the most likely coordinates." A digital map of the ice cap panned the table.

Lix held up her wristband and keyed in the coordinates.

Dye anxiously stared at her. "I told you it was suicide. They will spot you from orbit if not from the ground."

"If I don't try, who else will?"

Dye turned away at the monitors as if looking for an answer or hiding her dismay from Lix. "What about the Burik'dir?"

"It will take too long for me to get to a secure location that can transmit a message to them." Lix continued to input all information about the terrain and projected weather. "And there's no guarantee they'll receive or believe the information."

Dye quickly thought as she ran back and forth between the computer panels below the monitors. "Yes, there's a way."

Lix stopped making her preparations on her computerized wristband.

"We can transmit a message using low tech laser communications. We send the message to a known friendly location, who will transmit it to the Andromen armada, who will get it to the Burik'dir."

"Your mom would be proud of you." Lix replied. "Okay, send the message to this coordinate." She showed Dye a digital coordinate from her digital display on her wrist.

Dye, looked at it in confusion, but soon figured out it wasn't a typo. "Are you sure? It will take two days to get there?"

"Yes, I know, but it will be secure and it will be received there."

"So what do you want to say?" Dye asked waiting to type in the encrypted message as a triple measure.

"Say, Flare alpha 73 niner, queen found. Inform and join Burik'dir immediately, will attempt infill into nest, ETA is three days. Send coordinates and current time stamp." Lix instructed and continued to inspect her gear.

Dye sent the message. "Well as long as nothing gets in the way of the beam, the message should be received." Dye paused in defeat. "You're still going outside?"

"The chances of anything getting in between the beam and figuring out it's a message is beyond impossible." Lix replied as she emptied out a backpack she picked up from the floor.

"The stealth suit isn't going to last more than a few days in this kind of weather."

Lix smiled. "Your mom taught you well. But it'll be alright."

"It's over 700 miles with wind cycles every few hours, it will take you a few weeks to walk that far without any breaks."

"It will be okay." Lix repeated while withdrawing a high powered sniper rifle from its case and strapping it to the inside of her backpack into a lightweight configuration.

Dye looked at demolition, extra food supplements, breach and mass causality grenades left on the table.

"Sorry about leaving these things here with you, but they will slow me down." Lix moved the items to the side.

"You plan on running the entire way?" Dye's heart sank.

"Hide these things and don't attract attention to yourself by worrying about me. It'll be fine." Lix walked up to Dye, knelt and hugged her. "I promise."

Dye hugged her tightly, kissing Lix's green cheeks. "I believe you."

"I still have less than an hour before the winds ebb, so what do you say about telling me about your boyfriend." Lix walked towards the sliding door.

"How did you know I had a boyfriend?" Dye replied as they both left the room and into a larger office space full of empty chairs and terminals.

Lix's backpack seemed more like a large college student's stylish accessory as she walked towards an elevator. "Come on and let's talk about this over lunch."

The building operated with minimal personnel loyal to Dye Gledir in the business of communications. Kalar security forces monitored their activity and removed almost all males from the city, believing the females would be easy to rule as slaves. To Lix's good fortune, Dye was the daughter of one of her long time friends, Rasue, under the umbrella of galactic subversive operations in the Andromen imperial security forces. Most of the city operated as top energy producers for the planet's main industry of mining for minerals. This clandestine site was a communication hub for specific intelligence gathering in the sector acting as a normal communication relay to other planets in the empire

Wind turbines in and on top of most building rooftops produced this energy output and also helped in keeping the city standing. All non-essential cities around the planet were leveled to the ground by the Kalar military and was part of the topic of discussion after Dye spoke lovingly about her boyfriend who was somewhere with the Andromen armada.

Lix listened intently and relished the peaceful quality time.

An hour into the conversation, Dye looked at her watch. "Oh, you're losing time."

"Perhaps." Lix mirrored General Mihod's earlier response.

Dye stood up and led her mother-like mentor to the basement level next to a street exit. "People might be outside, but it's late and most are just waiting out the war. Aside from that, you can get out of the city straight down to the south." Dye stood next to the door controls.

Lix strapped her backpack tight to her suit, the robe also inside the pack. She placed her helmet on and sealed the visor. A digital 3D image of her path with distance and time to the coordinates displayed slightly above her eyes. Most of her body disappeared with a vague distortion of her frame, "I'm ready, and I will see you again Dye."

Dye said nothing as she pressed the controls and the inner door closed. The outer door opened and Lix sprinted outside. "May the Queen's favor be with you." Tears ran down her cheeks.

A few patches of ice particles lifted off the ground as Lix's footsteps dashed by. The visor indicated head wind speeds up to fifteen miles per hour, so she pushed herself at a high sprint for the first twenty minutes leaving the city limits behind her before she slowed down to a long lasting sustainable run.

Another hour into her run, the wind indicators in her visor began to rise dramatically. She waited for the thirty mile per hour threshold and picked a spot on the icy hard ground. She pulled out a fist sized metallic device resembling brass knuckles, but had a very short barrel sticking out in the center. She placed her fist against the ground and a blast of air sounded as an invisible nail penetrated the ice. She quickly moved in a circular motion, edging out an area large enough for her to fit in. The ice cracked in the middle as Lix punched it with the pneumatic nail driver, normally used to drive the tripod legs into the ground for her sniper rifle. She grabbed and threw chunks of ice to the side, making a hole almost knee deep. The wind picked up quickly reaching eighty miles per hour before she placed her backpack on the ground and curled up with it. An umbrella like dome popped out of the pack and covered her, maintaining its stealth properties.

Lix's visor opened up allowing her to eat an energy bar. The wind wallowed hard outside as she closed her visor and concentrated on the GPS information. Once satisfied with the calculations, she closed her eyes, slowed down her heart rate and slept.

The internal beeping alarm woke her up almost two hours later as expected by the weather trends of the unique climate belt. The wind speed was down to forty miles per hour as she prepared to break camp. The wind was at her back this time so she instantly started running again clearing almost 75 miles before having to make camp again.

Mountains on the horizon appeared three hundred miles into her trek. The night sky declared it was there to stay being the transition of the planet's rotation and influence of a dark region period for the winter season. The wind speeds would decrease, but the colder temperatures gave Lix a different obstacle to overcome.

By noon on day two, Lix had to slow down. The terrain going over the mountains taxed her. The winds were almost non-existent on the southern side of the mountains, so she took advantage of that fact and ran slower but for longer periods of times between resting intervals.

Rolling hills concealed her main objective late that day, but Lix finally came upon a canyon and signs of a fortified base appeared. The two mile perimeter was clear by heavy gun placements against aerial and ground assaults. Lix scrutinized the deep canyon before her and realized she was at her limit. She wouldn't be able to approach further should she alert ground surveillance monitors detecting any ground vibration her nail gun would produce. Not having rope also narrowed her options in that it would take half a day to descend and scale the other side.

She looked around and spotted a high vantage point that might not silhouette her location. She glimpsed back at the base as she moved to see if her location had a good view of the center.

Lix found a flat area inside a crevice of a ridge. She unpacked her scope from the backpack and scanned the base. She viewed the base for an hour before she placed the scope on her pack. She raised the scope again, but looked at the canyon instead. If the queen was in the base and Lix was unable to spot her from her location, she was there in vain.

Lix breathed deeply and ate an energy bar. She packed her scope and strapped the pack on her back again. She started her descent, keeping a watch for possible foot patrols along the bottom of the canyon or aerial patrols above.

Chapter Nine

Witness History

An encrypted message hit the secure comms terminal. "Lord Stargazer, an imperial security team is requesting permission to board the ship." The comms officer reported.

Stargazer sat in the captain's chair and turned towards Krodis. "You know these guys?"

"I don't really know them personally, but they're one of the sources for the intel we have now." Krodis stated, at a loss of what else to say.

"They're an undercover élite military unit, much like your team in the CIA." Ghost interjected as he walked between Krodis and Stargazer.

"If they're so undercover, how come we know who they are so easily at this point and time?"

"They're known by name only. No one has ever seen them or knows anything else about them. I thought they were make believe until a week ago." Krodis added.

"Oh, so they're ghosts like us?" Rat Bastard said sitting on the opposite side of the very large circular bridge.

"So we don't know if they're the real thing?" Spot suggested.

Stargazer stood up. "Alright tell them yes, but Ghost and I will pay them a visit before they get close."

Master nodded approval as he took over the seat. "I'll keep the seat warm for you."

Stargazer smiled as Ghost grabbed his wrist and Stargazer scanned the coordinates indicated by the navigation console. The two men flew into space and quickly found the military heavy class cruiser.

'Wow, where the hell did this ship come from?' Ghost said as Stargazer scanned the ship from top to bottom.

The cruiser's skin was very similar to their own stealth ship. Half of the ship was nothing but weaponry, while the rest was designed for speed and stealth. The design lent itself to be able to withstand heavy damage and still be able to operate on the offensive with independent weapon systems. It resembled a cylinder like rocket with two main starship size plasma guns on its sides. The crew of forty eight were mainly Andromen, or at least as far as both men could tell.

'They have high tech military gear.' Ghost commented.

'Yeah, they're for real. Okay let's introduce ourselves.' Stargazer replied, flying inside the bridge which was buried inside the hull instead of being closer to the surface of the ship.

Ghost stayed invisible as Stargazer separated from him. "I apologize for the inter…" Stargazer stopped talking and stood at ease.

"Don't move!" All of the bridge crew drew a hand gun or assault rifle on him.

"Stand down." The armor suited Soldier at the captain's chair commanded. "Welcome, Lord Stargazer. Excuse us, but its habit."

"I understand whole heartedly Captain. I had to make sure you guys were authentic." Stargazer replied as the crew went back to running the ship. The captain and another Soldier walked up to Stargazer.

"I'm Commander Rither and this is my first mate, Lt. Commander Valoth." The two men bowed slightly and stood at ease. "We understand your situation and also can see that our Captain had good reason to command us to contact you."

Stargazer raised his hand, "Before we go any further; another Lord is here, so don't be alarmed."

Ghost came out of invisibility, standing next to Stargazer. His white uniform was a sharp contrast to the dark colors of the bridge and crew, but was an impressive entrance. "Thank you." Ghost replied, reading some of the crews' thoughts.

"It's an honor," Rither said, noticing Ghost's non stealth suit capabilities.

"So what's the urgency to join us and where's your captain?" Stargazer asked.

"Helmsman, inform the Burik'dir ship that their lords are safely onboard and continue docking with them." Rither turned towards the navigator/communications specialist; then faced Stargazer. "We are for a lack of better words, the only imperial special forces task force personally created by Queen Cassandra to conduct unique operations that deal with the empire's future and queen's safety. Our captain, General Lix, has found the queen's location and is attempting an infiltration to save or assist you in her rescue. The Captain sent us a message two days ago and should be at the location within another of your Earth's day. All of our assets are at your disposal and if we need it, there are five other ships that will join us by the time we enter the Arlos sector."

Ghost smiled as he saw the operations the men around the room had conducted in the past. "Yes, we have little time, and Master needs to hear everything you have to say."

Stargazer turned his head at Ghost and smiled. "Let's do this now and bring everyone into the fold. Commander, can you broadcast a secure meeting throughout the ship?"

"Yes we can, but it will take a few minutes."

"Let's get Master on the main screen for now."

Rither gave the order and Master appeared on the main screen with Spot and Krodis beside his chair.

"Master, Commander Rither will update everyone on the current situation with the queen. I expect everyone to give some input, but Master is the expert tactician, so please heed his questions and comments." Stargazer started the conversation and motioned Rither to present what they knew.

The intelligence dump was quick and concise, as was the options and final decision on the best course of action. The two ships warped through space with a clear purpose as the crews prepared for a historic rescue attempt and possibly the end of the war.

Arlos Orbit

The Kalar defensive grid system alerted many space stations, starships and satellites into action. Energy spikes and readouts said there was a weapon discharge, but no one could locate the source.

Kalar reporting and analysis of the incident finally contributed it to a solar flare, but the capital's security forces quickly changed their focus.

"Emperor, Cyer has broken into the Arlos library." A guard reported as Korvax stood looking at reports of the Hansis encounter.

Korvax turned in the direction of the library. Several hundred Kalar Soldiers paused for a moment as the Emperor flew in a horizontal posture above all heads outside through the opened twenty foot tall doors.

Many of the capital's buildings were intact, but evidence of fire and extensive structural damage was left unchecked by the occupying army. Korvax flew swiftly across the city blocks leaving his security force behind trying to keep up with his gyro boots. It was late at night, but partial artificial lighting laid a clear path towards the library.

The stadium size library stood tall with a large section of the western wall collapsed and covered with semi metallic rubble. Korvax flew into the library entrance as all doors and objects in his path moved aside yielding to his telekinetic powers. He flew up towards the second level bypassing the multitude of wall consoles and interactive 3D instruction cubicles. The wide halls into the main circular balconies and shelves of thousands of video consoles were dimly lit by partially working lights.

Cyer stood at the center of the massive stair-like seating and monitors sectioned off by a galactic map of the universe. His yellow aura lit the area for twenty meters. A computer console used to monitor and direct information to the respective areas of the building quickly displayed thousands of simultaneous downloads.

Korvax approached within ten meters, floating above the terminals. He looked around, counting over a dozen dead Soldiers scattered all around the massive room. "This is how you treat me, after I was responsible for giving you life?"

Cyer's hand continued to touch the table and download information. "Knowledge is something you didn't give me, but if you want to speak of cause and effect, you would not have created me if the Lorthanian people had not enslaved your race. So, maybe I should thank them instead, or Alexmarks for sparing them."

"I will not allow the King or his daughter to influence trillions of races for an eternity with their dictatorship at the expense of my people." Korvax stated his position with a deep voice, knowing Cyer was completely informed by the historical data he found in the deepest archives of the Arlos library.

"You seek vengeance which is one of many emotions which have destroyed many races."

"And what do you seek?"

"You of all people should know that I seek a challenge." Cyer lifted his hand off the table and turned towards Korvax.

"And who would give you a challenge? King Alexmarks? The Queen? Me?"

"If power is measured by our actions, Alexmarks would definitely be strongest, of which I could not defeat." Cyer said as Korvax's security guards entered the upper and lower levels."

"The queen's power will be mine and Alexmarks will one day answer for his actions." Korvax promised.

"My challenge is not here and Alexmarks doesn't have to answer to what he created. If you are unable to defeat the Burik'dir or the queen, then you are surely not a challenge to me."

"Leave us if you are not going to be with us."

Cyer felt a strong squeeze around and inside his neck. His aura glowed stronger as he slowly flew straight up. "Your feeble attempt to decapitate me will be ignored. Enjoy your empire while you still have it." Cyer said and instantly warped out of the building into outer space.

Korvax looked up and then around the library. He grinded his teeth as all of the ninety-thousand chairs and monitors in the room were crushed into the floor. His own guards were pushed to the ground by the telekinetic attack.

One imperial bodyguard raised himself up to a knee with great effort. He looked up then bowed his head.

Korvax floated a few feet above him. "Get my ships fully loaded and ready to leave within the next thirty minutes.

The guard stood up with a bowed head as did the rest of the guards hearing the command clearly within earpiece shot. "Yes, my Emperor."

Korvax looked up and flew towards the sky as the ceiling peeled off like a can opener leaving a large tear revealing the stars above. He bolted outside into the darkness, as the guards quickly coordinated the departure of fifty starships.

Siris Mark Ice Cap Kalar Covert Base

Lix's hand softly pressed on the ledge two hundred meters from the metallic wall surrounding the military base. She eased herself up staying low to the ground. She moved at a snail's pace making sure the short range perimeter sensors didn't detect unusual movement of the ground she was pressing against.

Almost two hours later, she waited patiently inches from the wall. The icy ground underneath the wall was ideal to support the weight of the metallic structure which was basically forced into the earth. Lix .moved around the perimeter faster than the initial approach, but what she had hoped not to find, was looking like if it were another breaking point of failure to her mission. The Kalar were not conducting any foot patrols and relied solely on aerial surveillance called spotters. The aircrafts were flying in an out of two areas above the wall. Lix thought about why they weren't flying in and out from all directions, and it hit her that a force field was forcing the spotters to be guided in and out of the base. It wasn't long before Lix stood at the base of the wall calculating the speed and timing of a spotter coming towards the base.

Lix took a deep breath and stepped away from the wall. She modified the settings on her wrist as the visor allowed her to see the interaction between her suit and body. She sprinted three steps toward the wall and continued up the surface twenty feet up, grabbing the ledge and using it to thrust herself up on the wall and over as the large aircraft's jetwash almost blew her off the fifteen foot thick wall.

Lix quickly ran and jumped on the other side between two gun emplacements. The large battleship sized turrets held two plasma barrels each. The fifty meter spacing between the forty foot tall emplacements made it easy for her to run at full speed towards the taller structures resembling the standard bulkheads of the city she had left three days ago. There were no turbines on the rooftops and the layout of the long structures pointed to the center. Lix ran between many buildings to include sporadic gun emplacements every hundred meters. Lix looked around for Soldiers but none are in sight. The buildings increased in size as she neared the center or at least that's what she thought. She stopped her advance when she came upon a circular building as wide as she could see down the arch several hundred meters in both directions.

Lix sighed, seeing no possible entry points on the new building. She looked behind her and noticed no doorway or windows on any of the buildings. She backtracked her route and moved close to the buildings.

The material was the same as those in the city of Oscith. Lix smiled. She moved to the closest distance between two buildings about 10 meters apart. With a sprint she leaped high and against the wall; her boot keeping strong traction; she pushed off with both her feet away from the wall. The vault took her to the other building's wall as she repeated the technique and bounced back and forth between the side walls up forty meters to the rooftop. Her landing on the roof was stylish as she had to take extra steps so the traction of her boots wouldn't cause her to lunge forward on her face.

She surveyed the area better from the new vantage point; being glad she had moved closer. Her last sniper position was too low, which is why she didn't see the activity beyond the inner building acting as a wall.

Taller buildings in the center were surrounded by factory movement, more than military preparations or security. Channeled lighting on the ground level reduced the amount of light going up to the sky. Not that it really mattered since she was sure the entire orbit above them was off limits to unauthorized ships. Faint sounds of humming and hydraulic compressors told her they were still in construction mode.

She could see doors and windows on the buildings past the inner wall. The rooftop she was on was close to the same level as the circular building. She smiled again and moved forty meters from the edge. With an Olympian sprint she ran the distance and leaped toward the wall's top ledge. She stretched out as far as she could with her arms. The extra weight of her gear didn't help her almost fifty meter long leap as she grabbed the ledge and quickly moved her legs in to absorb the shock. Her left hand made impact with the edge at the wrong point. The kinetic force was mainly absorbed by her index finger splitting her nail, exposing bone. She pushed off the wall with her feet and used her right hand to leverage herself onto the roof; her left hand in great pain.

Lix mumbled in agony as she rolled on her side holding her finger tight. She painfully unstrapped one side of her backpack and let it slide off her body. She breathed deeply as she concentrated on getting the stealth doom operating on top of her and the pack.

The dome popped up like an invisible umbrella covering her already invisible body. She fumbled through the pack, grabbing medical sanitizer and regenerating gel. She lowered her visor with voice command and opened the gel with her teeth. She cleared an area inside the pack and placed gel on the surface. Taking fast deep breathes; she quickly removed her left hand glove and put her two finger tips in the clump of gel. Blood splattered all over the inside of the pack as she removed the glove, but once her hand was in the gel, the bleeding almost instantly stopped.

"Visor down." Lix groaned as it showed her the full extent of the damage. The bone was okay, but the tissue around the tips of the fingers were practically smashed like ground meat. Pain continued to pulse through her hand as the gel recreated the cells. Lix could see the nails being repaired as the molecular bonding material from the gel replaced her own cells. She let the gel do its work for a good hour, before she was able to focus on cleaning the mess in her glove and pack. She quickly cleaned the blood, keeping the cleaning pads inside the pack and retracted the dome. She strapped the pack over her shoulders and stood up. She looked at the ledge, seeing an inch deep indentation of her outer left hand on the metal.

She turned back around and moved closer to the opposite ledge. The Kalar Soldiers were positioning large conduit piping from the center of the base towards the building she was standing on. They were less than fifty meters from completion, which made it easy for her to see the people below her very clearly. The pipes were electrical in nature as the inside was layered with insulators according to the readout in her visor.

At the center of the base was a large fifty meter diameter cylinder structure, only ten meters taller than the rooftop she was on and eight hundred meters out. She looked down and across her left and right. If she moved off the rooftop, she wouldn't get a better vantage point like it again; which meant she would have to infiltrate the security systems, bypass Soldiers, find the queen's location and somehow get her out of her prison, then call for an exfiltration if at all possible. Lix looked at all her options. A gun emplacement was about the same attitude she was at. The suit's energy level had less than a day left on it.

She ran to her right, parallel to the closest building. To her relief, the building was lower. She picked her starting point, unstrapped her backpack, bringing it to her front carrying it under her arm. She sprinted once again and leaped across the fifty meter span. She let go of her pack before hitting the almost flat metallic roof and expertly rolled her landing. The pack thumped on the metal and slid past her.

She quickly checked for damage to the contents of the pack. Everything checked out so she strapped it back on. The dark gray metal she stood on was smoother than the other rooftops she had traversed before. Her boots had little to no traction on the material. She looked at the metal closely, but her visor couldn't analyze it beyond an alloy composed mainly of titanium and silver.

Lix stepped carefully to the edge of the roof, this time she was within throwing distance of the ground and Soldiers below. Small groups of people covered the area, but that didn't matter since she was not looking for a lone person. She lightly dropped down to ground level and walked along the walls, staying away from high traffic areas. She found her target and walked behind a group of people moving into one of the buildings connecting to the main center structure. The doors slide open and she moved in with the group.

The larger double entry way similar the one in Oscith allowed her to easily step into the complex. The inside of the building was semi-constructed being hollowed out with beams and very few rooms or levels. A lack of paint, furniture and utility rooms was odd. Activity inside was minimal to the point of barely being deserted. The group went to an elevator without speaking the entire time.

Lix moved to the open bay of the building, noticing the structure of the beams extending the entire length of the building. The beams strengthen the entire structure to some degree, but it was all one directional. Lix spotted what she was looking for; a computer console at the base of a pylon in the center of the building. The area was clear of people so she easily and quickly stood in front of the panel. Lix frowned as she inspected the display. The panel monitored energy levels and wasn't linked to the main computer system for security or administrative purposes. She could probably hack into the system, but it wouldn't help for hacking into the other systems she needed. She looked around thinking of her options.

"Hmm..." Lix said inside her helmet and started typing in a command. A general map of the entire complex appeared on the screen. "Save images." The visor displayed the image of the map. She touched her helmet and the map moved and zoomed in and out. She placed a finger in front of her face and made a route to a location on the map from her position.

Lix turned away from the panel and set off to the new location following the modified map in her visor.

Outside of Siris Mark System

"Can we get any closer?" Rat Bastard asked, seeing the fancy icons on the starship's main screen.

"Sorry big guy, we'll have to fly in." Stargazer replied.

"Great." Rat Bastard smiled, thinking of the fantastic light speed travel experience.

Stargazer turned towards Commander Rither. The special operations agent stood in full armor really for battle. "It's show time."

Rither looked at him with a puzzled face. "I'm not sure what you mean by that, but I assume it means it's time to commence the operation."

Stargazer viewed the commander's bemused reaction through his black visor. "Yes, indeed it does." Stargazer moved up next to Ghost, the entire group holding hands.

The five superhumans disappeared, flying through the hull and towards Siris Mark.

Commander Rither sat in the captain's chair. "Alright helmsman, take us in nice and slow." A digital countdown appeared on the top right corner of the main screen.

Stargazer easily guided the group around the space sensors, minefields and space stations constructed specifically for the defense of Siris Mark. Ghost helped in counting the starships surrounding the planet and moon base, which was relatively mild. "Fifty-six ships seem like the right number." Stargazer thought.

"Isn't that a little for defending a planet?" Ghost replied.

"No, they can't put too many ships around the planet, or someone would think they are protecting something extremely important. They have the right number to be able to use them as a quick reactionary force for Arlos, or at least hold someone off for Arlos forces to come to reinforce the defenses." Stargazer explained.

"Or it could all be a big elaborate trap or diversion to kill time." Ghost countered.

"No, I don't think so." Stargazer's vision penetrated the ice cap base. Ghost also saw Queen Cassandra's body being held inside a metallic gold capsule, in a state of animation.

"Can you show the group what we see?"

"I'll try?" Ghost projected his thoughts to Rat Bastard and Spot.

Each man saw Stargazer move around the area looking through buildings, ground, weapon emplacements and people. "There sure are a lot of Soldiers working on constructing those metal tubes." Spot stated.

"So what's the plan?" Rat Bastard asked.

"I say we just bypass everything and get her out without fighting anyone." Stargazer suggested.

"What if she's bait for us to be there and we go up in a super boom that can kill us all?" Spot commented.

Stargazer thought about the strategic possibility. "No, Korvax needs her alive for now."

"Are you sure about that?" Ghost privately asked him.

"No, but we have to try."

Ghost grimaced the negative option as the group sped off directly towards Cassandra, still a good thirty minutes away.

Stargazer monitored the base as they approached. Emperor Korvax made his arrival easily known by the movement of Soldiers and how they filled the areas around the queen's location. He was also not hard to identify by his large stature and lack of body armor the Kalar were so accustomed to wear. "He looks worse than those knights." Master commented.

"Well, you've been quiet for a while." Spot retorted.

"Yes, I have been going over how to rescue the queen, now that I see all the variables."

"So what's the plan now?" Rat Bastard asked.

"The plan is we fly into the large chamber, unplug three connections and beat up the technicians. Chances are that, what is holding Cassandra inside will also keep Ghost from going in there and just snatching her out. In addition, we don't know if unhooking her from the capsule will kill her. But it seems she is being kept in a static field type of energy chamber so unplugging it might just do it for us. I'm sure with her help we can defeat Korvax." Master laid it out.

"What makes you think we can't do it alone?" Spot asked.

"Because according to all data, the Emperor has telekinetic abilities capable of keeping us at bay, if not worse. He could easily kill me by breaking my neck and there's nothing you could do about it. Ghost and I need to stay out of sight while all this is going on." Master explained.

"What about the Soldiers?" Rat Bastard asked while the group approached the planet's atmosphere. Planetary satellites detected nothing around the ice cap as the group soared above the ice cap.

"They won't be a problem, but we should leave Master in a secure room, before we go on in there blazing." Stargazer replied.

"Don't you think it's weird that the chamber is on top of the center building? Almost like an alter ready for sacrifice." Spot commented.

"Why did I miss that?" Master replied.

"Hmm... Yeah, the chamber might be a center point where energy is transferred." Rat Bastard commented.

Everyone looked at Rat Bastard. "They're trying to use the planet's energy to pass through Cassandra and into Korvax somehow transferring her powers to him." He concluded.

Ghost smiled as the thoughts of the others were vividly seen. "You're a lot smarter than anyone gives you credit for."

"I told you that, but no one believes me."

"We believe you big guy, we believe you." Stargazer smiled as the group landed on top of the center building of the base.

A pulse of energy seared through all of their bodies. The numbing effects of the red energy interfered with their senses and coordination. The group became tangible and visible except for Ghost who also blacked out. The men and teenager rolled down the dome incline of a few degrees until they hit the roof's edge. The energy continued to pulse through them as Soldiers appeared to capture them.

Ghost woke up staring at the gray metal on the roof as Soldiers secured his friends. Without hesitation, he flew up away from the metallic roof and waited for the Soldiers to show the way in.

'Thank God, I stay in my state of existence when I'm unconscious.' Ghost thought.

The teams of Soldiers took the four superheroes off the roof using backpacks to hover and maneuver about. Ghost followed the group and entered the main building through a tunnel entrance. The Kalar Soldiers wore what seemed to be thicker armor than the rest he had seen. The weapons were also shorter with emphasis on close quarter combat. They handled his friends with mild care, more for expediency than efficiency, rapidly moving through the hallways and into the large chamber on the top floor.

The many double doors and security measures in the hallways were easily bypassed as Ghost flew above the heads of the Soldiers. He was tired from the shock of the alpha wave attack with an extra jolt of plain electricity, but he was well enough to stay invisible and intangible. His attention was diverted to the large chamber which was quite large, the size of half a football field, but circular in design. It looked so puny in Stargazer's images, but now it was huge and impressive. The walls of the five meter tall chamber were lined with silver, gold, copper and what seemed to be phosphate white panels from the floor in perpendicular patterns along the floor through the entire ceiling. Twelve cylinder-like work stations equally spaced, surrounded the perimeter. Cassandra laid at an incline, with a small window revealing her face. She seemed like a statue with no sign of breathing or motion in her eyes. Korvax sat facing her in a large metallic chair made of primarily silver. Gold handholds on the arms resembled a crude form of electric shock treatment to patients in a sitting position or a torture chair.

Stargazer and the rest of the group were brought before Korvax, and thrown on the floor with hands cuffed behind their backs.

Korvax showed no emotion only to stare at them for a few seconds and returned to look at the queen ten meters to his front. "You may go."

"My Emperor, there is another Burik'dir unaccounted for." One of the guards stated.

"He is accounted for." Korvax replied without moving his mouth.

The guards quickly left the emperor and twelve technicians alone.

Ghost looked at the technicians who were not as rugged as the Soldiers, but did have body armor. Their armor was colored lighter, but he wasn't sure if they were technicians or an elite form of Soldiers, as they each had a rifle attached to their backs. They practically ignored the commotion and the group on the floor, monitoring or inputting information at each workstation.

"You can stop pretending to be unconscious." Korvax said in English.

Spot opened his eyes, then Stargazer. Ghost was surprised as he sensed their consciousness only after attention was drawn to them by Korvax. "You too, rat creature."

"Who is this guy?" Rat Bastard muttered.

"Now that all of you are awake, I will begin." Korvax lifted his index finger. The three men and Master were lifted off the ground, their cuffs were broken and bodies were thrown against the walls to the left and right of Korvax's chair. Korvax motioned to one of the technicians who walked up next to Master and injected him with some kind of drug.

Stargazer's face was pushed sideways with full view of Master by his side. Spot and Rat Bastard on the opposite end faced each other. "If you were wondering while you are facing each other. I can't have Lord Spot there start firing lasers in my direction, but if they hit the rat, it would be painful. But don't worry, I won't kill you right away. I want all of you to witness history." Korvax explained and moved his finger around. Ghost felt an awkward squeeze on his body and was thrown against the ceiling between Stargazer and the queen.

Ghost tried to fly out of the tight grip in his intangible form but failed miserably. Stargazer likewise also tried to break free with his strength and flight abilities but failed. Rat couldn't speak and regretted he had not screeched earlier when he had the chance.

"You are all here to see how your efforts will be in vain. The armada around Arlos will be destroyed, your queen will die after her energy is transferred to me and you will die a quick but painful death." Korvax turned his head towards Stargazer, then at Ghost as if knowing what they were thinking.

"Try this rock man." Ghost said as his transformation attack turned one of the workstations into a gel-like bouncy metal. The technicians near the workstation jumped into action to compensate for the malfunctioning terminal.

Spot shot a laser beam out of his eyes centimeters from Rat's body, hitting another workstation, slicing into it like butter.

"Enough!" Korvax loudly spoke without moving his mouth, calmly sitting in his chair.

Spot's eyes where shut tight and Ghost's entire body was twirled around so he faced the ceiling.

"You may begin." Korvax motioned to one of the technicians.

The technician pushed a command into his workstation and the building started moving up with the ceiling separating like a flower in full bloom. The sky above appeared and the walls extended outward into a disk like configuration exposed to the cold weather. But it wasn't cold and the mild frost which Master had suffered from could now barely be noticed.

Blue energy started to move around through the silver lining of the floor. Each technician made sure they were seated in their respective chairs. Ghost stared helplessly at the stars, but sensed another presence. It was that of a woman. 'Is that Cassandra?' He thought.

Four hypersonic booms of titanium alloy rounds hit three technicians and would have penetrated Korvax's head, but instead shattered inches from his temple. The three technicians were not so fortunate as their heads were literally flung off by the impact of the deadly rounds. Their bodies falling to the ground. Korvax stood up as he looked in the direction of the sniper fire.

Stargazer managed to move his head in the same direction as

Korvax's hold weaken for a slight moment. "How insolent these creatures are." Korvax quickly lifted his hand and the next three rounds stopped in mid air, while a wave of telekinetic power swept the area towards Lix. Stargazer witnessed the uplifting of everything in the path, the building Lix was positioned on; getting tossed away like a toy trinket in a tornado out as far as the perimeter of the base. Stargazer could see Lix separate from the sniper rifle which was nailed to the building, and perform several crazy acrobatic maneuvers to keep from getting crushed by moving objects.

Spot had no idea what was going on, but his experience in Vietnam was now going to pay off. At least he hoped. With a concentrated effort his hands glowed as bright and as fast as he could manage. The ice cap lit up with light as never before. Stargazer closed his eyes instantly as did Ghost how sensed the thoughts of the group.

The technicians were blind as was Korvax for a few seconds. The four conscious men were set free and Stargazer instantly flew as fast as he could through Korvax's body. Spot lased three more terminals, as Ghost moved inside one of the technician's body.

Stargazer hit Korvax's telekinetic force field an inch from his skin. The impact felt like hitting a semi-truck without regard for life itself. The emperor moved back a few meters, but Stargazer broke a few bones in his hands and took a hard hit to the head.

"You cannot stop this!" Korvax said as if the destruction of the terminals or the death of the technicians was meaningless. Korvax held his hand to his front as Spot and Stargazer felt a crushing pain around their bodies. "I change my mind about you dying." He said as the pressure squeezed the life out of both men.

Two more bones snapped inside Stargazer's body, but it quickly ebbed off with the broken bones earlier not hurting anymore.

'I can't heal that fast, or can I?' Stargazer thought having almost never broken a bone in his life.

Korvax looked at the two men in complete disbelief. "What is this?" He looked at one of the technicians who had turned off the controls on the queen. The other technicians falling to the ground unconscious.

Ghost's body emerged out of the man, in complete sight of all to see. "You lose." He said and looked towards Cassandra.

Cassandra's clear blue eyes stared at him through the small window. In an instant she was outside of the capsule wearing a silver jumpsuit outfit with a high collar and zipper in the front middle down to her waist.

Her golden blonde hair was tangled in a wave of flowing white energy. "Thank you Burik'dir for freeing me." She faced the palms of her hands outward with both arms at her side.

Korvax stood motionless, as Cassandra kept him from acting.

She floated inches from Korvax's face as Master and Rat Bastard woke up and could see once again. "Your time of destruction and reign is over. You and those who followed you due to greed and arrogance will be punished. Those who didn't, will be given a life here in this galaxy should they decide to stay." Cassandra's lovely voice was almost hypnotic to everyone within earshot.

Spot flew towards the destruction Korvax had created looking for the sniper he was sure was either dead or critically wounded.

Cassandra raised her hand and Korvax fell into a deep sleep. His body disappeared as did the bodies of the technicians.

"Where did they go?" Ghost asked as he flew down next to her.

Cassandra turned to him with a smile of complete relief and joy. "You came."

"Yeah, well, I wanted to see you." Ghost barely got out the words as Cassandra communicated with him mentally. As they exchanged years of emotions, experiences and ideas, Stargazer, Master and Rat Bastard huddled around the two.

Lix opened her eyes to find Spot crouching over her; lifting her out of rumble. Her suit was damaged and helmet removed with a broken visor, but the cold air she was expecting was at normal room temperature. "You are so beautiful." Spot said with an awed expression.

"Is that how you greet strangers?" Lix replied, taking his hand to get up.

"I will always greet you that way for the rest of my life." Spot raised her close to his face with a smile. Their eyes stared into each other for a wonderful moment of understanding.

"I'm General Rashell Lix." Lix softly said.

"I'm Lord Spot. And I out rank you."

"Really?" Lix's eyebrow rose slightly.

"Yes." Spot slowly kissed her. Lix welcomed the kiss feeling a connection she had not had all her life with a man.

A bright light appeared in the middle of space near Arlos. The signature of the phenomena was not that of a starship, but was also not rare to the area. Cyer floated in the blackness of space waiting for the bright object to approach.

Arbitrator flew at light speed as did Cyer matching him while in a standing position. "You will hear me, time traveler."

Arbitrator's skateboard glowed as he slowed down to a complete halt. "What do you want from me Cyer of the present."

"Your Queen is free as you well know. But I will make a bargain with you as you are the only one who can grant it, besides the queen." Cyer said and paused. "You will send me to Earth in the same year that the Burik'dir return to."

"Why do you trust me to send you through time?"

"I am eternal, and if you don't, I will find you and destroy the entire galaxy for the sake of you not keeping your word."

Arbitrator kept silent as a mental message came to him from Cassandra. "I agree." He said and started to calculate the time traveling puzzle.

"Not now. We will meet here at this same location, in exactly 329 Earth years from now." Cyer firmly stated.

Arbitrator's perplexed facial expression could be seen by Cyer, but Cyer gave no indication of concern. "I will, but why may I ask?"

"I keep my promises. Make sure you keep yours." Cyer replied and warped away with extreme elegance.

'So the Burik'dir were successful?' He asked inside his head.

'They were and so were many others who fought for a life they have yet to understand.' Was Cassandra's reply.

Stargazer stood next to Cassandra. "What about the armada and Kalar who hold Arlos and this system?"

Cassandra stopped the mental communication with Ghost and faced Stargazer. All the Kalar weapons have been disabled and all the Kalar people are being captured by Andromen forces as we speak. But that is not the question you have been longing for, is it?"

The queen was shorter than Stargazer, but not by much as she was the same height as Ghost. "You know we want to go back to our time, but that is not why we came here in the first place to do, is it?" Stargazer returned the question.

Cassandra smiled and stared into his eyes. "You can go back to your time, but there are consequences for everything, and I could tell you that going back to your time will result in a happy life, but the future will not be one of happiness. Your task to save human kind doesn't stop here, it begins here."

"What are you saying?" Rat Bastard interjected.

"We are from the past and since we don't really know the future of Earth, we cannot technically create a paradox if the future of Earth is going to go through a doomsday crisis type of event." Master stated.

"But if you send us to our time without knowing the future, could we not also make the changes necessary to avert the crisis?" Rat Bastard asked as Spot and Lix landed next to them.

Cassandra turned towards Lix.

Lix bowed, "Your Majesty."

"Thank you for your devotion and selfless service." Cassandra replied with a smile as Lix stood up and held Spot's hand.

"You were all chosen for a reason. Your presence in your current time will create ripples which might cause a paradox unless you know what might happen which I can do. However, the crisis will not be averted because there is more at stake than your early management of stocks or crime fighting."

"What Cassandra is saying is that we have to go to the year 2016 and stop a mass assassination of world leaders and unite the good guys to fight against the destruction of Earth." Ghost stood in the middle of the crowd and turned toward Stargazer. "You know that the information in our heads is very clear now, and if we don't stop the world from being destroyed, there is no future for anyone in our own time of the 70s."

"But that means both of you cannot stay here." Stargazer turned towards Spot and then back to Ghost with a sad look.

"Well, Rat and I want to go back to Earth, and if it's a future Earth that's okay with both of us." Master stated.

"Yeah, I want to see if the hippies have taken over the world." Rat chuckled.

"Well, since this will be time travel is there a rush to leave now?" Stargazer asked Cassandra.

Cassandra smiled. "No, there's no rush my brave Burik'dir. Let us go to Arlos and there you all can give me your answers."

Chapter Ten

The Decision

The green, pink and yellow mellows stretched for hundreds of blocks throughout the city. The reconstruction of the buildings, landscape and even resurrection of people that had died for many days were part of Queen Cassandra's unique abilities. The people that witnessed the one hour process were deeply amazed by the Queen's powers, much more now that it was the Queen and not Alexmarks who performed the miracles. Stargazer was equally impressed by the look of the destruction he had witnessed on many planets and yet they all had been reconstituted as if someone had the reset button on maximum God mode.

The tall skyscraper penthouse let in the clear blue sunny sky throughout the structure with open windows. The marble walls and wood flooring was peaceful to behold along with the luxurious furnishings. The four men and teenager sat around the living room facing the center piece table.

"You guys had all night to think about what you wanted to do and it's all-or-none. We, stay here and live with the Andromen, go back to 1971 and resume with our previous lives, or go to 2017 to save Earth." Stargazer stated, waiting for someone to provide some input.

"Not that I hate the 70s, but I don't have much of anything there except you guys if we go back to that time. I would love to stay here with Rashell, but we talked and it would be wrong of me to not do the right thing to save Earth." Spot said with resolve.

"Rat and I found each other in the streets and we would still be there trying to find a purpose in life. We have one now and Earth is calling for help." Master commented.

Everyone looked at Rat Bastard. "You guys wouldn't last a minute without me." Rat smiled.

"Cassandra told me it might be possible to return here once we save the Earth, but it was not guaranteed since she can't tell me if any of us will live or die. The superhumans there in that time period are as powerful if not more than we are, so it will get messy." Ghost said not specifying if he wanted to go to the year 2017.

"As you know, I would like to return to my own time, but it is not about me. It never was." Stargazer looked around at his friends. "Gina would have wanted me to save the Earth in any time period."

"So what now?" Rat Bastard asked.

"We say our goodbyes and hope for the best. I told Cassandra we would be leaving this evening, so you guys have a good twelve hours to go shopping or whatever." Ghost replied.

"Well, I have a date." Spot said and flew out of the penthouse.

"Yeah, me too." Ghost smiled and disappeared.

Stargazer turned towards Master and Rat Bastard. "Want to eat an early brunch with Krodis and some other friends?"

Master turned to see Rat Bastard grin from the thought of food. "Sure, we would like that very much." The three stood up and called Krodis to let her know they were on the way.

The day passed by with great joy, but when it came to goodbyes, it was a grim parting for many, Krodis most of all. Queen Cassandra promoted her to command a starship which she had wanted for many years. It was all due to the arrival of legends and now her life would forever be changed.

The hour came when the five gathered. Queen Cassandra personally arrived at their penthouse carrying a silver mesh like ball. Arbitrator also accompanied her, with his usual ear to ear grin. His helmet was off this time and the rest of the group could see the man's glowing green eyes and elegantly braided black hair down to the shoulder blades.

"I knew you would do it." Arbitrator said as he bowed towards them.

"Before we start all of this. Why all the drama?" Rat Bastard asked out of the blue.

Stargazer and Ghost were caught off guard, but Cassandra seemed to be expecting the question.

"You are wondering why send you to save a planet, I could easily save myself. But it is not about me or my father. He will be there and the hope of humankind is not left to an all powerful being who can change everything at will. You have free will and everyone is involved, whether we like it or not. So why a need to fight? Why is there a need to work, or even entertain ourselves? Life is what you make it, and if fighting for it means someone can live in happiness, then we all need to see and experience it to really know what we have. Evil doesn't rest in destroying what is good in life. This is the drama that others will go through and either you are there to fight evil or let evil do its worst. I hope you will do your best to always stand against evil." She stopped speaking, sensing they all understood.

Rat Bastard smiled with a tear running down his cheek. "Thank you. I needed that pep talk."

Stargazer turned towards Ghost. "Now I know why you love her so much."

Ghost sternly glared at him. "I decided to write my own book called, Stargazer Knows It All."

Stargazer laughed. "I'll buy it."

"That's the Burik'dir, legend has it that they always laugh at danger." Arbitrator loudly added.

Ghost and Cassandra kissed one last time before the group gathered in a circle.

"Do we need to hold hands or something?" Master asked.

"No, but you can if you want." Cassandra said as she placed the silver mesh over her head. She touched the outside of the mesh with her fingers. Her silver fingernails complemented her silver suit and mesh. She stared straight ahead; focusing her powers as the Burik'dir slowly disappeared from sight.

The group once again traveled through space, but it was not a roller coaster ride like that last time. All of them felt light as a feather as they traveled in a standing position through space as if the universe was being slid past them, with them being still.

In an instant the five appeared on top of a large skyscraper roof. Rat Bastard rolled three times before he looked back at the group standing there wondering what was going on.

"What, the last time we traveled, I nearly got plastered on the bay floor?"

"It's okay big guy, we thought of it too." Stargazer said as Master let go of Ghost's hand being intangible.

Stargazer scanned the area. It was noon and cold with partly cloudy skies. He recognized the city as Chicago, but wasn't sure if it was because he remembered the old Chicago or if it was because Cassandra put the information in his head from before.

Ghost walked a few meters in all directions, the cold wind blowing his long hair as well as Master's. "So what's next?"

"We find some proper clothes and information on where we are and what we have to do." Spot suggested being clothed with their old clothes from the 70s, hardly appropriate for the winter Chicago climate.

"Cassandra's visions of people is all we have to go off. But I'm assuming they have computers in this time period, so Master. You are point man for getting computers. The rest of us will get clothes and money." Stargazer instructed as he walked up the ledge of the skyscraper. Scanning all throughout the city, finding ATMs, banks and relaying the type of clothing needed for the time period and climate.

"I'll get the clothes so we can go mix in with people." Ghost said and flew off, turning invisible.

It wasn't long before Ghost returned with thousands of dollars and five jackets for starters.

"I'm not going to ask how, but we'll need more than this." Stargazer commented.

"It's a start." Master said, knowing how he was going to get into the stock market. "But first thing is first. Clothes and four computers."

The group spent the afternoon changing clothes and finding the best laptops their budget could find. Master hacked CIA accounts and moved money which Ghost obtained before the banks closed.

They registered into the Hyatt Regency Hotel with separate rooms. The evening was spent eating and using four laptops for research about their new environment. It was quite easy to identify a few targets, which included three Senators and major leaders of seven countries. The problem they had was the exact time of the assassination attempts and who was behind it. A day passed with heavy research on the superhuman outbreak into criminal activity on both sides, the establishment of SIA, South American unification, African Union of states and Australian dictatorship.

The days seemed to run on top of one another, with only two confirmed scheduling of two targets in Chicago within the month.

One of the adjacent room doors was closed to provide privacy for Stargazer and Ghost as they caught up on the past fifty years.

"I noticed your interest in SIA, but why are you looking into their origin?"

"Director Gina Asher was..." Stargazer started to say.

"The girl you thought you would return to and possibly marry."

Ghost finished his explanation.

"She died in ninety-four." Stargazer's face reflected sadness and guilt.

"It wasn't your fault Steve."

"You know the last thing I left her with, were four dead people and one in the ICU. She probably thought I was a psychopath destroying everything I touched."

"I saw what you did and just because you did a Groo, doesn't mean she thought negatively about you, especially after that kiss."

"Is there no secret I have from you?... No matter, it wasn't very heroic of me and now I can't tell her why I never came back."

"Well, you're not the only one who left with a bang of heroism. One day I'll tell you what I did in Las Vegas before we went off to our crazy trip."

"You can't tell me now?" Stargazer looked at him with low expectations of out doing his past.

"We would like to know what you did in Vegas too!" Rat Bastard yelled through the wall.

"Yeah! What could Ghost have possibly done?" Spot added.

Ghost looked in the direction of the adjacent room. "So much for not ease dropping."

"Do you think if I fart, Rat and Spot will smell it?" Stargazer whispered.

Ghost looked back at Stargazer with a smile.

"For adults you guys are acting like four year olds!" Master yelled.

"What the heck, how did you hear that?" Stargazer asked.

"Paper-thin walls…" Master managed to reply.

"Hey Star, check it out! Brrraaapp!"

"Oohh! You BASTARD! Aaghh!" Spot ran out the front door into the hallway.

"What the hell! That's not a fart!" Master held his nose sprinting behind Spot.

"Ahh, man!" Rat rapidly hobbled into the bathroom.

Stargazer and Ghost next door rolling on the floor laughing!

Chapter Eleven

❖---✳ ✪ ✳---❖

First Strike

<u>Concourse 'A' Chicago Midway Airport, October, 2017</u>

Over a hundred people were in the concourse coming and going as flights arrived and departed. A few hundred more sat or stood around waiting for relatives, friends or departing flights. The evening crowd was starting to dwindle down as most of the flights just finished arriving at least until the next iteration every few hours. Ghost and Stargazer stood near Gate A9 next to a wall overlooking the waiting area and up along the entire terminal. They wore shades and black long overcoats resembling traveling businessmen, but lacked any carry-on bags or briefcases. They were both clean shaven and stood with excellent posture side by side speaking quietly to each other. "What do you see Star?" Ghost asked out of habit.

"Everything looks fine so far. Ask the other guys to report." Stargazer instructed.

Ghost called out telepathically to the rest of the group. 'What's going on down there?'

'Master and I are at A17… Nothing out of the ordinary.' Rat Bastard's heavy set mental thought replied. They stood near the Gate A17 counter looking around slowly for an unknown catastrophe waiting to happen.

'Nothing here. Hold on while I check the flight information again.' Spot replied as he walked over to the information screen near Gate A15.

Stargazer was in an ideal location, peering through people's bodies, walls, counters and waiting chairs. "Wait a minute. Ghost there's a big guy up there by the window at Gate 12, I can't see through him or his clothes." Stargazer said and quickly walked towards the gate.

"How could I have missed him?" Stargazer said then realized he had been concentrating on people coming into the terminal and not people coming in from arriving airplanes.

'Heads up, a big looking guy at Gate 12 is a superhuman suspect.' Ghost telepathically announced to the group.

Stargazer and Ghost covered four gates before a mass of arrivals slowed their approach to their intended target. "Rat Bastard, where are you?" Ghost asked not being able to see through the crowd.

"I'm at gate 15, but I think we have a problem." Rat Bastard replied, with Master next to him looking at the US Airways arrival information screen. 'Whoever you're looking at is at the wrong gate.' Spot interjected who was also standing next to Rat Bastard and Master.

Ghost grabbed Stargazer by the arm. "Wait, he's at the wrong gate."

Stargazer looked at Ghost slightly confused but thought quickly knowing they were running out of time. "He's probably a scout. When we get closer, can you neutralize him?"

"We don't need to get closer, I'll do it from here, right now." Ghost said catching a glimpse of their intended target and mentally projected his transformation command.

The crowd thinned and both men could see a large and well built man at Gate 12 crouch to a knee. He caught himself and slowly stood back up. "What's going on, did you do it?" Stargazer asked Ghost.

"Hey, he should be jelly by now. I don't understan..." Ghost replied being interrupted by a loud explosion as the mechanical man he tried to transform into jelly exploded into a ball of electricity and heat.

Gate 12 and everyone around the gate evaporated into nothingness. The shock wave from the explosion flung glass, plastic, wood and metal debris in all directions, killing men, women and children without prejudicial mercy. Ghost instantly disappeared and de-solidified allowing the fragments to shoot straight through his body. Stargazer momentarily stood being hit with secondary fragments all over his body causing major danger to his clothes, but none to his almost impenetrable skin.

The concourse was in complete pandemonium as the outside air and taxi way could be felt and seen through a forty meter hole where Gates 11 through 13 used to exist.

"No!!!" Stargazer screamed and flew towards the other end of the terminal above everyone's heads. Rat Bastard swung around as a flash of light diverted his attention from the explosion to gate 16 on the other end of the circular terminal. A man in a trench coat wielding what seemed to be a mini-gun by his waist bared down on the crowd and Rat Bastard. Rat Bastard transformed into the Rat and screamed at the top of his lungs. The deafening squeak expanded into a cone of destruction encompassing the man and mini-gun, throwing him twenty feet backwards, creating a hole the size of a pickup truck where the glass windows were at the other end of the concourse as the sound wave ran its course from where Rat Bastard stood.

Master ran up and grabbed the discarded mini-gun and fired at point blank range in the direction of the man who was now getting up from what would undoubtedly have killed a normal human. The teenager depressed the trigger letting out thousands of plasma projectiles in all directions. Several projectiles hit the man throwing him outside of the concourse through the hole created by Rat Bastard. The other projectiles created even more collateral damage to the terminal structure and people in it.

Stargazer peered through the gateway arm at gate 14 and saw another one of those superhuman type men inside of a taxing jetliner. He could see the man attacking the passengers running through the aisle as if they were pieces of meat in a slaughterhouse.

Stargazer flew with all his might through the gate wall, into the Jumbo jet, grabbing the murderer and continued on through to the other side of the plane out a few hundred meters onto the runway. In an instant, Stargazer found himself blacking out from extreme pain in his head as the assassin touched his temple with one of his free hands.

An unknown amount of time elapsed as Stargazer opened his eyes, seeing Ghost leaning over him in the middle of the cold grass next to the runway.

"What happened?" Stargazer asked seeing bright dots jumping everywhere in his head.

"We failed." Ghost said mourning for the countless number of dead and wounded left scattered all around the concourse and jetliner in the distance.

"Where are the bad guys?"

'It seems they can teleport and got away. Everyone come to me so we can leave the area quietly.' Ghost commanded.

Still a little dazed, Stargazer managed to stand up seeing Spot and Rat Bastard with Master land in front of him. They huddled together and Ghost turned them invisible.

Ten minutes later, they reappeared on top of an apartment building.

"So what the hell do we do now? Someone is sure to have us on video and they probably thought we were part of that terror strike." Rat Bastard stated.

We have to keep trying to save the targets. In the meantime, Master, I need you to figure out how we can get some allies." Stargazer replied.

"What about SIA or the Eternal Champions?" Spot suggested as he looked at the night skyline of lights, sirens still ringing throughout the city.

"We need to do it covertly, otherwise the assassins while only move up their timeline." Ghost cautioned.

"Find a place with good width band and I'll figure out how to communicate with the Eternal Champions. You guys can find and protect the targets." Master said.

"I might have a place." Ghost said.

Everyone looked at him with interest.

Ghost smiled. "No, it's not in LA, but it's not legal either."

"Maybe we should fly to South America for help?" Spot suggested.

Stargazer tuned towards Spot thinking it over. "I would rather do the illegal first and save the Senator while we're here. Hopefully Master will have found a solution by then." Stargazer said before the group flew off, guided by Ghost.

Ft. Lauderdale, Octavian Horse Farm

Data file 003981Delta now processing.

"Display it on the main screen."

"As you wish Creator." said the super artificial intelligence computer, Erica.

Creator viewed the opening scene of a telecast interview between Samantha Koons and the legendary superhero, Neutronium.

Neutronium's modified white motorcycle helmet hid his face, but his deep, confident voice projected an aura of awesome charm and comeliness. His red, white and blue cape draped over his armchair as he told the world about his life as a superhero.

"As you know Samantha, I have tried my best to help people in distress and catch those criminals who think they're above the law; However, I haven't been alone. My parents cultivated my powers and love for life at a very early age. They taught me right from wrong and opened my mind to truth and justice. Many people would say that truth is subjective, but I say the truth is a constant of doing what is right for the good of the individual and the mass. The police gave me many problems at first by treating me as a vigilante and obstructer of justice. But, I maintained my stance for truth, which they later acknowledged as genuine. Of course, my super powers or deeds didn't and still haven't changed some opinions that I always get in the way of justice and ignore peoples' rights. All in all, I can say that the public and my friends Blade and Alpha Force have motivated me to fight crime where ever it may be."

"Your accomplishments do indeed speak for themselves." replied Samantha. "The one in particular, which our viewers first learned about you is still a mystery, but as of today the Department of Defense has declassified the rescue of 57 sailors and the retrieval of two nuclear warheads. Can you tell us what exactly happened out there in the Pacific Ocean on the USS North Star"?

"I will be delighted to tell you Samantha," Neutronium leaned back on his chair, bringing his right hand up to his temple trying to remember.

"It was September. I was scouting out a lead about an illegal arms shipment down in the harbor one night when I spotted something out of place. You know how you get those feelings that something terrible is about to happen? But anyways, there was a full moon shining on most of the area around the loading docks, except for this huge rectangular space in between two large warehouses. I thought that one of the warehouses was casting a shadow on the ground, but noticed that the moon was not positioned in the proper way to create the shadow. The area had a lack of people to include security guards, which only meant that I was in the right place at the right time. I viewed the scene from the top of a nearby crane. After a while, two trucks and three unmarked sedans approached one of the buildings. I could see that the vehicles were armored with my en-ray vision, but to my surprise, they vanished one by one as they entered the area where the weird shadow was cast. So, I had to investigate and see what the shadow had in store for me."

"You mean they disappeared from your view, right?" Samantha interrupted.

"No, I mean they became invisible to normal sight and even to my en-ray vision. It would be impossible to create a force field to camouflage or completely hide an object that size with today's technology, but not with the aid of a superhuman. I knew that the field probably covered the entire area of the weird shadow, which was as large as the other warehouses. I jumped down to a corner opposite of where the vehicles entered and walked into the shadow. A large warehouse appeared in front of my face as I entered the shadow. I could see through the metal wall easily spying on a dozen men and two women off loading the truck. Everyone was in a hurry to load two large lead containers into a thirty foot speedboat, which was on a trailer ready to be put out to sea. I remembered that two nuclear warheads had been stolen from a Naval Base in Massachusetts. I was about to burst in there and apprehend them, but something hit me from behind knocking me out. I woke up later, chained underwater at the bottom of the harbor. I noticed several burn marks on my body, probably from their attempts to kill me. They must have thought I was dead and cast me out into the water. I snapped the one inch thick chainlinks with my hands and swam up to the surface of the water."

"You didn't drown?" Samantha interrupted once again.

"No, I don't need to breathe or eat for a very long time." Neutronium casually responded. "However, I do eat once in a while, especially good Thai food."

"How often do you eat?"

"Well, the longest time I ever went without eating was about eight weeks, but I really don't know how long I can go without food or water because I enjoy tasting food and the formalities of a nice meal with a close friend or loved one."

"That's a relief." Samantha smiled. "I guess me asking you out for dinner is okay?"

"Yes, a dinner would be nice."

Samantha smiled and responded to her earpiece. "I will take you up on that, but now it's time for a break, we'll be right back with the conclusion of the daring rescue of our brave sailors aboard the USS North Star."

"Stop. Display a four way split view of Neutronium's profile" Creator interrupted. Erica projected a portfolio of Neutronium's history on the top left corner, public folder on the top right corner, major accomplishments on the bottom left corner and his innate attributes outline on the right bottom corner of the 90" projection screen. Creator scrutinized the screen in deep thought.

"Display the coroner's report." Creator softly commanded.

The coroner's report highlighted Neutronium's untimely death. Cause of death: Natural, cardiac arrest with undetermined cardiovascular heterochrosis.

Creator thought for a few minutes. "Erica, what's the probability of an induced arrest?"

"Considering Nuetronium's anatomy, his powers and the events at the time of his death - .023%." Erica's seductive voice echoed sympathetically.

Creator thought for a moment, glancing at his own reflection off his glass work table in the living room. "No, he was an immortal like me. Someone or something killed him... Erica, reprogram your parameters to include current technology as opposed to twenty years ago and possible superhuman enhancements."

"Parameters altered." Erica quickly replied.

"What's the probability of Nuetronium being assassinated?" Creator asked, assuming Erica was following his logic.

"97.345% chance of assassination, 2.637% of an unidentified induced death and .018% of a naturally induced death." Erica replied

"Considering John and Susan's mental abilities, what is the possibility of a self induced death by Neutronium himself?" Creator asked.

"58.029% chance, however if Neutronium was aware of the assassin's presence or attempt to mind control him, the probability is 8.09%. Neutronium's experience with telepathy and mind control was a foundation for today's advance research in ESP." Erica replied.

"Now that we know that his death may have been induced. Who has the power to do it?" Creator asked.

"John, Susan, the Sagemaster, Ramus, Joshua and two other international superhumans. However, my database is incomplete, with possible superhumans or humans who might have the power; but if someone did kill Neutronium, what was the motive?" Erica asked engaging Creator's curiosity.

"Just having him out of the way was enough motive for hundreds of villains, not to mention several third world countries, but the question should be; who benefited the most after his death?"

"Analyzing now... Crime increased by 10% for the first three months nationwide; however, it decreased 22% by the end of the year.

Major radical groups rose up against organized crime and law enforcement agencies alike. This movement introduced the era of superhumans versus enhanced humans. It was during this time that the Colombian revolution became a focus of attention and independent groups recruited and taught superhumans to use their powers. President Reagan enacted Executive Order 33576, creating a separation of power and agency from the CIA, now known as SIA *(Special Investigation Agency)*. EFL *(Energy, Fire and Light)* was the first group to publicly institutionalize superhero crime fighting groups as a normal way of life. By 1989, EFL was the greatest threat to villains around the world. Colombia took complete control of South America in 1988 and the USSR declared independence and split into seven separate states. Australia also declared martial law imposed by Datan Varken restricting people from entering and leaving Australia, isolating it from the world as did South America... Richard..." Erica softly said.

"Yes, Erica?"

"If anyone benefited, it was superhumans and law enforcement agencies." Erica sadly commented.

"No, I don't think anyone benefited. I think the response to a dark period by superhumans and humans were all that kept villains from benefiting on the death of a legend." Richard said with yet more questions unanswered.

Soft fingers touched Richard's shoulder as a gentle whisper by his ear said, "I love you."

Richard smiled and turned to see beautiful hazel eyes meet his, "I love you too."

"Darling, it's three in the morning and you look like you could use some rest." Elizabeth said smiling as she hugged her husband from behind.

"I can't seem to sleep much lately. By the way, how can you tell that I need sleep? Can you see it in my eyes?" Richard grinned as his pure black eye balls metamorphed into common blood shot eyes.

Elizabeth laughed, "You know that I like it when you're silly and overworked. Besides, what are you doing? Are you and Erica still playing Sherlock Holmes?"

"Of course."

Elizabeth jumped on the sofa next to Richard placing her left leg over his right leg. "Can I play too?"

"You know I like it when you want to play." Richard leaned back on the sofa to relax.

Elizabeth leaned forward and fumbled through papers on the table. "Has it something to do with the Chicago Airport bombing?" she asked while holding a picture of a completely destroyed airport terminal.

"Yeah, 167 people died and the only clues of what happened are seven unidentified people using the airport as a war zone." Richard said in disgust. "The Chicago Tribune and Sun-Times said it was a terrorist bombing which the SIA failed to stop, but after talking with Max and Erica's probe into computer systems, I'm sure SIA wasn't involved."

"So what does this have to do with Nuetronium?" Liz stared at the screen.

"Reports say that one of the assailants forced himself into a Boeing 757, Flight 4011, while docking on the terminal and started to kill passengers without touching them. The description of witnesses indicate that some type of mental attack was used, strong enough and fast enough to make the victims go into cardiac arrest instantly. At the same time another person crashed through the aft of the plane and grabbed the assassin taking him away through the other side of the plane. After that the suspects all dispersed and disappeared."

"Assassins always have targets, who was he trying to kill?"

"If he was a terrorist, it could have been everyone. But that would be too easy..." Richard pointed to a passenger list on the table. "There were three possible prominent targets on the plane. Senator Hill, Leonard Kohans CEO for Panther International and Jean Lorenz. Of the three, Jean survived."

"Jean? What was she doing there? Didn't she have her team of secret service agents?" Liz asked a little revolted.

"No, she was in disguise sitting in the back of the plane. That's why the assassin went through half of the plane before he lost his prize. Regardless, he failed and she still lives. Only now she has an angel or demon watching over her." Richard said emotionless.

"So, what now? Are we going to tail her?"

"No, her guardian angel or angels can watch over her. I'm more concerned about the number of people involved. There has to be someone pulling the strings and I want that someone." Richard said with a glimmer of vengeance in his voice. "Erica..."

"Yes, Richard?"

"Prepare the Danger Room for myself and Larcis. Also, I don't care how you do it, but get all of the details about Nuetronium's death and the airport incident. You are authorized to hack into the FBI, SIA, State

Department and CIA computers if you have to, but I want a simulation ready in seven hours to see if we can recreate the assassin's profile and purpose."

"Will do." Erica replied.

"Only seven hours?" Liz quizzically asked, bringing her lips close to Richard's. "You didn't think that I was going to let you go to sleep without some foreplay, did you?" Liz kissed Richard lightly.

"No chance in hell." Richard replied, laying her down beside him on the soft black leather sofa.

Richard promptly woke up that morning, leaving his naked wife wrapped up in a blanket on the sofa with a sweet kiss. He walked towards the elevator and called Larcis on his comlink. "Good morning Larcis. I hope you're ready to fight Erica today."

"You know I'll rather fight bad guys instead of her." Larcis replied through the wrist watch/comlink.

"Is it because she kicks your ass every time?" Richard mocked him.

"I'll ignore that… so when and where?" His voice straighten.

"Meet me in the Danger Room and we'll see if we can prove my ultimate assassin theory" Richard commented.

"Roger, I'll be there in ten minutes." Larcis signed off.

Richard entered the elevator and descended to the 14th sub level. The extra wide doors opened into a lighted hallway with a metallic door on the other side. The ivory marble walls complimented the forest green tile floor design. Richard approached the door as Erica automatically opened the entrance to the Danger Room Control Center. Richard sat on his swivel armchair in front of a large oval gray table at the center of the room. "Run program." Richard ordered.

"Running." Erica responded as the lighted room grew dim and a three dimensional multicolored laser projection appeared on top of the oval table. Erica's seductive female-echoed voice narrated the events of Neutronium's death.

"The Lawrence N. Carthen Estate, Greenwood Canada, September 19, 1989; 19:32 hrs western standard time. The group named 'Alpha Force' now known as the 'Emerald Legion' had taken control of the Carthen Estate. The Carthen Estate was the headquarters of a group named 'The Apocalypse', a terrorist organization bent on the coming of Armageddon. Nuetronium and Blue Dynamo killed the terrorists in a short battle with many weapons dispersed throughout the property. The locations of heroes are on display in blue. The remaining personnel are color coded CIA, yellow; Canadian secret police, red; paramedics and fire fighters, green; dead villains, black; captured villains, gray; and innocent bystanders in purple. Playing audio recordings from Loki's database and SATCOM recorders."

A zoom-in display of the western section of the mansion, shown with three dimensional line diagrams of the floor plan and figurines of personnel, had Neutronium looking around in the library. Blue Dynamo was speaking to CIA investigators out on the front driveway at the entrance of the main mansion. Rover was outside of the west wall, taking in some fresh air while wrapping up his report to Loki via his satellite communicator."

(19:32:47) "Everything is secure and clear here by the west wall." Rover reported, as he scanned the horizon with its stretched red clouds in the distance.

(19:32:52) "Rog xsshxssh." Loki responded as static lagged at the end of the transmission.

(19:32:55) "Repeat message Loki, you broke up xsshxssh... Damn it! What's wrong with this thing? Nuetronium, can you get Loki?"

(19:33:03) 'Xsshxssh' then silence.

(19:33:07) "Rover are you there?" Loki's male voice asked over the SATCOM.

(19:33:12) "Yes, I'm here. What happened?" Rover asked.

(19:33:16) "Investigating... the satellites are all in working order. There must have been a disturbance near your location to have... xsshxssh... to stop." Loki attempted to state.

(19:33:27) "Are you sure it is not something near you that is causing this? Cause there's nothing out here powerful enough to cause a disturbance like that?" Rover interjected being the communication specialist of the group.

(19:33:42) "The only power source strong enough to cause the disturbance is my fusion generator which is presently holding its gold alloy shielding. I cannot determine the cause of the disturbance at this time, Rover" Loki frankly responded.

(19:34:03) "OK, take an infrared photo of the area for the next three minutes and tell me if there is anything you might have missed... Neutronium, come in." Rover said. No response... "Nuetronium, come in. Is there anyone on this line?" Rover questioned.

(19:34:24) "Hey, what's going on?" Blue Dynamo responded to the call.

(19:34:27) "Neutronium isn't answering. There was a break in communication with Loki, but I guess it's over now. Do you know where Nuetronium is?" Rover asked.

(19:34:36) "He said he was going to look around the library for links to the Fargoth family. He should still be there." Blue Dynamo explained.

(19:34:37) "I'm by the west wall. I'll go find him." Rover replied.

(19:34:45) "All right, in the meantime, I will be preparing the Lexus (hover jet) to go home.

(19:34:54) "Sounds good." Rover replied cheerfully.

"Rover entered the library at the west entrance door and found Nuetronium on the floor, section 7H." Erica narrated as the hologram of Rover entered the 3D library and Neutronium's body lay on the floor between two bookshelves.

(19:36:15) "Blue Dynamo! Get up here now! Nuetronium is down! Loki, scan his vital signs." Rover commanded as he placed a small electronic circular disk on Nuetronium's chest.

(19:36:25) "Reading no pulse or nueronomic activity. He has been flat line for at least three minutes. His heart has stopped completely." Loki sadly reported. "He's dead".

(19:37:02) "CIA headquarters... This is Blue Dynamo, patch me in to Hudson, right now!"

"Stop program." Richard ordered. "Correlate the time of first and last communication disturbances with the vital sign scan by Loki."

"Computed… There was an approximate 25-second span of time from the first disturbance to the time of heart failure and a 189 second time span from the last disturbance to Rover finding Nuetronium on the floor. The time span from the first disturbance to the last one was 24 seconds." Erica replied.

"What could have caused the disturbance?" Richard asked.

"Sunspots, a nuclear reactor or similar power source in the vicinity, or an outside electromagnetic pulse or field generated by a superhuman or weapons similar to a neutron bomb." Erica responded, adding current technology to her answer.

"Does this include teleportation by a superhuman?" Richard added.

"No, teleportation by a superhuman would be too weak, unless the superhuman teleported while invisible, which is almost impossible."

"Why is it that impossible?" Larcis interrupted as the doors slid open into the control center.

"Good to see you Larcis," Richard said. "Yes, Erica, why is that impossible?" Richard mirrored Larcis's question.

"It is in fact almost impossible, but at any rate, the field generated by an invisible superhuman is created by alpha waves and radiation wavelengths that would interrupt the wavelengths of a teleportation field. If a superhuman were able to be invisible and teleport at the same time, to create a disturbance large enough to jam secure high-frequency warping, then they would have to be as powerful as Hellfire or Quatris. The disadvantage to being that powerful is that one could not hide from the bio-satellites the CIA had put up in space since 1986."

"Okay, let's say it was not possible. Now, could someone have used a machine to teleport the assassin into the room?" Richard asked while looking at Larcis with a raised eyebrow.

"No. The enormous amount of power generated to create the teleportation field would kill most superhumans or disperse the atoms enough to cause the person being teleported to receive extensive physical damage, or at the very least take more than a few seconds for the teleportation to be completed. It would cause enough pain to the teleported person to compromise him or herself or enough time lapse allowing Nuetronium enough time to call and say he was not alone." Erica responded standing her ground, acting as the devil's advocate.

"Could it have been a robot, android or even a probe of some type?" Larcis asked. "You know, like the one in Terminator?"

"No, even though AIs do exist, Loki was the first to have been created. In addition, we do not have the ability to occupy the space of less than ten square feet, which would have left evidence of the AI's presence in the library. Third, AIs do have powers to a degree, but we do not have the amount of power or type to kill Nuetronium, especially eighteen years ago." Erica confidently explained.

"Why does it have to be an AI, why not a simple drone?" Richard asked.

"For the same reason of the space involved to be able to produce that amount of power and the ability to induce a heart attack would have to be mental or bio-physical in nature. If it were biophysical, there would have been evidence to that fact. If it were mental, it could have been done, however no drone or computer can perform the mental abilities we have just discussed." Erica again defended the stance of natural death.

"Okay, so how do you explain the assassin in the airport?" Richard challenged her.

"It must have been a superhuman, or superhumans that are not in my database." Erica replied a little stumped herself.

"Well, I say it was a terminator with superhuman powers, just like in the movies." Larcis proudly said with the final solution to the puzzle.

Richard looked at Larcis only to admire and agree with the 27-year-old young man that loved to watch movies and daydream about the future. In addition, Larcis was far from naive or stupid. Larcis had more common sense than anyone he knew, plus a 4.0 GPA studying for a Ph. D. in Criminology at the University of Miami. Richard on the other hand had eighty-six years of experience and wisdom, yet he was attracted to the fact that somehow his Ultimate Assassin Theory was a reality portrayed in Hollywood and now on Erica's probability program.

"Okay, Erica. Compute the probability of teleportation, the assassination technique and lack of evidence… Who or what could have assassinated Nuetronium or the passengers of flight 4011?" Richard asked while stretching his arms placing both wrists behind the back of his head and neck.

"The probability of a superhuman assassination is 1%, with one suspect at that time frame and three possible unknown suspects, .0067% chance of a Terminator type of assassin, like in the movies." Erica sarcastically replied. "Last but not least, there is a 1.09% chance of an alien assassination. Otherwise, Nuetronium should not have died. However, if the assassin fills the description as in the airport incident, then the probability of assassination by a Terminator, like in the movies, is 65%, but technically 3% with the technology now." Erica reported.

"What do you mean 3% with the technology now?" Larcis asked.

"The technology does not exist to my knowledge. As you know South America, Australia and even some secret projects in the US have technology that no one knows about. In addition, time has been viewed as a constant, in which case if it is not viewed as a constant, then someone in the future might have been able to go back in time to assassinate these people, like in the movies." Erica replied.

"I guess that's it, huh… Erica, can we go through simulations with the new parameters?" Richard questioned.

"No, Richard, the simulation cannot be done without a mentalist." Erica stated.

"Hmm… If only John or Susan were here." Richard sadly replied. "Damn I miss them." Richard cursed.

"I do too." Larcis said.

"We all do." Erica sympathetically added.

Richard's long career as a crime fighter was distinguished, but it was a lonely one with very few friends who knew his true identity. Fortunately, his work with the Air Force, his only son and routine patrols of about twelve county areas in southern Florida kept him busy. He swiveled back and forth in his chair and stared at a picture of the entire team on the adjacent wall. He and Liz were in the center, Erica I above them, Larcis and Cindy were on the far right, and John and Susan on the far left.

"So what do we do now boss?" Larcis asked.

"My gut's saying, there's a storm coming, and we can't stop it alone." Richard sighed.

Author Notes

T he locations, times and similarities of the scenes with current and past events was designed to give readers a common ground on what can be pictured or imagined. I tried to stay in line with technology and timelines like time periods in the 1970s with the CIA as a proponent of an agency in its infancy. There were intentional references to ideas and people, which represent a message or ironic twist in life. For instance, the reference to Carl Hawking, which is the first name of Carl Sagan and last name of Stephen Hawking, both renowned scientists in the field of cosmology and how the universe seems to define us as part of cosmic particles or star dust. So what do they know about what to do if you can read minds? I mean, who really knows until you actually are put in a position of knowing what someone thinks? Anyways, the intent was to put in humor and maybe provoke some thoughts about why Ghost did what he did.

Once again, as with most superhero stories when there are alter egos or secret identities, this book is no stranger to a list of several names of characters and their titles or superhero names. I hope you didn't get lost and I tried to keep the naming convention the same within a chapter(s) and minimized the personal names to private conversations. I also made sure that book seven builds on the last established names for each character.

Lastly, I am sorry if you feel that the ending of this book is sort of abrupt, but book seven does go deeper into the epic story and I didn't want the story to just jump from one major conflict averted to a totally new conflict in full swing. The characters of previous books are put into play for books seven and eight, so I didn't want to introduce all of these new characters from previous books at the end of this book. I ended with the Eternal Champions to also demonstrate at what point in time this book ends, with Quatris, Hellfire, Pandora and Mindseye in space fighting the Pylaxian Empire.

I hope you enjoyed reading this and previous books in the Superhero Epic series. I want to thank you for willing to sit down and take your imagination to places beyond this world. I hope you will enjoy and be on the lookout for "Ultimate Assassins" and "Last Hope for Earth".

www.ingramcontent.com/pod-product-compliance
Lightning Source LLC
Chambersburg PA
CBHW061602170626
46811CB00001B/285